# Praise for *Gundog* and Gary Whitta

"Brutal, brilliant, and deeply compelling. An absolute must read."
**—The Nerdist**

"I read it cover-to-cover in a single day—the twists made it impossible to put down."
**—Nicole Perlman, co-writer of *Guardians of the Galaxy***

"Whitta is a master of suspense. Abomination grabs you and doesn't let go."
**—Hugh Howey, *New York Times* bestselling author of *Wool* on *Abomination***

"*Game of Thrones* by way of H.P. Lovecraft."
**—Cliff Bleszinski, creator of *Gears of War* on *Abomination***

"A well-written debut that skillfully blends science fiction, historical fantasy, and spiritual themes...a tense, nail-biting ride."
**—*Publishers Weekly* (starred review) on *Abomination***

"Brutal, brilliant, and deeply compelling. An absolute must-read."
**—*Nerdist Podcast* on *Abomination***

"[This] novel about a medieval knight battling an unspeakable horror is getting tons of buzz."
**—io9 on *Abomination***

"I enjoyed this book thoroughly, horror historical magic fun."
**—Felicia Day on *Abomination***

"Nothing can prepare you."
**—Naomi Kyle on *Abomination***

"*Abomination* is an unexpected love-hate/buddy picture fantasy tale with swordplay, knights, and magic—though one with a heaping helping of many-tentacled, acid-blood-filled, gut-chomping creatures. We'll take that sequel now."
**—The Barnes & Noble Sci-Fi & Fantasy Blog on *Abomination***

"*Abomination* is truly fantastic. It's everything I loved about *The Name of the Wind* and so much more."
**—Gale Anne Hurd, producer of *The Terminator*, *Aliens*, and *The Walking Dead* on *Abomination***

"An epic blend of black magic, badass monsters, broadswords, and bloodshed."
**—Nicole Perlman, cowriter of *Guardians of the Galaxy* on *Abomination***

"Bloody, unapologetic fantasy—this is history twisted by the hands of a master storyteller."
**—Chuck Wendig, author of *Blackbirds and Zer0es* on *Abomination***

"Whitta has done an incredible job weaving together historical fiction, fantasy, and horror. This is a book that stays with you."
**—Veronica Belmont, *Sword and Laser* podcast on *Abomination***

"Dark. Scary. Magical. Monstrous. *Abomination* is my kind of wonderful."
**—Adam Christopher, author of *The Burning Dark* on *Abomination***

"It's a story where the reader travels to some very dark places that Whitta has created, with elements of horror, action and (thankfully) humor that keeps you turning pages until you get to the last one."
**—Elliott Serrano, Geek to Me on *Abomination***

"The one-time editor for the acclaimed gaming magazine *PC GAMER*, Whitta has carved a name out for himself with his sensational screenplay for *The Book of Eli*, overseeing Telltale Games's *The Walking Dead* game and writing a draft for *Star Wars: Rogue One*. Now, Whitta's debut novel, *Abomination*, takes the writer deep into the world of dark fantasy."
**—Fangoria on *Abomination***

"*Abomination* looks to place [Whitta] even more prominently on the must-read map."
**—Daily Dead on *Abomination***

"One of the biggest debut novels of the summer is Gary Whitta's *Abomination*."
**—Dread Central on *Abomination***

"If you're looking for a true escape—from real life and from the standard fantasy tropes—then look no further."
**—Science Fiction Book Club on *Abomination***

"*Abomination* is an immensely satisfying combination of everything we love about fantasy and horror but so rarely see together in the same book. I cannot recommend it highly enough and will definitely be keeping an eye to see what Whitta produces next."
**—Charlie Hopkins, *A Reading Machine* on *Abomination***

"*Abomination* is remarkable for more than just the words between its pages, but also its road to publication, via Inkshares, a new publisher who offers authors a unique way to engage with their audience."
**—A Dribble of Ink on *Abomination***

"With *Abomination*, Whitta offers up a well-written, concise, quick-moving Dark Ages historical-fantasy tale of honor, redemption, and fortitude laced with horror elements that's perfect for today's audiences."
**—Geeks of Doom on *Abomination***

"*Abomination* is tons of fun."
**—Revolution SF on *Abomination***

"The abominations themselves are brutal and absolutely horrifying, which is a good thing. They are really nightmare-inducing and I certainly wouldn't want to come across one!"
**—Vicarious Caytastrophe on *Abomination***

"Whitta has woven a compelling tale of inner darkness and perseverance, and of betrayal and secrets, into a highly cinematic, visceral experience. It is wonderfully paced, with fantastic and vivid action. A thrilling read!"
**—Elan Samuel, *The Warbler* on *Abomination***

"Suspenseful, frightening, and gripping to the final line, *Abomination* is a modern masterpiece of fantasy/horror fusion."
**—VGBlogger on *Abomination***

# GUNDOG

Gary Whitta

This is a work of fiction. Names, characters, organizations, places, events, and incidents are either products of the author's imagination or are used fictitiously.



Published by Inkshares, Inc., San Francisco, California
www.inkshares.com

Edited by David Gatewood
Cover design by M.S. Corley
Interior design by Kevin G. Summers

ISBN: 9781950301591
e-ISBN: 9781950301607
LCCN: 2022952072

First edition

Printed in the United States of America

*For my parents, who taught me*
*to always stand up to bullies.*

Here's what I know.

The Mek came to us in peace. A machine race from some faraway star system. They came offering a new future for our people, our planet. Science, technology, medicine that would have taken us centuries to develop on our own, if ever. And all they asked in exchange was a share of our abundant natural resources: water, seeds, things their dying homeworld needed.

Most of my people's history was lost in the war that followed, but this much is remembered: We are a greedy and selfish species. For thousands of years before the Mek, we fought each other almost constantly, for every reason imaginable and some unimaginable. We made war over the land we all shared, over the fossilized rocks and oil beneath it, even over whose god was the greater. Hard to believe now, I know. In one story I heard, the world's most powerful nations went to war because one king had stolen the wife of another. So maybe it was naive of the Mek, who had surely studied us in advance of their arrival, to believe they would be met with the same spirit of goodwill in which they had come.

The greater miscalculation, though, was our own. Despite the Mek's obvious technological superiority, they were an inherently peaceful race; they appeared to possess nothing in the way of weapons or military capability. And so our planet's leaders decided, in their limitless cynicism and avarice, that what was being offered by the Mek, and much more besides, could simply be taken by force—without having to give anything in return.

They were wrong. Though the Mek were not a warlike species, we soon discovered that they had more than enough capacity to defend themselves. Gravely insulted by our refusal of their offer of peaceful cooperation and coexistence, and by our sudden declaration of war, they unleashed upon us weapons such as we had never seen, and repaid our insult by claiming our entire world, and all its resources, as their own.

Don't piss off the Mek when they come bearing gifts. That's a lesson my people learned real fast.

Our great superpowers joined together to fight back. Maybe there's some irony in the fact that my people, who had been ceaselessly fighting and killing each other for countless generations, finally united in the face of a common enemy. And for a while, we even made a real fight of it. Using technology salvaged from whatever Mek we managed to kill, we augmented our military enough to at least hold on. The war lasted the better part of ten years. But all we were doing was postponing the inevitable. It was always a losing battle—one city, one stronghold falling after another. Until only one remained.

My mother was among those ordered to defend that last city, twenty years ago now, when I was just a baby. She was a pilot of what they called a Gundog. The Gundog wasn't just our greatest weapon—it was our last hope. Built with some of that sweet stolen Mek tech, it was the most fearsome war machine my people had ever created, and an entire legion of them was deployed to defend the city.

It wasn't enough. The city fell. The Gundogs were destroyed. And what remained of my people were rounded up and enslaved in big labor camps—we call them townships now—to serve the Mek, who began to build their own cities on the ruins of ours before the dust even settled.

Many believe we deserve our fate. The Mek offered us a chance at something better. A bright future, free of poverty and hunger and disease. Everything we'd always dreamed of. But instead of looking to the future, we once again fell back into the ways of our inglorious past. Greed, selfishness, hostility, conflict. We pissed it all away. Started a pointless war and lost it. And condemned all who would come after to a lifetime of suffering and servitude.

That's it. That's all I know.

# ONE

THE MORNING ALARM sounded before sunup, as it did every day without fail. That was one thing you could say about the Mek: they were reliable, like clockwork—the most advanced clockwork anyone had ever seen. Their machine composition was so intricate that the military scientists charged with figuring it out during the ten-year war had barely begun to scratch the surface of what made them tick before it was too late. And now those precious secrets, obtained at such great cost and once thought the only hope of turning the tide, were lost forever. Obliterated by the Mek in the days after the war, along with the rest of human history and learning.

The alarm was a shrill, modulated tone, designed by the Mek to cause the greatest possible discomfort to the human ear. They had studied human anatomy and neurology well, both during the war and after, to maximize their every advantage over their enemy, and those efforts paid off in every detail, including this one. The alarm was essentially a sonic weapon that immediately brought on piercing headaches and nausea and didn't cease until everyone in every barracks hut was out of bed and dressed and lined up outside for the morning head count. From the alarm's first sounding to the time it was shut off was usually less than a minute. Few could tolerate it any longer than that. So there was no dawdling, even on the part of those too sick or infirm to be out of bed at such an hour. Others would haul them to their feet, dress them, and carry them outside if they had to. Anything to stop that sickening sound.

The alarm roused everyone except Dakota, who was already awake. She woke early every morning and dressed ahead of the alarm, then lay on her bunk, her eyes adapting to the dark, staring at the slats on the ceiling above. She had memorized every splinter and gnarl in the wood by now. What else was there to do? She wished she could sleep through the night, but some perpetual, indefinable itch at the back of her mind would inevitably wake her in the pre-dawn hours and keep her awake while she listened to the snoring of the others, or sometimes the cawing of a distant bird outside.

And now the alarm drove a metal spike through her skull and twisted her stomach into an agonizing knot, and she was immediately on her feet and moving quickly across the barracks to her brother Sam's bunk. He was sitting up, groggy from waking and wincing in pain from the excruciating sound. Most others in the barracks were by now already out of bed and hurriedly dressing, but Sam was slower than most. Weaker.

"Sam, come on. Let's go." Dakota put her arm around him and lifted him out of bed. He swayed unsteadily on his feet as she helped him dress; Sam was missing his right arm below the elbow and it wasn't easy for him to do it alone. Anyone who held up the head count and the cessation of the alarm would be in for a hard time at the hands of their barracks mates for the rest of the day, so Dakota always made sure that never happened. He was a few years older than her, and for years he'd protected her, kept her alive, running and hiding together before the Mek finally captured them and brought them here. Now, together in this township, she did the same for him. She was all he had.

Some fared better than others in captivity. The strong ones survived, and the weak ones, who were quickly identified by the Mek as a waste of rations, were "recycled"—that's what they called it—for fuel. Sam was somewhere in between. He had once been so strong—a tower of strength and resilience that Dakota had come to admire and had tried to emulate. For as long as she could remember, she had looked up to him. But these past few years in the Mek township… they had taken something essential out of him. Hollowed him out.

*Humans were not built to be prisoners, Dak,* he had told her over and over, when they were still living in abandoned farmhouses and sewers and half-destroyed apartment blocks, constantly moving from place to place, trying to stay hidden. *If it comes to it, I'll take care of us both. Better to die free than live in a cage.* Back then, he always carried a pistol with two rounds in it that he'd saved for just that purpose. But when that time finally came, when the Mek drones surrounded them in an open field with no hope of escape, he couldn't bring himself to put a bullet in his little sister. Instead he just fell to his knees and sobbed. And they were both taken and brought here.

In the years that followed, Sam became a living monument to what he had always told her. *Humans were not built to be prisoners.* Dakota's heart broke for him as she watched, each day reducing him to a little less than he was the day before. He had lost so much weight that Dakota scarcely recognized him as the strong, fit man he once was. His uniform coveralls hung baggy and shapeless on his skeletal frame. His eyes had grown sunken, his skin pallid. At night, she would often sit by the side of his bed and watch him sleep, and at times he looked to her like a dead man ready for burial.

When Sam lost his right arm a year ago, in an accident with a steel press while working in one of the township factories, that might well have been the end. But Dakota, who was fortunate to have been working just outside at the time and heard the cries, rushed in and saved him. Tied off the wound and cauterized it using the factory tools at hand, then carried him back to the barracks to care for him. She worried he was already as good as dead—the Mek considered a one-armed worker an inefficient expenditure of rations, and normally they would have recycled him the same day—but Dakota pleaded with the Mek supervisor to spare him, offering to split her rations with him until he was well enough to be productive again. Coming from anyone else, such a plea would have fallen on deaf ears, but Dakota had proven her worth to the township as an engineer and problem-solver many times over, and so—in a rare and ultimately pragmatic show of mercy—they allowed her brother to live.

Sam never again returned to full work. In the Mek's eyes, he was a cripple, capable of only menial chores and unworthy of a full ration of food. So to keep him alive, Dakota continued to split her rations with him—to this day.

But the toll that these past years as a slave laborer had taken on his body wasn't the worst of it. It was what it had done to his spirit that crushed Dakota the most. All the fight had gone out of him. His quick-minded improvisation, which had saved them from Mek detection time and again during their years as fugitives, and the gleam in his eye as they sat by night around makeshift fires and he told her stories of humanity's valiant last stand against the Mek... all that was gone. Only this emaciated shell remained.

Twice she had caught him close to ending his own life, once with a sharpened piece of metal he'd snuck from the factory, and later with a bottle of some dire Mek chemical stolen from a maintenance shed. Both times she managed to talk him down, persuade him to keep living, if not for himself then for her, because he was all she had in this whole miserable world, and if he left her, who knew how long she would last before following him. But she knew that despite his promises, the greatest threat to his life was not a Mek or another accident, but his own deliberate hand. So she continued to keep a close eye on him. Often, while he was supposed to be working the gardening plot or ferrying supplies, she'd catch him just staring at the horizon, or at nothing, and she'd know what he was thinking. She'd make her way over as quickly as she could—before a Mek watcher could get to him first, to give him a low-voltage jolt to spur him back to work—and give him a smile or a touch of her hand, some reminder that he hadn't yet lost everything.

Now she finished helping him dress, and together they joined the line of workers quickly filing out of the barracks into the floodlit night. Dakota hadn't seen the true dark of night, the stars in the sky, for years, blotted out as they were by the Mek light towers that blazed from dusk to dawn, keeping the entire township awash in stark fluorescent light that made everything in the world look artificial, antiseptic, alien. There were shutters on the barracks doors to keep the light out so workers could sleep, but out here in the open, it barely seemed like night at all, at least not the kind Dakota remembered. Still, it would be sunup soon, and then the lights would shut down and stop humming, and there the blue sky of day would be, the sun and the clouds.

Not even the Mek could take that away.

She stood still beside her brother, waiting as the Mek drone moved from one end of the line to the other, scanning each face, making sure everyone who checked into the barracks hut the night before was still present and accounted for. Only when every drone surveying every hut was satisfied did the morning alarm fall silent. Everyone exhaled in relief, their headaches and stomach pains abating, then at the sound of another alarm, this one a short but unpleasant electronic squawk, they made their way to the canteen huts for their breakfast ration, the Mek drones registering and recording their every move.

* * *

By the time breakfast was over and everyone was reporting to their work assignments, the sun had just started coming up, breathing light and life into the day. There was a cool breeze, and Dakota took a moment to stop and close her eyes and feel it waft over her, the briefest sense-memory of freedom. Then she heard the telltale *clik-clik-clik* of a Mek drone approaching and got moving again before it could jolt her.

Most everyone in the township worked to serve the Mek. They toiled in factories and foundries and on assembly lines, turning the metal ore and other raw elements that arrived by automated convoy from other townships into the refined materials and components the Mek used to build more of their cities, build more of themselves. But Dakota was different. She worked to sustain the township itself. Her specialty trade was everything. She fixed the plumbing when the pipes froze in winter or the toilets backed up; she patched fried electrical panels to keep the hut lights on; she decontaminated the water supply when it became undrinkable, as it so often did from the Mek's toxic exhaust chemicals leaching into the groundwater; she kept the barracks huts' dilapidated heating and ventilation systems running; she repaired broken windows and leaking roofs… basically everything that needed to be done to keep the Mek's slave labor force from freezing to death or dying from poisoning or dehydration.

Still, many did die. There was no township doctor, no one old enough to have that kind of training or experience, and people frequently succumbed to illnesses and injuries that would have been routinely treatable before the war. The Mek could easily have provided medical facilities based on their vast knowledge of human physiology, but somewhere along the way one of their impenetrable algorithms had calculated that it was more efficient to tolerate the mortality rate than to expend resources to curb it. There was, after all, a never-ending supply of people to replace those who were lost. New workers arrived in the township via Mek prison vehicles on a regular basis.

Dakota was an exception in that regard. Though no human was truly valuable, she was considered less expendable by the Mek than most, as she had come to know every quirk and foible of the township's run-down utilities, better even than the Mek themselves, and if she were to die, many more might follow before she could be replaced. More than the algorithm deemed acceptable.

As she went about her day, she was always careful to not let Sam out of her sight for too long. He'd recently been moved to an outside gardening detail, tilling crops that helped supplement the worker food supply, so she too tried to stay outside as much as possible, making busywork for herself if necessary. The Mek watchers would jolt her if they thought she was procrastinating, but today was easy. A barracks hut roof had sprung a bad leak, letting the rains in. Dakota might have needed only the work of a morning to patch the leak, but she had convinced a Mek supervisor that it would be more efficient to re-shingle the whole roof, further convincing the Mek that it would take her at least two weeks—twice her actual estimate. She wanted to be up there as long as possible, not only because it gave her a good view of Sam and his garden plot, but also because she liked it up there. Being up off the ground, closer to the sky above, felt to her like a sort of freedom, even though the roof of the hut wasn't even as tall as the township's perimeter fence, which could be seen in the distance, towering over everything, an ever-present reminder that even the briefest feeling of freedom was an illusion.

"Need a hand?"

Startled, Dakota almost hit her thumb with her hammer. She turned to see Runyon standing on the ladder she'd used to climb up here, peering over the edge of the roof at her. He was one of the youngest workers in the township, eighteen or nineteen she guessed, although she'd never really given it—or him—very much thought.

"Thanks, I'm good," she said, turning back to the shingle she was working on. After hammering a few more times, she got the feeling she was still being watched and turned again to see Runyon still there on the ladder, looking at her. She glared at him, and this time he seemed embarrassed and looked away.

"Do you need something?" she asked curtly.

"Finished with my detail early, thought I might help." There was a quaver in his voice, like he was nervous, though Dakota couldn't imagine why. All she knew was, the last thing she wanted was someone to help her make this work go faster.

She turned back to her work again. "Go ask a supervisor. I'm sure they'll find something for you to do. Or just wait there—they'll find you." And true enough, she heard a Mek observer approaching at roof height, closing on Runyon. Its sensors had detected him out of place and inactive, and even now, Dakota had no doubt it was charging its electrified prod to jolt him.

She was surprised by what Runyon did next. He should have raced back down the ladder, but instead, he stayed a moment longer even as the drone drew closer.

He spoke quickly. "There's story time at the rec hut tonight, right after dinner ration. You should come. I'll be there. Will you come?"

Before Dakota could answer, the drone moved within just a few feet of Runyon, a moment from jolting him, and he slid down the ladder and raced back to his assigned area. She shook her head, took another roof nail from the box, and went back to work as the drone turned and moved away.

# TWO

AFTER DINNER RATION, Dakota lay on her bunk, nursing the blisters on her hands. They weren't bad; worse was the cut she'd gotten on her palm from a sharp sliver of wood hiding under an old shingle as she'd torn it away. She'd wrapped the cut as well as she could with a band of cloth torn from her coveralls, but she could only hope it wouldn't get infected.

She looked across the hut at the only other person there. Sam was on his bunk, asleep. Neither had spoken a word to each other all day, save for Dakota urging him to get up out of bed that morning. She missed him so much, or at least missed the man he once was. The stronger sibling, the protector, the one who sang her songs at night and made the nightmares go away. Now he was living his own waking nightmare, and there was nothing she could do to help.

She walked over to his bunk and sat by him, watching his chest move gently up and down with each breath. She reached out, stroked a stray lock of hair away from his face, and tucked it behind his ear. Those little things, it seemed, were all she could do for him.

His eyes opened, and he looked up at her.

"I thought you were sleeping," she said, half a whisper.

"I was," he said. "I was dreaming about you, and then I woke up, and here you are."

She smiled. "You see? Dreams do come true."

He darkened—probably reflecting on how little truth there really was to that. Dakota spoke quickly to keep him talking, rather than let him sink into some bleak hole of his own making.

"Tell me about your dream."

"It was that time, do you remember, when we were living in that bus terminal."

Dakota smiled again; she remembered that as one of their happier times together. That old bus station was half-destroyed, and it reeked of urine and spent ammunition, but it was good shelter and it had taken the Mek a long time to find them there, which was all that mattered. They'd spent almost two weeks there, longer than they'd ever been able to stay in any one place, enough to make themselves something like comfortable, and in a strange way, it had almost begun to feel like a home. Dakota was distraught when Sam told her he had seen Mek surveyors on the horizon and that they had to leave.

"I remember," she said.

"We made a chess set out of those old nuts and bolts and spark plugs we found around the place, and drew a board on the ground with chalk," said Sam. Some light had returned to his face at the memory of a happier time.

"And you always won," said Dakota. Though she remembered that she had *let* him win on more than one occasion.

"I wish we could be back there again," said Sam, that worrying, vacant stare returning now.

"It's not good to think too much about the past," Dakota said. "There's nothing for us back there."

"There's nothing for us here, either," said Sam.

Now Dakota was really starting to worry about him. He must have seen that register in her expression, because he reached out to touch her arm.

"I know you don't like to look back, but it's what makes me happy," he said. "Thinking about those times when it was just you and me."

Her hand closed around his. "It's still just you and me. It always will be."

Sam raised his head and looked around the empty barracks. "Where is everyone?"

It took Dakota a moment to remember what Runyon had told her earlier. "Story time in the rec hut."

"Oh, yeah. That kid Runyon, he asked me if you were going."

"He asked me, too."

"You know he likes you."

Dakota felt her face flush, which annoyed her. Relationships between workers weren't forbidden, but that kind of attention was the last thing she needed, least of all from a callow boy, so skinny he looked like he had to walk around in the shower to get wet. She had enough to worry about as it was.

"Why don't you go?" asked Sam.

"You know why."

"You're imagining things."

"Am I?" said Dakota. "You've seen the way some of the other workers look at me. They don't like me. They think I'm a Mek pet. They don't want me socializing with them."

"When's the last time you even tried?" Sam asked.

It was a good question. Dakota could hardly remember the last time she'd had much of a conversation with anyone besides her brother. Trying to shoo Runyon down off her damn roof earlier in the day was about as sociable as she'd been in . . . forever.

"I'll go if you go with me," she offered. What might be good for her would surely be good for him, too, and besides, she didn't like the idea of leaving him alone in the barracks.

"I'm too tired," he said. "I can barely keep my eyes open. I'm fine, really. I just want to sleep, maybe find that dream again. But promise me you won't just sit here and watch me. Promise me you'll go, and you can tell the stories to me after."

She squeezed his hand again. "I promise."

* * *

One night every week, the Mek allowed free socialization within the township's recreation huts for an hour between dinner ration and lights-out. Another Mek algorithm had determined that a small amount of recreation time, properly regulated, was ultimately beneficial to production. Few wasted the opportunity to come and talk and sing songs and drink shine from a still that they had somehow managed to keep hidden, trying to forget their troubles.

As she approached the rec huts, Dakota could see the flickering of gaslight in the windows, could hear the sounds of talk and laughter and song. This was how much of the old world must have been, she imagined, though she was too young to remember, born nine years into the ten-year war. And though the thought of joining the gathering filled her with trepidation, she felt an equal sense of attraction to the warmth and companionship within. She had been starved of these things her entire life, though they were as essential to human survival as water and air.

She waited by the door for a moment, gathering herself, before pulling it open and walking inside.

Dakota felt as though every single face turned to stare at her. That was an exaggeration, but in truth, many did, their silent glowers questioning why she was there. She did her best to ignore them as she made her way through the crowded room to an unclaimed seat, continuing to avert her eyes until her onlookers got bored and returned to their conversations. Apparently no one felt passionately enough about her being there to make something of it, perhaps because they remembered what happened the last time someone tried to goad her. An older woman, in her late twenties, big and stocky, had stepped right up to her and spat in her face and called her the daughter of a traitorous whore. Shortly after, that the woman was relocated to another township with a different work remit, one where the loss of an eye wasn't an impediment to productivity.

So Dakota sat quietly, alone, and people-watched. There were so many faces, and so many of them alike. At twenty-two, she was among the youngest there, while the oldest person in the township was said to be just over thirty. She'd never seen anyone older than that inside the fence, though she and Sam had come across many older men and women during their years on the run. Those poor souls were nearly always terrified, barely able to speak beyond begging Sam and Dakota to let them join their group, share whatever shelter they had. It always crushed Dakota to have to turn them away, but Sam made no room for sympathy, knowing it would get them all killed. Older people were a priority target for the Mek, shoot-on-sight, everybody knew that, although there were conflicting theories as to why. The most common one was simply that only those in their physical prime were considered proper fodder for laboring in the townships. Some Mek algorithm determined that beyond a certain age you were in inexorable decline, slower and weaker every day, an entropic organism with no capacity to be easily repaired or refurbished like a damaged Mek. Fit only for recycling.

Someone at the head of the room, where a fire crackled in a stone hearth, was just finishing a tale about a time before the Mek, long before anyone present was born. Dakota caught only the end of it, something about a time when countless innocent men and women and even children were marched to their own cremation not by the Mek but by their fellow human beings, and the nations of the world rose up in alliance to defeat those who would perpetrate such an atrocity. It was a popular story, one that highlighted humanity at both its best and worst, and the teller always swore that it had been told to him by his own father, who had read about it in a proper history book. But as captivating as the story was, most dismissed it as fable, its crimes too monstrous to be true of human nature, its valor too improbable, especially the part about the young men wading out of boats onto an entrenched enemy beach only to be mown down en masse by machine-gun fire, yet still they came, wave after wave, until they took the beach and began to drive an enemy once thought unassailable toward ultimate defeat.

Some held fast that it was all true, every word. But Dakota, who had heard the story before, agreed with the majority that it was little more than a fairy tale.

"You came!"

Dakota looked up to see Runyon standing there, a big grin on his face like he'd lucked into a triple ration. In the walk from her barracks, she'd forgotten this might happen. All she wanted to do was sit and listen quietly, not get drawn into an interaction she knew would only exhaust her.

"Uh, mind if I sit down?" Runyon asked.

Dakota gestured to the space on the bench next to her as blithely as she could, trying to indicate that though he wasn't unwelcome, he wasn't particularly welcome, either. Runyon seemed to understand at least the first part of that and happily sat down next to her, slightly closer than she would have liked. She shifted over, opening a more comfortable distance between them.

"So, what made you change your mind?" Runyon asked.

"I didn't," said Dakota. "My brother insisted I come."

"Ah," said Runyon. "How is he? Your brother?"

Dakota turned and looked at him. No one ever asked her that. To everyone else, Sam was a liability, a slacker, someone who had gotten preferential treatment from the Mek because his sister was deemed to be of special value to the township. No one else gave a shit about Sam. And yet here was this kid, asking after a man he barely knew and certainly had no reason to care about.

"He has good days and bad days," said Dakota, realizing instantly that she had already told him more than she wanted to. Her brother's welfare was their own private business—no one else's. She should have just said "fine" and been done with it.

"Well, that's better than nothing, I guess," said Runyon. "My brother lost his foot to gangrene a few years ago. The Mek recycled him."

She scowled at him. "A foot's not the same as a hand. Sam still works, he's productive, and his ration comes out of mine. So if you want to accuse me of—"

Runyon threw up his hands in surrender. "That's not what I mean. I know some of the others think that way, but that's not me. That's not what I was trying to say at all."

"Then what *were* you trying to say?"

"I guess just… count your blessings? I'm sorry."

He lowered his hands, and Dakota could tell he felt genuinely embarrassed. He wasn't ill-intentioned—quite the opposite, she now realized. He was just naive.

Another storyteller was taking his place by the hearth. Dakota recognized him. His name was Sellers, and the rumor, much contested, was that he was the oldest person in the township. Someone actually born before the Mek arrived, though too young to remember anything of that lost world. As he prepared to speak, Dakota shifted uneasily in her seat and thought seriously about leaving because there was only one story he ever told, and she'd heard it enough. She waited, though, to be sure. It had been a long time since she'd been to story time. Maybe Sellers had a new story by now.

"Let me tell you," Sellers said to a rapt audience as the fire crackled behind him, "about the Gundogs."

Dakota got up to leave; as she feared, it was the same old story. But she was stopped by Runyon's hand on her arm. He looked up at her with those sad puppy-dog eyes of his.

"Don't go," he implored. "This one's my favorite."

"It isn't mine," she replied, though the truth was that she didn't dislike the tale itself, only when someone other than her brother told it. They always got something about it wrong. Besides, it was their family's story and no one else's.

Yet somehow, though she fully intended to leave, she found her feet rooted to the spot. Something deep within her wanted to stay and listen. And so she sat back down, even as she struggled to understand why.

And so they listened as Sellers told his tale, the same way he always told it. About the final battle, mankind's last stand against the Mek, at a place called Bismarck. It was the only human city still standing, the city to which all remaining military forces had retreated after falling back again and again, suffering loss after loss to the overwhelmingly superior Mek. Still, at the time, it had seemed there was hope. Humanity's greatest scientists had at last begun to unlock the secrets of the Mek's technological superiority, reverse-engineering captured drones and surveyors and battle units. And what they learned they incorporated into a weapon known as the Gundog.

The Gundog was an armored vehicle, taller even than the township's perimeter fence, that strode across the land on two great legs like a colossus. The stolen Mek technology made it a more fearsome weapon than anything yet deployed against them, a taste of their own medicine. Piloting the Gundogs were the best and bravest warriors, those who had proven themselves against the Mek in battle after battle. In those desperate final days, the military had only managed to build a dozen or so Gundogs, but still it was hoped that they were potent enough to hold the last city and save the millions of innocents cowering within.

For six days and six nights, the Gundogs gave the Mek a fight like they had never seen. In that short time, more Mek battle units were shredded and smashed into junk than in the entirety of the ten years preceding. And for a few glorious days, it seemed as though the city might actually hold. But though the Gundogs were the Mek's match in terms of armament and battle strength, the enemy had an overwhelming advantage, an advantage that was probably the defining factor of the entire war: the ability to quickly repair and remake themselves. Mek reclaimers roamed the smoking battlefield after each engagement, collecting damaged and destroyed battle units, then made new ones out of the scrap metal, spitting out fresh Mek fighters almost as fast as the Gundogs could bring them down. Nothing was wasted. Everything got recycled and re-deployed.

"One by one, the brave Gundogs fell," said Sellers, approaching the end of his story. By now most everyone in the room was leaning in, spellbound. He was a good storyteller, Dakota had to admit. Almost as good as Sam. "Until only one remained. The Mek came in overwhelming numbers, and still that last Gundog stood its ground, fighting to the last, until it was overwhelmed, swarmed by the rampaging Mek. And so too, then, went the last city.

"Some say the rusted shell of that last Gundog still stands outside what we used to call Bismarck. The Mek erected their own city on its foundation, after destroying everything we had built, but the last Gundog they left standing. As a tribute, some say. A salute to their enemy's courage and defiance. A monument that will stand for all time."

There was a long pause before anyone spoke, just the sound of the fire in the hearth spitting and crackling.

"Bullshit."

That had come from near the back of the room. Everyone turned to see. A man back there, Dakota didn't know his name, emerged from the shadows where he had been listening.

"You have a problem with my tale?" Sellers asked.

"That's all it is, a tale," said the man. There was an angry look about him. "We all know about the Gundogs, the last stand. What you never say is what really happened there. That they *didn't* fight to the last, but *ran*. Fled before the Mek when the battle started to tilt against them, cowards to the last. That's why the last city fell, why there's no monument outside Bismarck. Am I the only one who knows this?"

There was a murmur of agreement around the room, and now Dakota really wanted to leave. She'd heard this version of the story before, too, and liked it even less than the other. She was about to stand, but her path to the door was now too crowded to get there without making herself conspicuous, and all she really wanted at that moment was to be invisible.

"I understand why you tell it your way," the man went on. "But it's a lie, and one that gets people riled up for no good reason."

"It's a tale of heroism," offered Sellers meekly, looking around as if becoming aware that the room was slowly turning against him.

"What good is that to any of us now?" asked another man, standing from his table. He stabbed a finger at Sellers. "What good was it even then? We lost the war, and anyone who hears that story and gets some damn fool idea about standing up against the Mek only gets themselves recycled."

There was another ripple of agreement, this one more emphatic than the last. There was some truth to what the man had said; every once in a while, a worker who couldn't take life in the township anymore snapped and tried to escape, or gave way to anger and attacked a Mek observer. Whether or not the old war fables Sellers and others liked to tell played a part in any of this was debatable, but there was no denying that defying the Mek only ever ended one way—with immediate extermination and recycling.

"That's not the worst of it," said a third man, also rising to his feet. Dakota knew this man's name, and she wished she had taken the risk of trying to leave when the thought first struck her.

"The Gundogs were *worse* than cowards," said Carmichael. He shot a glare at Dakota from across the room. "They were traitors. Like all the rest of them, the entire bloody generation before us who started that war. The Mek came to them in peace, and they bit the hand that tried to feed them. Now we all suffer because of their shortsightedness and greed. That's the legacy they left for us before we were even born." Carmichael glanced again at Dakota, his unspoken accusation plain. "If any one of them was still here to answer for what they did, I'd sooner kill them than any Mek I've ever met."

And that got the biggest agreement from the room yet—not from everyone, but enough that it was damn near a roar. As much as the township hated the Mek, they hated their own forebears more, their parents and grandparents who had responded to an offering of peace and goodwill by making war. Everyone here lived with the misery of that choice every day. And what made it worse was that those to blame were no longer present to be held accountable. They were all dead now, either killed by the Mek during the ten-year war or rounded up and exterminated after. Instead this next generation, too young to have played any part in the war, remained to pay the price.

The chorus of approval stopped suddenly at the sound of a chair toppling backward and hitting the stone floor hard. All heads turned to Dakota. Many had no doubt been expecting this from her since she first entered the room. And every one of them was surprised that it was not she who had sprung to her feet. It was Runyon. Dakota was still seated next to him, tugging at his arm, beckoning him to sit back down. But he was having none of it. He was no longer looking at her, as he had been for much of the evening, but across the room, at Carmichael.

For a moment there was silence, everyone wondering what would happen next. Runyon was known around the township as quiet and meek, more a boy than a man. This was entirely out of character for him.

"Her parents weren't traitors," he said, putting a hand on Dakota's shoulder. She shrugged it away, but Runyon was undeterred. "And they weren't cowards, either. They fought in the war because they had to, everyone back then did, but they didn't *start* it. You can believe what you want, but whatever the truth about the war is, no one here deserves to carry the stigma for it."

For a moment there was silence.

Then Carmichael sneered. He was not about to be put off by this weakling boy.

"If her parents weren't cowards—if she isn't one—why does she need you to speak for her? Or are you just trying to get in her good graces so she'll finally fuck you?"

Dakota bolted from her chair and vaulted over the table in a single move, closed the distance between her and Carmichael, and before he could even react, she slammed him against the wall so hard it shook.

She pinned him there with her forearm across his chest.

"My parents aren't here to answer you," she spat, "but I am. My mother fought for the last city. She stood against the Mek when there was no one else left. Insult her again, and we'll see which of us is the coward."

Dakota was scarcely more than half Carmichael's size and weight, but her sudden anger had given her enough strength to make her more than a match for him. He tried to push back against her, but she just pressed him harder against the wall. She could see the wheels turning in his head as he weighed his options. All eyes were on him. If he backed down now, in front of everyone, he'd never hear the end of it. But he'd also surely heard the story about the woman whose eye she'd gouged.

In the end, he decided to press his luck.

"Maybe she wasn't a coward," he said boldly. "Maybe she didn't run away. Maybe she struck a deal with the Mek. A collaborator! Maybe that's why you and your cripple brother get special treatment around here, because she—"

Dakota drove her fist into his stomach, taking all the wind from him and buckling his knees. Then she was raining blows down on him in a blind fury. Others rushed to drag her away, and Runyon waded into the fray in an effort to protect her. For a few moments, it was chaos.

Then the rec hut's door blasted off its hinges, and two Mek enforcers floated inside, blasting a piercing sound wave worse even than the morning alarm. They ordered everyone to disperse back to their barracks, and jolted anyone not obeying quickly enough.

The night was cold outside, and bright as usual, the blazing tower lights casting everything in that horrible antiseptic pale blue. As Dakota hurried back to her barracks hut under the watchful eyes of the Mek drones, she heard someone running up behind her.

"Hey." It was Runyon. "Are you okay?"

She whipped around to face him. "I *was*. What the hell was that? What did you think you were doing back there?"

Runyon seemed at a loss for words. "I was… just trying to stand up for you," he managed. His voice was quavering, far more than when he had confronted Carmichael.

"Well *don't*," said Dakota. "I don't need anyone to do that for me. Don't ever—" She stopped. "What happened to your eye?"

Runyon reached up to touch his left eye, then quickly moved his hand away, wincing. It was red and swollen where someone had landed a fist or an elbow during the melee. "It's nothing," he said.

She was about to say something when she saw a Mek drone moving toward them, its jolt prod at the ready. They'd been stationary for too long, and almost everyone else who'd been ejected from the rec hut was already back in their barracks.

"Put some ice on that," she said quickly. Then she turned and walked away.

# THREE

DAKOTA COULDN'T SLEEP at all that night. Her mind was filled with racing thoughts, anxieties, questions. A walk might have helped, but by night, that was impossible—the hut doors and windows would be locked until the morning alarm, and even if they weren't, she'd be lucky to get ten feet outside before a Mek sensor picked up her movement. So she just lay on her bunk, tossing and turning, trying to will herself to sleep.

"What's wrong?"

The voice was barely a whisper. She opened her eyes to see Sam kneeling beside her bunk.

"Nothing," she said, keeping her voice low. "Go back to sleep."

"I will when you will."

Thin slivers of light from the Mek towers bled through the edges of the window, revealing Sam's kind smile—the smile she had grown to rely on so much during their years in the open. But she could tell he was worried about her. That had been the pattern of their lives together for as long as Dakota could remember—taking turns worrying about each other.

"What happened tonight?" he asked. "I heard the commotion."

"Couple of guys had too much shine, got into it," she said casually.

But Sam could always tell when she was lying. So he said nothing, just sat there, waiting for the truth to come.

"Sam," she said finally, "how much do you know about what really happened at Bismarck?"

"What do you mean, *really* happened? I've told you the story a thousand times."

That was barely an exaggeration. It was the story Dakota had most often asked Sam to tell her in their time before the township, when they hunkered down by night in old subways and parking structures, listening to the sound of distant gunfire. She'd lie with her head in his lap and he'd stroke her hair and tell her about the last city and humanity's last stand outside of it, about the Gundogs, and about their mother, who was the last of them still standing, still fighting the Mek even after the rest had fallen. It was often the only thing that got her to sleep.

"Some people say that Mom and the others ran away when the battle was lost," said Dakota. "That there's no Gundog still standing outside the last city."

"They only say that because they're jealous," said Sam. "Because that's what *their* folks did in the war—surrender or hide or run. Mom was a hero; she died fighting for something she believed in. And they have no idea what that must feel like."

"But how do you *know* she was a hero, Sam? I mean know for sure? You weren't there, and you're too young to really remember."

"I remember what Dad told me before he died, and that's enough."

"Tell it to me again," she said.

He smiled down at her, then shifted his position and sat on the side of her bunk. "Come here," he said.

She placed her head in his lap while he stroked her hair and told her the story one more time. And before he was halfway done, she was sound asleep.

* * *

The next morning after breakfast ration, Dakota was on her way to the roof she'd been working on, when a Mek supervisor approached and re-assigned her to replace the broken door to the rec hut. Normally that job would have taken her the better part of the morning, but since she couldn't keep her eye on Sam from down on the ground, she managed to get the new door fitted and hung in just over an hour. The Mek supervisor scanned the door suspiciously, as if not trusting the quality of work done in such haste, but it ultimately conceded that she'd done the job satisfactorily and allowed her to get back to her roof.

As she climbed the ladder, she wondered if she'd made a tactical error. She'd stretched her time on the roof by working as slowly as she could get away with, but now she'd clearly demonstrated that she could work much faster than that. Once that data was fed into the algorithm, would the Mek grow to question her honesty? The thought frightened her. The trust they placed in her was the only thing keeping her brother alive.

She resumed her work, picking up where she had left off the day before. But it was distractingly hot today, and there was no shade on the roof; she was finding it difficult to concentrate. Her mind insisted on returning to the same nagging thoughts that had kept her awake the night before.

Why had she stayed to listen to the Gundog story when every instinct had told her to leave? For that matter, why had she gone to story time in the first place, when all she really wanted was to stay with Sam? And why—this one bugged her most of all, like an unscratchable itch—why was it not the insults directed at her own family that had provoked her into sudden violence, but the vulgar crack about Runyon's intentions toward her?

Runyon and his stupid swollen eye. It wasn't even that bad of an injury, yet at the sight of it last night, she had been tempted to take him back to her barracks and tend to it herself. Why did she even care? *He's not even—*

She hit her thumb with the hammer and cursed loudly enough that several workers below looked up at her. She turned away, embarrassed and annoyed, as she shook out her hand. She'd gotten herself good; that thumb was sure to hurt for the rest of the day, at least.

She took a swig of lukewarm water from the plastic bottle on her belt, then centered herself by watching Sam working in the gardening plot below. He must have felt her gaze on him, because he turned and looked up at her, then propped his rake against his body and waved. She smiled and waved back.

She was about to get back to work when she heard a familiar sound behind her: the grinding of mechanical gears indicating that the township's main gate was opening. She turned and watched as the Mek enforcers floated over to the entrance, taking up positions to discourage anyone from trying to make a break for it while the gate was open. And their presence was definitely discouraging. While the observers and utility drones could give you a jolt strong enough to drop you into a convulsing heap, an enforcer could simply vaporize you outright, from fifty meters away. Dakota had seen it happen before, and so had most of the others, so when the enforcers took up positions, any workers who found themselves in the vicinity were quick to find somewhere else to be.

A Mek transport—an armored train comprising five short windowless cars, held off the ground by some kind of magnetic repulsor tech—floated into the township, the gate closing behind it. Just about everyone was watching now, as curious as Dakota was to see what was inside. The Mek usually tolerated this—too many idlers to jolt all at once, Dakota supposed—and a convoy delivery rarely took more than a couple of minutes, so the work stoppage was minimal.

Sometimes these transports brought raw materials for the township's factories and foundries. Sometimes they carried a general resupply of parts, food and water. And sometimes they brought in new workers, either captured out in the world—though Dakota wondered how many free people could possibly be left twenty years after the war—or transferred from another township under orders from the algorithm.

The transport came to a halt, and the Mek enforcers converged around it. That was enough for Dakota to know what was inside: new workers. Sure enough, when the train car doors slid open with a mechanical hiss, men and women shuffled out from the darkness within, squinting against the bright sunlight.

It was easy to tell which were freshly captured and which were transfers from another township. Transfers wore the uniform coveralls issued to all township workers, while the new workers wore whatever ragged clothes they had been captured in. But even if they had all been dressed alike, Dakota would have been able to distinguish the two groups simply by their demeanor. The new captures always looked terrified and uncertain. They didn't know exactly what fate awaited them here, but they'd heard the horror stories. Transfers, by contrast, looked resigned, numb. Their wills broken long ago by years of Mek confinement.

One man, barefoot and dressed in a torn, oil-stained sweater and filthy, ragged jeans, stumbled and fell as he exited the transport. A drone was on him instantly, grabbing him with its pincers and hauling him back to his feet before moving him along with a jolt. The man was stick-thin, severely emaciated—another obvious sign of a new capture. Though the food the Mek served in the township was unappetizing, it was calorie-dense, and no one was ever malnourished; whereas those on the outside were often reduced to surviving on berries and bracken, as Dakota and Sam once had.

Dakota found herself thinking, just for a moment, that maybe the poor man was better off here. Judging by his current condition, she doubted he'd have lasted more than another week on the outside, whereas here at least he'd have food and clean clothes. But she dismissed the thought as quickly as it had come, ashamed for having even entertained it. She remembered the words of her brother, repeated so many times during their fugitive years, when Dakota, in her gnawing hunger and despair, had suggested that it might be better for them if they simply surrendered to the Mek.

*Freedom is better,* he would tell her. *Freedom is always better.*

With typical Mek efficiency, the drones sorted the prisoners into two groups. The transfers were escorted directly to the barracks huts that would be their new homes, while the new captures were taken to an imposing concrete slab of a structure known to all as the orientation building. Everyone had to go through orientation after their capture—a week-long process in which new arrivals were rigorously familiarized with the rules and operating procedures of the township. That was the stated purpose, anyway. In Dakota's view, orientation was more about weeding out the weak and the troublesome before they could become a liability. Most new arrivals would leave that building ready to work hard, obey orders, and do whatever was necessary to survive under the township regime. But some would never leave it at all. They were recycled.

As the two groups were led along separate paths to their destinations, Dakota noticed one young man who stood out from the rest. He was in the transfer group, but instead of wearing the standard coveralls, he wore baggy cargo pants, lace-up running shoes, and a faded T-shirt that read "OLD NAVY ATHLETIC DEPT. 1994," whatever that meant. She reckoned him to be about twenty-five or twenty-six, although something about him suggested a soul much older. His hair was wild and unkempt, but he seemed to be in good physical shape, and his eyes were keen and bright as they darted around. That was what truly made him stand out, more so than his strange clothes. He seemed alert, observant, alive—so different from those around him, with their haunted, barren expressions. Dakota had never seen anyone quite like him, except perhaps Sam in his younger days, before Mek captivity stole all the fight out of him.

As he surveyed the township, he glanced up at the roof where Dakota was working and stared directly at her. Suddenly feeling conspicuous, she turned away, pretending to busy herself. And when she dared look back again, he was no longer looking at her. Instead, he seemed to be surveying every township worker in the vicinity, pausing to examine each face before moving on to the next. He was still doing it when a Mek drone gave him a jolt to spur him through the door of his barracks hut with the other transfers.

The gate opened once more, and the transport, now empty of its human cargo, exited the township. The whole thing had taken less than two minutes. And yet, for the rest of the day, Dakota couldn't stop thinking about the alert young man who had caught her looking at him.

# FOUR

FOR THE NEXT few days, Dakota found herself surreptitiously watching the strange newcomer. The morning after his arrival, he had emerged from his barracks wearing newly issued uniform coveralls, but even dressed the same as everyone else, his behavior set him apart. Dakota began to form a picture of someone who had been in Mek captivity for a long time. Not because he was particularly cowed or compliant—quite the opposite—but because he seemed so familiar with the rhythms and routines of township life, in particular how the Mek regulated and policed them. He knew exactly how long he could idle or how far he could stray before attracting the attention of an observer, and he used that knowledge to make himself known around the township very quickly.

In fact, in just a few short days, he must have introduced himself to almost a hundred different workers. Most people shrugged him off, for fear of attracting unwanted attention, but that was what was so strange about it. Why was he making the effort at all? New arrivals typically kept their heads down, at least for the first few weeks, until someone else, usually a more veteran worker, made the first approach. Yet this man was casually making the rounds like he'd been there forever.

Dakota didn't know what to make of it, but she suspected it couldn't be anything good. From time to time, a worker would arrive who ingratiated themselves with others, then reported to the Mek what they had learned in exchange for preferential treatment. A spy, essentially. But if that was what was going on here, the man was being unusually brazen about it.

Not that it mattered, because that wasn't really what was bothering her about him anyway. What bugged her was that she couldn't take her eyes off of him. He wasn't like anyone she had ever seen, inside the fence or outside. Few people made her feel nervous or self-conscious, but something about him did. The way he carried himself, confident but guarded, gave the impression that even while he was hard at work, his mind was somewhere else entirely. Dakota supposed he was much like herself in that way—but while she knew why she was so often distracted, his motivations remained a mystery.

And that was what he was to her: one big mystery.

By now, Dakota had completed her roof assignment, but she had managed to get herself another job where she could keep her eye on Sam. She was managing the tool shed, where workers in this section checked out whatever was needed for the day's labor. It was her responsibility to keep the tools in good repair and make sure none went missing. The shed was located close enough to Sam that she could see him, at a distance, working in his little plot of garden, and as an added bonus, he was required to come to her at the start and end of every day to check his tools in and out. Sometimes he'd even fake a problem with a hoe or rake, creating an excuse to see Dakota and get it replaced. She appreciated these little efforts he made to check in with her whenever he could.

Working in the she also allowed her to listen in on gossip and make a few discreet inquiries, which is how Dakota learned the strange newcomer's name: Falk. He had gotten himself a job as a water carrier, which meant he walked around their section of the township with a ten-gallon tank strapped to his back, dispensing water to thirsty workers from a hose. It was a job nobody wanted, hauling around such a heavy load, particularly in this hot weather, which countered the idea that he was collaborating with the Mek in exchange for favors. But it did very conveniently facilitate what appeared to be Falk's apparent goal of talking with as many township workers as possible.

Exactly one week after his arrival, she was seriously considering setting her nerves aside and asking him what he was up to. But then he made the decision for her, at least indirectly. While she was at her shed, checking out a pipe wrench for an irrigation worker, she saw Falk speaking with her brother—and that was all the nudge she needed. She still had no idea what the man's plan was, but if there was any possible danger to it, she didn't want Sam anywhere near him. So she left her shed and jogged over to them, still clutching the pipe wrench, just in case Falk needed to understand that she meant business.

She found Sam and Falk in the middle of what sounded like harmless small talk.

"Hey, Dak," said Sam. "What're you doing over here?" He looked around for drones. She was out of her designated area, and the Mek would soon be there to jolt her back to work.

"I don't want you talking to him," Dakota said. "We don't know who he is."

"Let's fix that," said the newcomer. "Hi, I'm Falk." He extended his hand.

Dakota just glared at it. An uneasy silence fell over them both, until Sam saw fit to break it.

"This is my sister, Dakota," he said. "I call her Dak."

"Nice to meet you, Dak," said Falk. He seemed utterly unfazed by Dakota's unwelcoming demeanor. "I was just asking Sam what happened to his arm."

She was about to tell him to leave her brother the hell alone, when a Mek observer approached. She raised her hands to acknowledge its authority and started walking back toward the tool shed, glancing behind her to make sure the drone was moving Falk along, too.

* * *

At the end of the workday, when Dakota was making sure all the tools that had been checked out that morning had been checked back in, a rap sounded at the door. She swung around to find Falk standing there in the open doorway, silhouetted against the waning daylight.

"You and I need to talk," he said.

It took Dakota a moment to respond, and even then the words caught in her throat. This man made her nervous in ways she didn't understand, and that scared her.

"No, you need to go to your barracks if you don't want to get jolted," she said. "There'll be a Mek here any second."

"Actually, we have about twenty-five seconds," he said. "I need to know what happened to your brother's arm. Did the Mek take it?"

Dakota struggled to find words again. None of this made any damn sense. "What? No. He lost it in an accident. Why would they—who *are* you?"

She saw the Mek drone coming now, off in the distance. At the rate it was moving, it was about fifteen seconds away. Falk's prediction had been surprisingly accurate.

"Do you remember if Sam had a tattoo?" Falk asked. "On the inside of his forearm?" He tapped his right sleeve to indicate where he meant.

That stopped Dakota cold. *How the hell—*

"How do you know that?" she asked.

The drone was about ten seconds away now. Falk didn't look around, but surely he could hear it coming. Still, he didn't move.

"Because I have it, too," he said, rolling up his sleeve.

Dakota's mouth fell open. There on his forearm was an abstract diagram, a haphazard assemblage of lines and dots. To anyone else, it would have been meaningless. But it shook Dakota to the core because she had seen that exact same tattoo many times before. On the inside of her brother's right forearm, before he lost it in the steel press.

"What—what is it?" she asked. Her voice was shaking.

The drone was just seconds away, its jolt prod crackling. Still, Falk refused to move.

"It's a map," he said, rolling his sleeve back down.

"A map to what?"

"Liberation."

And that was the last thing he said before the Mek jolted him in the back and he fell to the ground, his body twitching. All Dakota could do was watch in silent shock as the drone grabbed him and hauled him away.

* * *

Another restless night followed. How was Dakota supposed to sleep after that? She had so many questions and no chance of getting answers until tomorrow, when she'd see Falk again. Hopefully. If the Mek decided to move him to another section…

How strange, she thought, that she had come to view Falk so differently, and so quickly. In the space of just a few days she had gone from feeling intrigued by him, to being suspicious of him, to thinking of him as a possible danger to her family—and now she was lying awake, counting the hours until she could talk to him again. There was nothing she hated more than an unsolved riddle, and Falk was several of them rolled into one. How did he know about Sam's tattoo? Why did he have one of his own, exactly the same? How could it be a map? What did he mean by liberation? So many questions, and no damn—

*Stop it, Dak.*

There was no point driving herself crazy. She would find no answers here, tonight.

Unless…

She looked across the darkened hut to her brother's bunk. He was snoring gently. She could tiptoe over and wake him, ask him about the tattoo. She'd asked him about it before, many times during their years on the run, and he'd always brushed off her interest, saying he didn't know what it was or even remember how he got it. But Dakota had always suspected he knew more than he was telling her.

And now she felt certain of it. It seemed inconceivable that he had been lying to her this whole time, but what other explanation was there?

Yet now he would *have* to tell her the truth. Because if he didn't, Falk would. And if Sam had been keeping secrets from her… he'd want to be the one to come clean. Not have some stranger come along and do it for him.

But now wasn't the time. As badly as Dakota wanted to talk to him, she couldn't risk doing it in the barracks, in the dead of night, even at a whisper, because there was too much risk that someone would overhear and decide to earn themselves a better work assignment or a double ration by passing it along to the Mek. She would have to wait.

Dakota had never been very good at waiting.

* * *

At breakfast ration, Dakota took a double dose of the stim drink the Mek gave them to keep them alert and active. It tasted foul and it made her jittery, but she was so tired, and she needed her wits about her today. She hadn't yet spoken to Sam other than to say good morning and help him dress and get ready for the morning head count. There hadn't been an opportunity to talk more, and besides, during the night, she'd made a decision. She wouldn't risk upsetting Sam with what he might take to be an unwarranted accusation. She needed more information first.

From Falk.

As she walked to the tool shed, she looked for him everywhere. But there was no sign of him, which filled her with dread. Her life, both before and after Mek captivity, had trained her to always assume the worst. And in the township, there were so many worsts to choose from. What if he had been moved to a different section? The township was vast, and she might never find him. What if the Mek had put him in the punishment block? He might be there for weeks. What if he was hurt—or even dead? The last time she'd seen him he hadn't even been conscious. Other prisoners had died from jolts that weren't intended to kill; it was rare, but it happened.

She found herself looking toward the recycling structure. If anyone had died overnight, there'd be black smoke coming from its two giant chimneys. There was none. But still, what if—

And then there he was, and she felt her entire body slacken with relief. He was alive, still in her section, still with the same assignment, carrying the heavy plastic tank on his back, the water sloshing about as he walked. Surely his rounds would allow him to come to her today, to linger long enough to tell her something more about the map on his arm.

So for the rest of that day, she kept an eye on him, whenever his rounds took him within her field of vision. Something was different about him today. He wasn't chatty; in fact he didn't talk to a single worker as he dispensed his water. He just went about his business.

And then Dakota realized why.

*He's already found who he was looking for.*

Yet he never made his way over to her, didn't even look in her direction. Dakota's impatience grew, and the extra stim drink didn't help. Her frustration and anxiety rose to the point that she was considering excuses to leave her designated area and go talk to him.

But finally, while passing by on his rounds, he looked at her. Right at her. And gave a conspiratorial nod intended just for her.

She froze, and her heart stopped for a moment.

Falk got the attention of the nearest observer drone and made the signal to request a bathroom break. A light nestled within the drone's face turned green, granting him permission. Falk set down his water tank and walked to the lavatory hut, sneaking another glance at Dakota as he went. She understood and made the same signal to the observer. When she got a green light as well, she hurried over to join him.

"How'd you sleep?" he asked as they walked together.

"I didn't," she replied. "Tell me about the map."

"Can't risk telling you too much yet," he said.

"You can trust me."

"It's not a question of trust. You ever been interrogated by the Mek? I have. Believe me, you'll tell them whatever they want to know."

"Look," she said, talking fast now. "You can't just come marching in here all mysterious and asking about my brother and then showing me some secret map and talking about *liberation*, whatever that means, and not expect me to—"

"Okay, slow down," he said. "Did you drink too much stim or something?"

"I may have had an extra one look that's not the point you need to tell me something that makes sense or I'll—"

Falk stopped. They'd arrived at the lavatory hut, with its different entrances for men and women. They'd have to separate.

He glanced around, kept his voice low.

"My father was a Gundog pilot. Like your mother. They both fought at Bismarck, in the last battle. Before they died, they left something for us. Call it an inheritance."

The Mek drone was floating toward them. Falk disappeared into the men's lavatory, and Dakota had no choice but to go on into the women's, where she took what felt like the longest piss of her life.

"What do you mean, inheritance?" she asked as they walked back from the lavatory hut together. "You mean that map?"

"Yes. I mean that map."

"What is it? Where does it lead?"

"You'll find that out when we get there."

That stopped her dead in her tracks. "What?"

"Keep walking. Eyes everywhere."

She resumed walking, caught up with him. "Are you talking about escaping? Because that's impossible."

"It's not impossible. I've been in six townships before this one. I escaped from them all."

That took a moment for Dakota to process; it seemed barely believable. But something about Falk's demeanor, his uncommon confidence, told her it was true.

"Okay, but you got recaptured every time."

"That was by design. Each time I escaped, I'd make my way toward another township, get myself captured close by so they'd put me in that one. Until I found who I was looking for."

"You mean me?"

"Actually, your brother. But I'm a little worried about him now that I've seen him. Would he be up for this? Seems like he's not… all the way there, in himself."

That hit Dakota hard, because she knew it was true. Sam hadn't been the man she'd once known for a long time now. Still, her first instinct was to defend him, protect him, as she always had.

"He kept us alive for years when we were on the outside," she insisted. "Whenever I felt like I couldn't go on, he was strong enough for us both."

"That's who he was *then*," said Falk. "Who is he now? I've seen that look before, in a lot of folks, in every township I've been in. All the fight gone out of them. If I'm taking you two with me, I need to know there's fight in you both. In *you* there's plenty. I can see that. But can he honestly say the same? If he can't, I can't afford the risk."

Dakota hated how right he was. But she couldn't lie, so she changed the subject.

"Why do you even need us?" she asked. "It's your map, your plan. Why not just go do whatever the hell this is by yourself?"

"Because when we get where we're going, it's going to take two of us. I can't do this alone. I had a brother, and we were supposed to do this together, but the Mek..."

He didn't need to finish the sentence. Dakota knew how it ended.

"You have to tell me more than this if I'm going to trust you," she said. They were almost back at Dakota's tool shed and had little time left to talk.

"Your brother was told everything I was, back when we were kids," said Falk. "Why don't you ask him?"

"If that's true, why hasn't he ever told me?" asked Dakota.

"Maybe you should ask him that, too," said Falk.

And then he veered away from her, back to where his water tank was waiting. Dakota walked the rest of the way to the tool shed in a daze, her mind filled with more questions than ever.

# FIVE

AS DIFFICULT AS it was, Dakota sat on what she had learned for three days and nights without saying anything to Sam. He had even asked her what she and Falk had talked about later that same day, and she had lied, said they were just chatting. She had so much to say, so many questions, but it wasn't a conversation that could be had quickly, and it wasn't easy to get enough time alone with him. The Mek were always watching.

The opportunity to talk finally came when it was once again story time in the rec hut. Their barracks emptied out completely; word was, that the guys with the secret still had cooked up a fresh batch of potato shine and there was enough for everyone. So for the first time in a week, Dakota and Sam were alone in the barracks. He was lying on his bunk, reading an old book, when Dakota came and sat beside him.

He glanced up at her. "What's up?"

Dakota kept her voice low. No one really knew how sensitive Mek audio sensors were.

"What was that tattoo you used to have on your arm?" she asked.

He lowered the book. "What's brought this on?"

"Just answer me. The truth this time, please."

He sat up. "I already told you the truth, every time you asked about it. I don't know. I don't remember."

"Falk says you do know."

"Falk? The new guy? You believe him over me?"

"Actually, yeah, I do," she said.

"Why?"

"Because he has the exact same tattoo. And he knows exactly what it is. It's some kind of map, isn't it?"

There was a pause as Sam took that in. Then he reached up and pinched the bridge of his nose. "Shit," he said.

"The truth," said Dakota. And her tone made it clear that neither of them was going anywhere until she got it.

"Okay… look," he said finally. "There's a reason I never told you. My whole life, all I've ever tried to do is keep you safe. And that map would only have put us in danger."

"Where does it lead?" Dakota asked. That was the question she wanted answered more than any other.

"I honestly don't know. I swear, I really do remember very little of this. I was only six years old when Mom gave it to me, right before she left for the last battle. She said that it led to some place called the Four Faces, where there might be a way to fight back against the Mek. That's all I know."

"And you never did anything, never said anything?" Dakota asked, horrified. "Those were Mom's last words to you, and you just *ignored* them?"

"Mom never meant for me to go there *alone*," said Sam. "Dad was supposed to take us there when the time came, but he died not long after he got us out of Bismarck, and then it was just us two kids all alone. What was I supposed to do? Take you on some suicide mission across hundreds of miles of Mek territory? And to do what? Restart a war we'd already lost? No. I put you first, I kept you alive, and I'm not going to apologize for that."

"If you wanted to put me first, you should have told me the truth," Dakota said. "We've never lied to each other. Never."

"I knew if I told you, you'd want to go," said Sam. "I'd never be able to talk you out of it, and you'd wind up getting yourself killed. You've got too much of Mom in you, Dak. That's always been your problem."

"Maybe yours is that you don't have enough," Dakota snapped. She instantly regretted it as she saw in Sam's eyes how much that stung. She lowered her gaze, ashamed. "I'm sorry. I didn't mean that."

"It's okay," said Sam. "Maybe you're right about that. Even at my best, I never had the same fire in me that you did. And I haven't been my best for a long time."

There was a long moment of silence before Dakota spoke again.

"Falk says he knows how to get out of here. He wants to take you and me with him."

Sam eyed her skeptically. "He said that? That he wants to take us both. Not just you."

"He'd *have* to take us both, Sam. There's no way I'd go without you."

Sam gave that some thought, and when he finally spoke, he sounded unusually certain. "No, that's exactly what you should do."

"Don't even say that," said Dakota. "No matter what, it's you and me. It's always been that way, and it always will be. If we both go and make it out of here, it'll be just like it used to be. Making our way together."

Sam shook his head. "You said it yourself, Dak. We can't live in the past; there's nothing for us back there. I'm a cripple. I'd only slow you down. And I just don't have it in me anymore. I spent it all already." He reached up and touched the side of her face. "I want you to go. For both of us."

Dakota felt tears forming in her eyes. She gripped his hand. "I don't think I can."

"I *know* you can," said Sam. "You've always been the stronger one, even when you didn't know it. And now that you know the truth—that maybe there's something out there to find—you're never going to be able to stay here. It'll eat away at you, a little more every day, until you wind up like me. I won't let that happen. I couldn't bear to watch it. It'd be the end of me, too. Dak, look at me."

She looked at him.

"I'm sorry I never told you the truth," he said. "But maybe this is how I make it right. I'm asking you to go. Please. Do it for me. Go with Falk, to the Four Faces, and whatever it is that Mom left for us there. And when you find it, come back here and smash these Mek motherfuckers into junk. Promise me you'll do that."

Dakota was crying now and found it difficult to speak. But she managed the only words she needed.

"I promise."

# SIX

OVER THE NEXT three weeks, Dakota stole every moment she could with Falk to plan their escape and what would come after. He managed to get himself transferred to a labor detail that required him to check tools in and out from Dakota's shed regularly. They took their lavatory breaks together as many times as they felt they could without alerting the Mek's observers; too many times and the algorithm would detect a "suspicious behavior pattern" and intervene. And they attended story time in the rec hut, the longest stretch of social time they were allowed. They sat in seclusion near the back of the room, where they ignored the stories being told at the hearth and made up one of their own—a story they hoped would end with them finding the Four Faces and the secret that had been left for them there, twenty years ago. Neither of them had any idea what that secret might be, nor how it could possibly ignite a new war against an enemy that had already conquered humanity. All they knew was they had to try. To do any less would be to dishonor the memory of their parents, who had died fighting for their freedom.

Falk taught Dakota how to read the map on his arm, which was actually two maps overlaid atop one another. The dots represented stars, which Dakota hadn't seen in years because of the Mek tower lights that blazed all night long. The lines and other symbols were landmarks—rivers, mountains, what remained of roads. By aligning the stars with the landmarks, it was possible to navigate a path to the Four Faces, which Falk explained was not marked on the map—you just had to keep following the path and you'd know it when you saw it. That was how his father had explained it to him.

But first they had to get outside the perimeter. Dakota had always thought it impossible, though over the years, she'd seen no shortage of workers desperate enough to try. Most simply fled through the gates when they opened to admit a transport; few of them made it even fifty meters before being vaporized by a Mek enforcer or tower gun. Some tried to stow away aboard the transports themselves, but the Mek sensors always detected them. The closest anyone had ever come to escape was the man who scaled the fence during a freak power outage that rendered the Mek's perimeter defenses inert. He was gone the whole night, and many in the township were just beginning to believe he might actually have made it until, just after the morning alarm, his body was dragged back by a Mek search party and taken to the recycling structure. It would have been easier for the Mek to leave the body where it fell, but Dakota figured their algorithm told them it was better to bring it back to the township for all to see, as an example. If true, they calculated correctly—that was three years ago, and no one had tried to escape since.

Until now. Falk claimed to know of a particular flaw that existed in the design of each township perimeter. There was a gap about two meters wide where the coverage areas of the closest Mek sensor stations were supposed to overlap but didn't—and due to some tiny quirk in their programming, the sensors failed to recognize the error. If you knew exactly where to stand, Falk said, you were invisible. He had spent the final few days of his water carrier detail surveying as much of the perimeter as he could, and he believed he had found this township's blind spot. He had even tested it by standing at the spot by the fence for a full two minutes. Not once did a Mek come by to move him along. That was where they would get out.

Dakota's tool shed detail proved to be invaluable, for there was much in there that they could use. As long as she marked an item as "checked in" at the end of the workday, it wouldn't be missed until the following morning, and by then she and Falk would be long gone.

Or at least, that was the plan.

The first step in that plan—getting out of their locked barracks at night—was the easiest part. Dakota had once been assigned to repair a damaged lock on another hut's window shutter and discovered that the mechanism slid open and closed via a surprisingly low-tech electromagnet. The lock wasn't even alarmed. For an alien race that had conquered all of humanity, the Mek were sometimes surprisingly sloppy when it came to details. So Dakota had palmed a small magnet, a battery, and some wiring from the township factory, and improvised a device that could slide the bolt open from the inside. This was all during her first years in captivity, when she still gave serious thought to escaping with Sam. But though the device worked, she never used it, because the window shutter was the easy part. It was the two hundred meters of open, floodlit ground between the hut and the fence—not to mention the fence itself—that was the problem.

Except, these things weren't problems at all. Not according to Falk.

"The Mek sensor stations around the perimeter pick up on everything," Falk explained to her one night during story time, the last one they'd have together before their planned escape attempt. "Motion, sound, even your heartbeat. But the drones that patrol the interior at night only track thermal output."

"Isn't that enough?" Dakota asked. "We can't stop our bodies from generating heat."

It was amazing, she thought, how close she and Falk had become during these past few weeks, and how much she now trusted him. Every experience in her life had taught her to trust no one—except Sam, of course. In their years on the run, every now and then they'd forget that lesson, trusting some kind soul they'd encountered. They were betrayed every time. Held at gunpoint for their food and supplies, or sold out to the Mek by those looking to save their own miserable hides. Every one of those betrayals hammered the point home, until Dakota had found it almost impossible to put her faith in anyone.

And yet here she was, risking everything on a man she'd known for less than a month. Maybe it was the promise of finding some kind of connection with the parents she had never known that had made her lower her defenses. Maybe it was because he was as careful and as guarded as she was. Or maybe it was his eyes, the way he looked at her.

She allowed herself to entertain that last thought for only a moment before batting it away. *Don't be ridiculous.*

"How close is your wash hut to your barracks?" Falk asked, and Dakota had to bring herself back to the conversation, remember where she was. Something about body heat.

"It's close," she said. "Two huts over." The wash huts, where workers cleaned up at the end of the day, were just big communal showers. As the township fixer, Dakota had spent a lot of time in them over the years because even the Mek hadn't come up with a reliable way to avoid plumbing problems. Something was always leaking or blocked, or the water was freezing cold or scalding hot.

"Mine's the next hut over," said Falk. "That's good. All we need to do is time our runs from our barracks to the wash hut to avoid whatever drone's patrolling between them."

"And then what?" Dakota asked. "How is the wash hut going to help us?"

"To be invisible to the thermal sensors, all we have to do is drop our core body temperature," Falk explained. "So we're going to stand under freezing cold showers for at least five minutes before we make a run for the blind spot. But we have to move fast: the effect will only last a minute or two before our bodies heat back up."

She stared at him. "Are you kidding me?"

"Do you want to get out of here or not?"

"We'll freeze to death," said Dakota. "Do you know how cold it gets out here at night?"

"I do," said Falk. "I've done this before. Look, it's not going to be pleasant, but it's the only way. Unless you know a better one?"

She didn't.

# SEVEN

EXACTLY FORTY DAYS after Falk first arrived in the township, he and Dakota attempted their escape.

Everything they'd have to do to get from their barracks to the fence and beyond was planned out in precise detail. If something went wrong, it wouldn't be for want of preparation. The hardest part, as Dakota had feared, was saying goodbye to Sam. They kept it short, as they both knew the longer they spent, the more agonizing it would be. She was reminded of the time she dislocated her shoulder tumbling down a rocky hillside while running to evade a Mek patrol, and Sam had had to pop it back in. It hurt so much Dakota wouldn't allow him to touch her, so fearful was she of the pain of resetting the joint. He told her then, *The quicker we do this, the less it will hurt. You're strong, you can do this, don't be afraid.* He told her the same thing now. One last gentle kiss on her forehead before they both retired to their bunks, Dakota trying not to cry. She had to keep a clear head, because this night, more than any other in her entire life, she would need all her wits about her.

It had been difficult to work out how to synchronize the escape with Falk, as he was in a different barracks and there were no clocks, no way to gauge the passing of time save for the movement of the sun in the sky and the various Mek alarms. And after lights-out, there was no sun, and no alarms. This wasn't a challenge Falk had been forced to deal with before, since all of his previous escapes had been on his own.

But Dakota had an idea. About an hour after sundown, the Mek tower lights would blaze from partial to full brightness, and every time they did this, they made a sound, a kind of mechanical *ker-chunk*. For the past few nights, Dakota and Falk had stayed awake in their bunks listening for it, to make sure they could both hear it. That was the sound that would allow them to synchronize.

Dakota now stared at the wooden slats on the ceiling above her bunk, waiting for that sound. She was trembling, adrenaline coursing through her body like it had when she was a child hiding from Mek scouts. Life in the township had been miserable, boring, deadening, but not dangerous. At least, not in the physical sense. If you knew the rules and abided by them, there was little chance of anything happening to you other than an occasional jolt or possibly a work injury. After years of just barely clawing for survival on the outside, Dakota found it strange to realize that this moment, tonight, was the first time her life would actually be at risk since she and Sam had arrived there six years ago.

And it was certainly at risk. So much could go wrong. What if her makeshift electromagnets—she'd scrounged the parts to make new ones for both her and Falk—failed to open the window shutters? What if she mis-timed the drone patrol route past her hut and was spotted? What if this shower trick of Falk's didn't work? What if the blind spot in the perimeter wasn't exactly where he thought it was? What if, what if, what if, what—

*Ker-chunk.*

There it was, the telltale sound as the Mek tower lights switched to full illumination. That was the one downside to this stage of their plan—the bright light that would unavoidably flood in when she opened the window shutters could alert someone in her barracks, who might then raise the alarm in hopes of being rewarded with an extra ration or easier work detail. But there was nothing she could do about that except hope for the best; Falk would already be up and moving, counting on her to do the same.

She retrieved her electromagnet from inside the stuffing of her pillow and silently swung her legs off the bunk. The floorboards in her barracks tended to creak, but not in the area around her bed—one small blessing. As quietly and as carefully as she could, she crept to the nearest window.

She lifted the magnet up to the spot where she knew the locking bolt was, and then moved it from left to right. It took two tries before she heard the bolt on the other side slide open.

Then she waited for the sound of the Mek patrol drone outside. If the Mek followed a predictable pattern—and they were nothing if not predictable—then once it came and went, she'd have twenty seconds before it came this way again.

She heard the Mek coming… and then going.

She had to move now.

She pushed open the shutter, feeling a wave of relief when it didn't creak, and in one nimble move she vaulted over the ledge into the starkly lit compound, her boots crunching on the dirt. Quickly, she re-closed the shutter, slid the locking bolt shut, and tossed the magnet into the crawlspace beneath the hut.

And then she ran.

Her wash hut was only two buildings over, but that short sprint across open ground—fully exposed, heart pounding—felt like an eternity.

She made it to the wash hut and slipped inside. It wasn't locked and had no windows, leaving it pitch black inside. But over the past several days Dakota had counted the steps and turns from the hut entrance to the showers. Walking blind, she followed the mental map she'd made, and she was relieved when she reached out and felt the metal water valves on the tile wall. She turned the cold valve on full, wondering if Mek security would detect the anomalous activity in the plumbing system in the middle of the night and send a drone to investigate. Falk had assured her they wouldn't, and she trusted him, but right now, in the moment, all she could think about was what could still go wrong.

She tested the temperature with her hand—it was about as cold as water could get without turning to ice—then braced herself and stepped, fully clothed, beneath the shower head.

The water hit her like a thousand ice-cold needles, and it was all she could do not to shriek. It was worse than she'd feared—and Falk had told her to fear the worst.

She started counting. Falk had taught her how to do an accurate five-minute count using a trick he'd learned. *One Mississippi, Two Mississippi, Three Mississippi* all the way to sixty, and then repeat it five times over. Dakota had no idea what Mississippi meant, but she found that reciting it over and over helped keep her mind off the agony of slowly freezing to death. By the time she hit *Sixty Mississippi* for the fifth time, she was chilled to the bone, feeling numb in her extremities, and shaking like a leaf. She was barely able to command her trembling fingers to turn the water off. She took short, shallow, gasping breaths as she shuffled her way back through the darkness to the door.

When she opened it, the cold air on her sopping wet skin hit her like another sheet of ice. But she stepped outside, squinting her dark-adapted eyes against the bright lights of the Mek towers, and made her way down the hut's steps.

Until a familiar sound brought her to a dead stop. The sound of a Mek drone.

She looked behind her to see it floating right toward her from no more than ten meters away. She was too terrified to run, for all the good running would have done her, and found herself instead thinking, in her final moments, how miraculous it was that she had even made it this far, that at least she'd had the courage to try, that she would die on her feet and not on her knees.

She stiffened, straightening her back. *Okay, you Mek piece of shit, let's get this over with. And by the way, on behalf of the entire human race, go fuck yourself.*

She closed her eyes as the Mek drew within kill distance…

…and then simply floated right on past her, continuing its patrol like she wasn't even there.

Falk had been right. With her lowered body temperature, it hadn't registered her presence at all. Their plan actually work.

She darted off toward the arranged rendezvous point, still marveling at her close encounter, and arrived at the northeast corner of the maintenance building, the closest structure to the blind spot. She was so goddamn cold. And as she stood there, staring at the floodlit fence line a hundred meters away, shivering like she'd never feel warm again, only one thought went through her mind.

*Where is Falk?*

For her, everything had gone exactly as planned, but it had to go well for both of them or it was all for nothing. She couldn't possibly do this alone. Only Falk knew precisely where the blind spot was. Only Falk had the map. She found herself contemplating how stupid this whole idea was, leaving her beloved brother behind to follow a man she barely knew based on a promise and a tattoo. She wondered if she still had time to make it back to her barracks and slip back inside, pretend none of this had ever—

"You made it."

She whipped around to find Falk standing right there behind her, his coveralls soaked through, his body shuddering with cold.

"Any trouble?" he asked.

"If there was, I wouldn't be here," she said.

"Good point. Dumb question. You ready?"

She nodded. It was far too late to back out now.

"Stay close to me. Remember, the blind spot's barely two meters wide. You have to stay *right* next to me or we're both dead. You understand?"

"Yeah."

"On me," he said.

And he ran, sprinting like a jackrabbit for the perimeter fence. Dakota had to race to keep up.

Twenty seconds later Falk was sliding into the dirt at the fence, and Dakota arrived right behind him. The spot he'd chosen looked entirely nondescript, just another stretch of endless chain link like any other, but if Falk was right, this was their way out.

"That run heated us up, so we've got maybe thirty more seconds before those drones know we're here," Falk said. "Work fast."

Dakota pulled a pair of wire cutters from her coveralls—another prize from the tool shed—and started snipping away at the chainlink. She could barely believe this was happening. Not only were they right up against the fence, where no one was ever permitted to go, they were also directly beneath a Mek light tower, with drones patrolling not twenty meters away. Every alarm in the township should be sounding. They should already be dead. And yet…

"Work faster," Falk urged, sounding anxious. Dakota was already going as fast as she could, but her hands were still trembling and unresponsive from the cold, and more than once it took her a couple of tries to get the wire cutters to bite down on the metal links. But a few moments later, she'd cut enough to push a flap of fence aside, just enough for her to crawl through, and then Falk behind her.

"Go," he said. "Run!"

And together they ran. Leaving the bright lights of the township behind, slipping away into the dark of night.

# EIGHT

THEY MOVED QUICKLY that first night. They knew that within minutes of morning alarm, just hours from now, when they failed to appear for headcount, the manhunt would begin. Fast-moving surveyors from across the entire surrounding area would be hunting them. Satellites in orbit would be tasked with scanning the surface for them. Every asset the enemy had in this region would be brought together in common purpose: finding and recapturing the escapees. And unlike humans, the Mek never tired, never slowed, never quit. The harsh truth was, even after the miracle of their escape, Dakota and Falk's chances of staying at large for very long were marginal at best.

And yet, Dakota felt as though she had left all her concerns behind her. They were free, and her fears and doubts faded along with the township lights receding into the darkness behind them. Just being outside the fence was exhilarating. The night air was drying her clothes and hair as she ran, and the blood and adrenaline rushing through her body warmed her more by the moment.

She had no idea where she was. When she and Sam were first brought to the township, it was in a windowless Mek transport. They had been captured near someplace called Idaho, but the transport was fast and had traveled for hours, so the township could have been anywhere. All she knew was that right now they were moving through a forest. Leaves crunched underfoot as they ran, tree branches whipped and scratched at their faces, and a few times, Dakota stumbled and nearly fell as her foot caught on a tangled root or rock.

After what felt like an hour of ceaseless running, Falk motioned for them to stop in a clearing. "We should rest for a bit," he said, his hands on his knees as he bent forward to catch his breath.

Dakota slumped down on the wet grass and collapsed onto her back, her heart pounding so hard the sound of it throbbed in her ears.

And then her eyes widened in astonishment. She was looking straight up at the sky, and there, above the treetops waving gently in the wind, was something she hadn't seen since she was a child.

*Stars.*

At first she didn't believe it; she thought it must be an illusion, an old memory summoned up by her fatigued mind. But as she gazed upward at the countless shimmering pinpoints of light, she knew it was no trick of the mind, just a sight denied to her by the Mek captors for so long that she could barely conceive of it as real.

She laughed quietly to herself. For that one perfect moment, she was overwhelmed with joy—and all her time in the township, every dismal memory, every sorrow, was momentarily wiped away. It was just her and the infinite above.

Her reverie was short-lived. Falk rose and stood over her. "That's enough rest," he said. "Time to move."

* * *

The forest grew thicker as they went on. It made for slower going, but as Falk pointed out, it was preferable to moving over open ground, where Mek surveyors and satellites could more easily spot them from the air.

"What were you laughing about back there?" he asked as they moved together, side by side. They were walking briskly now as neither was able to keep up a running pace the whole night. The pale light of the moon shafted through the trees, affording them enough visibility to see each other and keep from losing their footing.

"Oh, nothing," she said. "Just the stars in the sky. It's been such a long time since I've seen them, I'd almost forgotten what they looked like."

"They look kinda like freedom, huh?" said Falk, and Dakota looked at him, amazed that he saw them exactly the same way she did. Perhaps it shouldn't be that surprising; he'd been in and out of townships for years, so he would know more than most the difference between the antiseptic glare of a Mek night sky and the clear, ink-black beauty of a natural one.

"My brother told me once that every star in the sky is a sun just like ours," he said. "They're just so far away that all we see of them is that little pinprick of light. Some of them even have planets that go around them, just like this one."

Dakota looked up at the sky again. The stars were less visible here through the treetop canopy, but she could still see some. "I wonder which one of them the Mek came from," she wondered aloud.

"Well, whichever one it is," said Falk, quickening his pace, "we're gonna send them the fuck back there."

* * *

The forest started to thin out just as the first light of day was breaking on the horizon to the east. That was a bad combination: less cover and less darkness to hide in. Falk pointed that out, but Dakota didn't need it explained to her; she knew all that and more from her years in the open with Sam. She knew every way to hide, every way they might be exposed, every way the Mek could find them if they forgot themselves for even a moment and did something stupid to give themselves away.

But the real danger daybreak signified, they both knew, was that morning alarm back at the township had sounded. By then, their absence had been discovered, and the Mek were searching for them.

"When you escaped before," she asked Falk as they walked together, "how hard did the Mek come looking for you?"

"It's always pretty bad at first," he replied. "If we can make it through the next couple of days, it should start to get easier. The algorithm's all about efficiency; if the Mek can't find us right away, they'll recalculate; eventually they'll figure a couple of township workers aren't worth so many resources that could be better tasked elsewhere. Things will slowly go back to normal."

*Back to normal*, Dakota thought. So just the "normal" amount of hiding in terror from the "normal" number of Mek surveyors that "normally" roamed the open world looking for humans to capture or kill.

But then, maybe normal wasn't so bad. She and Sam had survived that kind of normal for years before they were caught; this time they only had to last as long as it took to reach wherever the hell Falk's map was leading them. Still, her doubts were starting to return, dawning on her like the rising sun.

"What do you mean when you say the Mek can be better tasked elsewhere?" she asked. "What else is there for them to do anymore, other than keep us locked up? The war's long over."

"If you really believed that, you'd be back at your tool shed right now, not here risking your life with me," said Falk. "There are still humans out there in the world, you know. Some of them are still fighting."

"Really?" Dakota was genuinely astonished to learn that. It seemed beyond belief, twenty years after the fall of the last city.

"I mean, fewer and fewer every day, but yeah," said Falk. "I fell in with a few of 'em over the years. Just small groups, guerrilla fighters, hit-and-hide tactics. Sometimes they'll manage to take out a rover or a surveyor or even a transport. Barely makes a dent in the big picture, but still, they do what they can."

He looked east, toward the sun. "That's the one thing the Mek will never understand about humans: we never really know when we're beaten. Maybe that's how we'll win in the end."

# NINE

FALK HADN'T EXAGGERATED: their first full day of freedom was brutal.

They saw their first surveyor as they were emerging from the forest about an hour after dawn, roving across a distant hillside. In that at least they were lucky, seeing it before it detected them. It was barely visible, just a speck on the horizon, but the early morning sunlight glinted off its metallic carapace, alerting them to its presence. Dakota and Falk knew from hard-won experience that they were only just beyond the range at which a surveyor could detect the presence of a human, and they retreated back to the trees and crouched there, prepared to turn and run deeper into the forest if it moved much closer. But instead it moved away, continuing on its assigned patrol route. They both breathed a sigh of relief, waited a little longer just to be sure, and got moving again.

They were crossing open country now, which was dangerous, but they had little choice. It was all wide open here, great plains that seemed to go on without end. The day was clear and bright at least, which made it easy to scan for distant Mek drones—though it also made it easy for the Mek to spot them from the air or from orbit.

Still, all they could do was keep moving, keep hoping.

"How do you know we're going in the right direction?" Dakota asked as they traipsed through the tall grass.

"I checked the map against the stars last night," Falk replied. "We're lined up right, headed east. And those mountains up ahead, they're right where they're supposed to be." He pointed to the rugged range on the horizon. "It'll be hard going across there, but better cover, more difficult for the Mek to spot us."

"But how do you know we're meant to be headed east when we don't even know where we started from?"

"I've got a general idea," Falk answered. "The township you were in was in a territory that used to be called Wyoming. Who knows what the Mek call it now, sector something-or-other. The place we're looking for's in the next territory over. I don't know what that one's called."

Dakota had learned much about survival over the course of her short life, but geography meant little to her. Occasionally on their travels, she and Sam would come across an old road sign or a name marker outside a destroyed town, but those names were meaningless, just artifacts of a lost world. Even when they came across an old map, they'd never bothered with it; maps showed you how to get to places you wanted to go, and there were no places anymore, nowhere left to go. Only the empty landscape, the townships, the Mek cities. And those were easy enough to avoid without maps or road signs; you could see their towering pyramids on the horizon from miles away.

As she recalled those times, Dakota found herself thinking about how much she missed Sam. This was literally the first day in her entire life that she'd been apart from him. She'd come to rely upon him for so much over the years—and he upon her—that she felt like one half of a whole, somehow incomplete without him. She worried about him now. Would the Mek back at the township be interrogating the other workers, trying to find out if anyone had known about the escape? Surely they'd question Sam first, the brother of one of the escapees. She remembered what Falk had said about Mek interrogation and horror filled her; what might she have consigned Sam to by escaping and leaving him behind as the Mek's only link to her? What might they do to—

"Get down!"

Before Dakota could react, Falk was dragging her down into a ditch and gesturing to her to be quiet. They cowered in the dirt, Falk listening intently, Dakota wondering what the hell he'd seen or heard.

A moment later, a Mek fast-mover shot across the sky high above them, leaving a black contrail in its wake. Dakota watched from her prone position, huddled next to Falk, as it moved away as quickly as it had come.

They waited a while longer, silently, before daring to move. Then at Falk's nod, they rose from the ditch and scanned the surrounding plains.

"Do you think it saw us?" Dakota asked.

"I guess we'll know soon enough," said Falk, brushing the dirt from his coveralls.

"You don't see fast-movers that often," Dakota observed. "Maybe the Mek sent it to look for us."

"Maybe," said Falk. "Nothing we can do but keep moving. Come on."

He offered her his hand and helped her climb out of the ditch. Together they kept walking toward the distant mountains.

"How did you even know it was coming?" Dakota asked. "They don't make a sound."

"They do, it's just real high-pitched," said Falk. "Guess I'm lucky: I got the ears to hear it. And you have to know what to listen for. These guys I ran with for a while a few years ago, they kept a dog with 'em because dogs can always hear Mek coming. Dogs can hear things humans can't. If we had one with us, we'd have known about that fast-mover long before I—"

He stopped. Listening. Dakota's heart was in her throat.

"Shit, it's coming back," said Falk, looking in the direction the fast-mover had gone. They were too far from the ditch to seek shelter there again now. "Run."

As Falk took off, Dakota looked back in the same direction. And now she saw it, the Mek flyer in the distant sky, just a black dot but getting larger, and quickly, approaching at high speed. It must have seen them after all, or had at least gotten enough of a reading to rouse its suspicions, make it swing around for another—

"Dakota, run!"

Falk's voice shook her racing mind back to the here and now and she started running, trying to catch up with him. There was no hope of stealth now, nowhere to hide, nowhere to run. They *couldn't* outrun this thing, but she kept running anyway because that's what Falk was doing, and running felt better than standing still and simply awaiting her fate.

The fast-mover shot overhead, and Dakota watched, aghast, as it dropped a half dozen metal spheres from its belly just up ahead. She knew exactly what would happen when those spheres hit the ground, what was hiding within them.

"Scuttlers!" Falk called.

The spheres were still falling, moments from the ground, and Falk was now veering away to the left to avoid running straight toward them. Dakota followed, her tired legs carrying her as fast as they could.

The first sphere hit the ground hard and cracked open like an egg, its shell designed to break apart neatly on impact, and from within arose a six-legged metal creature, a newborn spider emerging from its sac. The Mek scuttler's armored shell gleamed in the sun as the other spheres impacted around it, each giving birth to its own oversized metal insect.

As she ran, Dakota stole a glance over her shoulder to see all six of the scuttlers now fully emerged and spread across the plain, just a few hundred meters away. They were already moving fast, scurrying like giant crabs in pursuit of their prey.

*This is it,* thought Dakota in that moment. She and Sam had had close encounters with scuttlers before. They were faster than humans, they were heavily armored, and they carried a beam weapon that could fry you with one shot. She'd once seen a single scuttler take on a dozen armed humans, killing every one of them without suffering so much as a scratch. Some it vaporized with its beam, others it tore to pieces with its powerful mechanical limbs. The sight of that monster slaughtering so many, so quickly, and with such ruthless efficiency, remained a recurring nightmare for years after.

And now she and Falk were facing not one, but six of them, closing the distance fast.

*At least we tried,* Dakota thought. *At least we'll die on our—*

"This way, come on!" It was Falk again, frantically ushering her toward some kind of sewer grate set into the side of a hillock. He pulled on the rusted metal grille, but it wouldn't budge. Dakota raced to join him and tried to help, both of them tugging on the grate with everything they had, trying to wrench it free. She didn't dare look back now because she knew the scuttlers were close, mere seconds away, just by the awful metallic chittering sounds they made.

She felt an intense heat burn the left side of her face as a section of mossy hillside just in front of her burst into flaming, molten slag. One of the scuttlers had fired its beam weapon, missing her by no more than a fraction of an inch. She doubted she'd be so lucky a second time.

She and Falk yanked on the grate for all they were worth, and with one final effort, it came free of its housing, weakened by decades of rust and disrepair, leaving behind a hole just big enough to crawl through.

"Go, go!" Falk grabbed Dakota and practically pushed her through the opening. She scrambled inside, her world suddenly black, and fell into the darkness, landing a few meters below in a shallow pool that stank of putrid shit. Definitely a sewer. And then Falk was there, splashing down next to her. He groaned, seeming to have hurt himself in the fall, but Dakota helped him to his feet, looked up to see daylight shafting through the aperture above. The scuttlers were up there, clawing and thrashing at the opening, but they were too big to squeeze through. Dakota and

Falk took off down the tunnel, racing blindly, desperately into the dark, leaving their pursuers behind.

* * *

It was hours later before they finally felt confident the scuttlers hadn't been able to follow them into the sewer. Still, they didn't feel remotely safe. Their position had certainly reported, and the algorithm, making trillions of calculations per second, would have plotted dozens of moves ahead. Did the Mek have access to the schematics of these old sewer systems? If they did, they could find another way in, or at least lie in wait at every possible exit point. Maybe Dakota and Falk were already trapped. Maybe they would die down here, in the dark. But for now at least, they were alive, if only by inches.

After what felt like an eternity of fumbling and splashing through the sewers, they came to an intersection where two tunnels converged into an open area, a tiny bit of daylight coming in from a grate high above. The grate was wildly overgrown with plant life, hopefully enough that it was invisible to the Mek. As a place to rest, this seemed to be as good as it was going to get.

The two of them sat quietly for a while, gathering their thoughts. But the silence was beginning to make Dakota uncomfortable. She felt the need to say something, anything.

"What's the Old Navy?"

Falk looked up at her from the shadows, snapping back from wherever he'd been.

"When you first arrived in the township," she went on, "you were wearing a shirt that had Old Navy written on it."

"You can read?" Falk asked.

Dakota made a face. What kind of question was that? "Of course I can read. My brother taught me."

"Sorry," said Falk. "It's rare, that's all."

"Was Old Navy the type of military your father was in? My mother was in the Air Force."

"Oh," said Falk. He sounded somehow weaker than usual. "No, it was just a shirt I found. I don't remember where."

Silence again. Dakota was beginning to sense that something was wrong. She felt the need to keep Falk talking, if not for his own spirits, then for hers. Plus there was still so much she wanted to know, and now she could actually talk to him at length, not like back in the township when the best she could do was steal a moment with him here and there.

"What did you mean when you said the map led to liberation?"

She could see Falk sitting there, across from her, in the semi-darkness, but he wasn't looking back at her. Just staring at nothing in particular. It made her nervous.

"Falk," she repeated.

"Huh?"

"What did you mean when you said the map led to liberation?"

"You know as much as I do. That's all my father ever told me."

"He also said there'd need to be two of us. Why?"

"I don't know!" he snapped, too loud. He quieted again, glancing up at the grate. Sound could carry through the sewers, and Mek could be nearby, listening. "Dammit, could we just—could we just sit quietly for a little while?"

Dakota decided not to push. It was unusual for Falk to snap at her like that. For a while, neither of them spoke.

"I'm sorry," Falk said finally. "I didn't mean to bark at you like that."

"It's okay," said Dakota. "It's just, back in the township, you sounded like you knew more than you wanted to say. I figured now that we're out…"

"I really don't," he said. "My father never wanted me to know too much in case the Mek ever interrogated me about it. He just said it'd all make sense when I found the Four Faces. If I made it sound like I knew more, I'm sorry. I didn't mean to deceive you. It's just…" He trailed off.

"Just what?"

"It's just… I was afraid. Afraid to do this alone. I would have if I'd had no other choice, if I'd never found you, but once I did, I really needed you to believe in me, or you might not have come."

It was too dark in the sewer to see much of Falk's face, but Dakota could tell how vulnerable he was in that moment. It was there in the tremor in his voice, the way he was looking not at her but at the wall behind her. She wasn't certain if it made her feel worse that he wasn't as assured as he'd always seemed, or better because he seemed more human, more… like her.

Finally he looked her in the eye. "I'm still afraid," he said.

"We both are," Dakota replied.

She reached out and put a hand on his shoulder, a small gesture of comfort, but he recoiled from her and drew breath sharply between his teeth. Dakota knew that sound; he was in pain. Had the fall into the sewer been worse than it looked?

She saw now that he was clutching his arm. Maybe he'd dislocated it. If so, she knew how to help.

She stood up, took a step toward him. "Let me see that."

"It's nothing," he said, and he angled his right side away from her, trying to hide where he was hurt.

"Don't be silly, show me," she said, coming closer. And he couldn't hide it anymore. Even in the dim light, she could see what had happened to him. He hadn't hurt his arm in the fall. It had happened before that, outside. His upper right arm had been grazed by a Mek scuttler beam, another near-miss but closer than the one that had passed by her face. Even a graze from a scuttler beam was a grievous wound. The outer side of his arm was horribly burned, layers of flesh deep. It wasn't bleeding, the beam had cauterized the wound instantly, but it was oozing some kind of clear fluid.

Dakota had seen burns before. She'd treated Sam for a particularly bad one after he had tried, against her advice, to examine a downed Mek drone. That was how they learned the Mek were fitted with self-destruct mechanisms to prevent human tampering. She'd pulled him away just in time, but the heat flash from the explosion had badly seared his hand. But the burn on Falk's arm was worse. Far worse. And she knew that a bad burn was the worst possible kind of pain. How he had managed to hide what must have been agony for the last few hours was beyond her.

She unzipped the top half of her coveralls, revealing the drab olive-colored tank top beneath, and started ripping away one of the sleeves. "You should have told me about that earlier," she said. She didn't try to hide the sharpness in her tone; she was genuinely annoyed.

"I didn't want to worry you," he offered meekly.

"Don't go mixing up brave and stupid," she said. She finished tearing off the sleeve and started working it into a bandage.

"It's not that bad," Falk said. "It's just a burn; I'm not going to bleed out. I'll be fine so long as it doesn't get infected."

"The longer you leave that exposed, the more chance there is it'll get infected," she said.

What both of them knew but didn't dare say was that it was probably already infected. They were in an ancient sewer surrounded by every kind of filth imaginable—literally the worst place in the world to be with an open wound.

"Stay still; this is going to hurt," she said, and she began winding the sleeve-bandage around his arm.

He flinched, screwed his eyes shut tight against the pain.

Dakota finished as quickly and as carefully as she could. "There," she said when she was done. "That'll have to do."

Falk examined the dressing. "It looks good. Thanks."

Dakota sat back down. "We can't stay here."

"No," said Falk. "We'll start out in a little while, try to find some way out of here while there's still some light. Then we'll wait for dark and head for the mountains. Sound like a plan?"

It sounded like a plan.

* * *

COMMAND UNIT REPORT
UNIT RANK: WAR COMMANDER FIRST CLASS
DESIGNATION: MEK-39487651-28743
FILED 1176/8492 MKST 36:45.843

>This unit is tasked by the Master Algorithm with overseeing the recovery of two prisoners from Labor Township * * *7424 (Sector 11) on 1175/9873 MKST 52:88.732

>Escape subjects are designated * * *81-47676 DAKOTA BREGMAN age 22 and * * *39-90983 STEPHEN FALK age 26 subject files appended to this report

>Positive subject identification by aerial scout unit traveling overground on foot at grid-ref E48EA-94116 on 1176/8492 MKST 31:93.751 standard ground units deploy subjects escaped via subterranean drainage system remain at large this unit assigns additional units to conduct search operations in Sectors 12/13/14/17/21

>This unit travels to Labor Township * * *7424 (Sector 11) to conduct preliminary investigation to acquire information about Subject BREGMAN and Subject FALK

>The Master Algorithm calculates termination of subjects is permissible if this unit should determine live recovery impossible or inefficient expenditure of resources this unit is thereby granted broad operational discretion

>STAND BY

# TEN

DAKOTA AND FALK spent the next few hours making their way through the sewers, attempting to put as much distance between them and their pursuers as possible before choosing a place to re-emerge. Though it seemed they were safe from the Mek down there, at least temporarily, Dakota couldn't wait to get out. The smell was close to unbearable, and she felt more confined than she ever had in the township. More than that, though, she needed to get Falk out of there. He was worsening, and every second in the rank, germ-filled environment only increased his danger of infection. She wished she could give him real medicine and a proper dressing, but right now she would settle for fresh air and sunlight.

Eventually they came across what seemed like a suitable exit, a large circular outlet covered by a rusted metal grille. They reckoned they were at least a few miles from where they'd escaped the scuttlers, unless they'd somehow gotten turned around in the darkened maze, which was certainly a possibility. The sky outside confirmed their sense of the passage of time; it was late in the day, nearly dusk.

After wrestling with the grate, they were able to get it to budge—Dakota did most of the work, as Falk's bad arm was next to useless—but they didn't remove it all the way just yet. They loosened it just enough to peek out, to discover that on the other side was nothing but a sheer drop to a broad river coursing ten meters below.

"Well, shit," said Falk, echoing Dakota's feelings exactly.

He propped himself against the sewer wall. "Let's rest for a while before we do this, let it get a little darker first," he said.

In the fading light shafting through the grate, Dakota could see that he was exhausted. Despite her eagerness to get out of the sewer, she nodded. Her lack of sleep last night, and then a full day on the run, was catching up to her. She was tired, too.

"You just have the worst luck, huh?" Falk said after a long moment of quiet.

"What do you mean?" she asked.

"I mean, saddled with two guys in a row with only one arm. What are the odds?"

She frowned at him. "That isn't funny."

He looked down, glum. "Sorry."

Now she felt bad. He'd tried, however clumsily, to find some humor in a bad situation. "No," she said. "I'm sorry. It's okay."

After another long silence, Falk tried again.

"Do you remember your mother?" he asked.

"No," said Dakota. "I was only two when she died. But I've seen her. My brother used to have a photograph of her with my dad and him when he was a baby."

"What happened to the photo?"

"The Mek took it when we were captured."

Falk nodded. He understood. The Mek took everything.

"If I close my eyes, I can still see it, though," Dakota went on. "I looked at that photo so many times, it's like it burned into my brain."

"Take a look at it now," said Falk. "Tell me."

She closed her eyes, and there it was, right in front of her. "My mother's beautiful," she said. "She has long, dark hair that she wears tied up in back, and she's tall. My dad, he's a big man, stocky, close-cropped hair and a mustache. He's handsome. Sam… well, Sam looks like a baby." She smiled as the image grew more vivid in her mind. "My mom and dad, they both have the same look. Proud, but… sad. Like they knew something bad was coming."

Dakota couldn't be sure, but based on Sam's age, the photo was probably taken four or five years into the ten-year war, and from everything she'd heard, the second half of the war was far worse than the first. The Mek would bring more and more reinforcements from their homeworld, deploy battle units on every front, and make it impossible for Earth's increasingly desperate military forces, already stretched thin, to hold them back. From that point on, it was just a matter of time. Maybe her parents already knew that when the photo was taken.

"What were their names?" Falk asked.

"My mother was Rosalind. My father always called her Rosie." That was true as far as she knew, what Sam had told her. "My father's name was Fred."

She looked at Falk and saw a sadness in his eyes. "What about you?" she asked. "What do you remember about your parents?"

Falk seemed to think deeply for a moment about his answer, then looked outside. "It's dark enough now," he said. "We should go."

* * *

Dakota and Falk stood at the open sewer outlet and looked down at the fast-moving river below.

"You up for this?" Falk asked.

It wasn't herself that Dakota was worried about. "Are you?"

"Let's find out," he said, and without another word, he jumped.

Dakota watched in astonishment as he plummeted into the river.

She hesitated to follow. She hated the water, always had, but the current was already carrying him away. If she didn't go now, she risked losing sight of him.

So she jumped.

She felt the air rush past her, saw the water coming up to meet her, and then everything disappeared as she hit the surface and sank beneath it, her world reduced suddenly to a dark blur and a deep-bass rumbling in her ears. The cold water bit into her skin, sending a shock running through her; it wasn't as bad as the township shower, but it was close.

For a frightening moment, she couldn't figure which way was up. She'd gotten turned around during the fall, and there was no sunlight to guide her back to the surface. Lost in the dark, she panicked, twisting frantically, thrashing her arms and legs—and then finally she broke through, one hand finding the surface, her head rising above it.

She was facing backward as the river pulled her along; she turned herself around and was relieved to see Falk up ahead. He'd made his way to the riverbank and was climbing out. Dakota tried to swim over to the same bank, but she wasn't closing the distance fast enough; she was going to pass him right by. Falk moved quickly; with his good arm, he held out a fallen branch to her. She lunged for it and grabbed on, the rough bark cutting into her hands, and Falk heaved her ashore.

The two of them collapsed onto their backs beside one another, taking in deep gulps of air.

"That wasn't so bad… was it?" said Falk between breaths.

All Dakota could do was laugh.

* * *

Fortunately, the river had deposited them at the edge of a forested area. They traveled through the moonlit night under the protection of the foliage, shivering as they went, still soaked through. Before dawn came, they needed to find a place to hole up. Moving by day carried too much risk of being spotted, and they were both deathly tired and in dire need of rest. So when, just as the sky was starting to lighten, they came upon a dried-up stream bed traversed by a crumbling stone bridge, they decided it would have to do. It wasn't much, but down in the gully, covered by the bridge above, they were at least sheltered from the elements—and the Mek. They even decided it was worth risking a small fire; if they didn't warm themselves soon, they might well freeze to death. Dakota gathered the wood and tinder, and the rocks to spark the flame, as she'd done so many times with Sam, while Falk nursed his wounded arm beneath the bridge.

It was strange, Dakota thought, as she built the fire, how her relationship with Falk had come to mirror her relationship with Sam. As with her brother, she had at first depended on him, seeing him as the leader, the protector, the one with all the answers. And then those roles had reversed. Falk, like Sam, had been weakened, and Dakota was responsible for keeping him alive.

It was foolish to have ever thought of Falk as some kind of storybook hero; she knew that. But that was nonetheless how she had come to see him during their time in the township. A man with no fear, no uncertainty. He'd reminded her of a part of herself she'd almost forgotten. The fighter, the survivor, the one who dreamed of saying *no more running,* instead turning around and taking the Mek head-on, whatever the outcome. Falk embodied all that and more. So perhaps it wasn't surprising she had begun to mythologize him, to make him into more than he was.

But he was just a man. Braver and more competent than most she'd met, but still just a man, as fallible and mortal as any other. And now he was badly hurt, and afraid, and so it fell to her to make sure they fulfilled their parents' last wishes by finding what had been left for them at the Four Faces—whatever the hell that even was.

When she had the fire going well, spitting and crackling, she and Falk huddled close to it, enjoying a warmth that their bodies had almost forgotten.

"That feels good," said Falk.

Dakota looked at him across the fire, and it occurred to her that this was the first time she'd really stopped to look at him since the township. With his face lit orange by the dancing light of the fire, he appeared drawn. But the fight hadn't left him. It was still there. Buried a little deeper beneath fatigue and pain and fear, but still there. And not going anywhere.

"Did you really escape from six townships?" she asked.

"I, uh… may have exaggerated a little," he said, looking up from the fire. "Really it was four. Sorry, I guess I was trying to impress you. I needed you to believe that I knew what I was doing, so you'd trust me enough to help."

"Escaping from four townships is plenty impressive. You didn't need to exaggerate," said Dakota. Then she asked another question, one that had been on her mind for some time. "Why did you go to the trouble of finding us at all? You said whatever it is we're supposed to do will take two of us, but why did you need Sam? Or me? You already have the map; you could have picked anyone you wanted."

Falk gazed into the flames. "I certainly thought about that," he said. "Would have been easier, for sure. But… I don't know." He looked down at the strange map imprinted on his forearm. "I've always felt like I wasn't supposed to do this with just anyone, but with someone who this—whatever this is—was meant for. Same as it was meant for me. Maybe that's dumb. But I believe in fate. It's brought me this far."

Dakota thought about that. "But the map *wasn't* meant for me. It was meant for Sam. And you're not here with him, you're here with me."

He looked up at her. "Maybe that's fate, too," he said.

She looked back at him from across the fire, and for that moment, it was only them in the world.

Falk looked away. "So yeah, four escapes. Or five, now."

"Four and a half," said Dakota with a smile. "We split credit for this last one."

Falk allowed himself a smile, too. "Fair enough."

They slept then, for the first time since their escape. They lay beneath the crumbling bridge, their bodies pressed together for warmth, and though they were alone in the hostile wilderness, defenseless and hunted by a merciless alien race that had conquered their entire world, Dakota had never in her life felt safer.

* * *

She rose shortly after dark and foraged for food. As she crept around, careful to stay quiet and hidden and always watchful for Mek, she remembered her lessons from her time on the run with Sam. She knew which berries and acorns were safe to eat. When she returned with her haul, Falk was still asleep, so she let him rest a while longer as she ate her share. She liked watching him sleep; it was the first time she'd seen him at peace. After he woke, she surprised him with the food she'd gathered and watched as he hungrily ate it down. Then it was time to move again.

Rejuvenated by their much-needed rest, they continued at a brisk pace through the moonlit forest until they arrived at the outskirts of a small town. Though most everything from the old world had long since been picked over by scavengers—or destroyed by the Mek—there were still sometimes treasures to be found in places like this. So under cover of darkness, they headed toward the town to explore.

It was less a town than a place that had sprung up by the side of the road, a waypoint for travelers on the way to their actual destination. There was a dilapidated gas station, some restaurants, shops. A few houses. Dakota's optimism about finding something of worth waned as she got a good look at the place.

"Should we split up?" Falk asked. "Maybe get this place searched faster?"

"No," said Dakota firmly. "We stay together, always." Sam had taught her that rule, and she'd never forgotten.

"Right," said Falk. "Sorry. I'm used to doing this alone."

"It's okay," said Dakota. "Just stop apologizing." Was it her imagination, or was he beginning to seem more nervous, more self-conscious around her?

"Sorry," he said.

She shot him a look.

He smiled.

* * *

They didn't make out that badly. The gas station and the stores had nothing left, but in one of the restaurants they found packets of sugar and ketchup, which they feasted on. And best of all, one of the houses had a cellar with clean rags and a quarter bottle of bleach. Falk bit down on a rubber hose they found down there while Dakota cleaned his wound and wrapped it. She was relieved to find that, while the burn was still horrific, it didn't look infected, and surely they'd have seen the signs by now. Things were actually looking up, down in the rank cellar.

It was also as good a hiding place as they were likely to find, and with the new dawn not far away, they decided to stay until the following nightfall. They were both bone-tired, and some more rest in a place of relative safety would be well worth the delay. Dakota was sure the obsessively efficient Mek algorithm would have agreed.

They ate more of the ketchup they'd stuffed in their pockets, and though the plumbing didn't work, they managed to coax some water out of the pipes by taking them apart and draining them into a bucket. It tasted foul, but it beat death by dehydration. Best of all, Dakota found an old chess set tucked away on the back of a shelf. She'd never seen a real one before, and it took her a while to work out which piece was which. Her whole life, a queen had been a spark plug, a bishop a bolt with two nuts threaded onto it. But once she had it figured out, she taught Falk how to play, just as Sam had once taught her.

"Again," he said after his seventh defeat in a row.

She'd shown him no mercy. It was his own fault; he'd insisted she not go easy on him.

"Your problem is you never know when you're beaten," she said with a smile.

She began to reset the board. When she was done, she saw that Falk was looking at her, a half smile on his face.

"What?" she said. "Why are you looking at me like that?"

He shook his head. "Nothing."

"Don't give me that. Tell me."

He shrugged, still smiling. "I wasn't going to say anything, but you should go look in the mirror. Honestly, it wasn't even all that funny to me until you started beating my ass at this dumb game."

There was a cracked and stained old mirror on the wall above a sink. Dakota went and looked. It was the first time she'd seen her face since leaving the township. And it didn't look the same.

The face that stared back at her now had been neatly divided down the middle. On one side, her skin was its usual color; on the other side, she was a bright pink bordering on red.

"What the hell?"

And then she remembered. The Mek scuttler that had missed with its heat beam. The shot had been close enough to give one entire side of her face instant sunburn.

Falk was laughing now. She whipped around. "You think this is funny?"

"What can I say? The world's gone to shit," he said. "My standards for what's funny are real low."

She turned to look at her reflection again. Falk was right. She looked ridiculous.

And then she was laughing, too. She and Falk had, from the beginning, been comrades. Now they were friends.

# ELEVEN

IT WAS IMPOSSIBLE to reckon the passage of time down in the windowless cellar, so every now and then, Falk and Dakota took turns going upstairs to peek outside. When at last night had fallen, it was time to go. They made one final sweep of the cellar to be sure they hadn't missed anything of value and found nothing other than an old marker pen, which Dakota stuffed in her pocket.

She led the way out of the cellar, and they crouch-walked silently down the hallway and across the ransacked living room. Falk popped his head up to take a quick look through the broken windows, and when he saw nothing but the abandoned shops and gas station under the pale light of the moon, he gave Dakota a thumbs-up.

Dakota reached up and was just about to turn the knob on the front door when a stark, antiseptic light flooded in from outside.

Adrenaline shot through her like a bolt of electricity as she recoiled. Only Mek made that kind of light; it was the same cold hue that blazed all night long inside the township.

She froze, her back flat against the wall, and gestured to Falk to stay quiet, though of course he already knew.

The Mek was right outside. If it was a surveyor or an enforcer, they were as good as dead, detected already. But as the drone moved around the house, its searchlight spilling in through the windows, Dakota caught a glimpse of it. She knew that shape well, knew all the Mek types well enough to write her own field guide, from every kind of battle unit to the rarely seen but terrifying commanders, hideous anthropomorphic machines that walked about on two legs and even had something approximating a human face, though it was obscured behind a visor of translucent glass. So she knew with certainty that the machine outside was a rover, about as low-end as it got. The Mek produced them in mass numbers, more than any other. They were formidable enough once they spotted you, fast and well-armed, but they were only equipped with basic audio-visual and motion sensors that you could get past, if you knew how. Basically, don't move and stay the fuck quiet.

And so Dakota and Falk did just that as the rover continued to probe outside. Dakota wondered if it was just a routine search, part of its usual patrol route, or if something had alerted it. Had it seen their movements? Heard them? What if these rovers had gotten smarter during the years she'd been incarcerated, upgraded to some superior model with better sensors?

She closed her eyes, aware that nothing she did now mattered. Fate would decide what happened next. And though she knew it was unwise, she moved her arm a few inches along the wall until she found Falk's hand. She took it in hers, felt his grip tighten, and knew they agreed: if they were going to die here and now, then let them do it together.

After what felt like an eternity, the light turned and moved away. The living room was plunged into darkness once more.

Dakota exhaled. But still, neither of them moved. They waited, hands clasped tightly together, for more than an hour.

And then they were out the door and running like hell, into the dark of night.

* * *

The town wasn't far from the mountains, and they found an old zigzag trail that went into the foothills, and they started to climb. It was never wise to stay on any kind of road or pathway for too long, as the Mek watched those most of all, but they followed it for a bit before charting their own course. They were careful to move through crevasses or ravines where possible, and never atop ridge lines or along bare rock, where they'd be exposed to Mek eyes and ears. Both of them had used mountains to travel stealthly before, and they knew that even the best Mek sensors couldn't penetrate millions of tons of solid rock. So as long as they kept themselves walled in, they had a decent chance of remaining undetected.

They spent the better part of a week that way and never saw a single Mek, except for one fast-mover that shot high over them on the second day but never came back. They found shelter in the mouths of caves and beneath rock outcroppings, drank from streams, and made surprisingly good time over the rugged terrain—Falk estimated at least ten miles per night. Dakota even caught fish for them to eat, showing Falk how she'd learned to do it with a tree branch whittled down to a fine point.

When they came out of the mountains on the fifth day of their trek, things got harder. Falk had checked his map against the stars twice the previous night, and the land markings now, and he was pretty sure they were close to their goal, maybe fifty miles. But they'd no longer have the cover of the mountains, just open plains of grass and fields as flat as floorboards. They waited at the edge of cover and watched for signs of Mek activity, but to the surprise of them both, by the time darkness fell, they had seen none.

"What do you think?" Falk asked.

"I think maybe we're lucky," said Dakota. "I don't think the Mek are looking for us this far out. Or they figure we're already dead."

Falk nodded. "I agree. Doesn't mean there's no Mek out there though. There's still the standard patrols. Let's be careful."

They walked the edge of the tree line until they found an area with foliage dense enough to keep themselves at least somewhat concealed if they stayed low. It wasn't much, but it was all they had. Falk led the way after dark, and they spent the rest of the night losing count of the number of scrapes and scratches they got from the brambles and prickly shrubs they pushed through.

Just as dawn was lightening the sky, they came across the broken asphalt of a two-lane highway.

"I don't like being anywhere near a road during the day," said Falk as they lay prone in the bushes, peering out. "But if we're quick, we're across that highway and back into cover on the other side in seconds, and we can cover a bit more ground before we rest. You good?"

Dakota nodded.

Falk counted down from three, and they were both up and sprinting across the highway.

But even as Falk ran ahead and leaped over the corrugated crash barrier on the far side of the road, something caught Dakota's eye and caused her to suddenly stop. Normally she'd know better than to stand in the middle of open ground with clear skies above, leaving herself vulnerable to detection. But she couldn't help herself.

Falk saw that she had stopped in the road and hurriedly made his way back to her. "What's wrong? What is it?"

She was staring up, transfixed, at a rusted road sign.

"It's me," she said.

Falk looked up at the sign, too. The top of it was gone, either rusted through or damaged by some past battle, but the words beneath were clearly legible, save for a few letters that had fallen away.

**WELCO E TO S UTH DAKOTA**
**THE L ND OF INFINITE VARIETY**

* * *

COMMAND UNIT REPORT
UNIT RANK: WAR COMMANDER FIRST CLASS
DESIGNATION: MEK-39487651-28743
FILED 1179/8312 MKST 58:21.712

>This unit arrives at Labor Township * * *7424 (Sector 11) to conduct standard interrogation of prisoners related to escape of subjects * * *81-47676 BREGMAN and * * *39-90983 FALK all prisoners are advised to report to command building immediately after morning alarm for questioning by Township administration units interrogations ongoing

>This unit is advised that subject BREGMAN has older sibling * * *81-47675 SAMUEL BREGMAN age 27 also resident in Labor Township * * *7424 BREGMAN S is instructed by Township administration to report directly to this unit for interrogation

> Labor Township * * *7424 remains under enhanced security status after escape of 1 additional worker at 1178/4829 MKST 36:45.843 details to follow

>STAND BY

# TWELVE

IN THE END, it was a Mek that got them, just not in a way that either of them could have expected.

Falk had pulled Dakota from the naked exposure of the highway and into the scrub on the other side, where he told her they'd crossed the old territory boundary from Wyoming. That was good news; going by the map, their destination wasn't far across the border, and if they continued to make good time, they might be there in only a few days.

But Dakota couldn't stop wondering why she had the same name as the place they'd been headed this whole time. By coincidence or intent? In a world in which a mysterious man had somehow found her in a vast nation under alien occupation, coming to her with a treasure map printed on his arm and promises of a freedom always thought impossible, she was no longer willing to believe that anything happened by accident.

They continued through more swaths of prickly scrub brush, heading toward another small town that Falk had spotted on the horizon. Beyond that were more mountains, big ones—and according to Falk's map, their destination lay somewhere within those peaks. They were so close.

The arrived at the town and found it was bigger than the last. A place people had once called home rather than just passed through. It was a ghost town now, of course, and though Dakota had never seen a town look any other way, the sight of empty human settlements always filled her with unease, a horrible sense of wrongness that a place once so full of life should now be hollowed-out and barren.

"Wait for dark, then go house to house?" Falk suggested.

Dakota nodded.

* * *

On the edge of town was a small strip of stores, but there was nothing to be found there. More interesting were the houses on the shallow hillside above. The first few had nothing, stripped down to the floorboards and wall studs, but eventually they found an unmarked can of food and a weatherproof jacket. After shaking out the moths and dusting it down, Falk insisted that Dakota take the jacket; she'd been a sleeve short ever since she sacrificed one to wrap his wounded arm. The jacket was a size too big, but it felt wonderful around her, soft and warm.

Though they didn't know it, the next house they checked would be their last. Dakota and Falk were searching the downstairs when Falk stopped outside a closed door and gestured for her to join him. She crept over.

"I think there's somebody inside," he whispered. "I can hear them moving in there. Scratching around."

Dakota listened, and then she heard it, too—the scratching.

"It's probably just a cat or something," she said, though she was getting a bad feeling. "Let's move on to the next house."

"What if it's someone who's hurt?" said Falk. "Like a kid or something? We can't just leave them."

"If they're hurt, there's nothing we can do for them. I'm serious, Falk—let's go."

She tugged on his arm, but he wouldn't move.

"Hello?" he called through the door, and Dakota felt a sudden panic. Sam had taught her better than this, and she gesticulated wildly at Falk to cut it out.

But there was no response to his call, just more of the same scratching.

Falk reached for the doorknob.

"Do *not* go in there," Dakota whispered.

"It'll be okay," said Falk, and he opened the door.

They were hit by the smell of motor oil and something, acrid and sour and familiar. There had been gunfire in there, and not long past. And then the door swung wide, and they saw it. A Mek rover, resting in the corner with its underside exposed. Like an overturned beetle, it twitched its metallic limbs in the air as if trying to right itself. But it was badly damaged, leaking oil and other fluids that pooled on the floor. There were bullet holes in the walls around where it had fallen.

"Someone took it down," said Falk. He took a step closer, fascinated.

"We should go," said Dakota. "More will be coming."

"I don't know," said Falk. "Look how much the oil's soaked into the floorboards. It's been here a while. Maybe its radio's damaged. You ever see a downed Mek before?"

"Yeah," said Dakota. She'd seen plenty. "Don't get too close; it's still dangerous."

"Pretty sure it's dead," he said, still transfixed. "I never saw one like this before, all shot up. Not this close."

"You said you'd been with people who've done it," she said.

"Never actually saw it though, just heard tell. Maybe there's some way we can take it apart, gets its weapon. You're a mechanic, right?"

He stepped forward eagerly to get a better look, and Dakota could manage no more than "Stop! They have a—" before Falk's approach triggered the damaged Mek's proximity sensor, activating its self-destruct mechanism. It exploded, the blast knocking Dakota clean off her feet and through the doorway, into the hall. She hit the wall hard and collapsed to the floor, dazed.

Her vision was blurry and her ears were ringing and the doorway was coughing out thick black smoke. She staggered to her feet and covered her nose and mouth before rushing headlong back into the room, blinded by the smoke but following the sounds of Falk's hacking and spluttering. When she found him, she grabbed his arm and dragged him from the room. It took tremendous effort in her disoriented state, but she pulled him all the way outside, onto the house's front path. She looked back. The explosion had started a fire, and the blaze was already raging in the room where they'd just been.

She pulled Falk farther from the growing inferno and stopped beneath a tree. She slumped back against it, exhausted.

"Are you okay?" she asked.

"I think so," he said, lying prone next to her. "Nothing hurts."

Only then did she see that most of his left leg was gone, shredded just above the knee.

She clapped her hand over her mouth. Falk saw her reaction and craned his head forward to see what was the matter.

"Oh," he said when he saw. "Fuck."

"You're going to be okay," she said, lying to them both. She tore the lining from her jacket and fashioned it into a tourniquet. She was fighting back tears as she tied it around the stump of his leg. There was no way to know how much blood Falk had already lost, but if she'd tied the wound off well enough and quickly enough, there was at least a chance he could—

"You can't stay here, Dak," he said. "You have to go."

"I'm not leaving you," she said, her voice faltering.

"Listen to me: I'm done. You can't carry me, and even if you could, I'm useless. This is as far as I go." His whole body was shaking.

"Shut up, shut up! Just give me a minute to think!" She was crying now, unable to control it.

He grabbed her arm, made her look at him.

"Dak, listen! There's no way the Mek haven't seen that fire. They are coming. You have to go *now*!"

"I can't," she sobbed. "I can't."

"We've come so far," said Falk. "Don't let me down now." His voice was growing weaker, his eyes dimming. "Whatever's waiting for us is so close. Don't let all of this be for nothing. Please, Dak. Go."

"I can't do this without you," she sobbed.

"Yes. You can." He took her hand and tried to squeeze it, but his grip was weak. "You have to."

Dakota wiped the tears from her eyes. The house was burning down to its frame, on the verge of collapse. Even at this distance, the heat was almost too much to bear.

"I just need to get you away from here," she said. "Then we can figure this out, okay? Let's just—"

He wasn't looking at her anymore. His eyes were closed and his body was no longer shaking. He fell still.

Dakota almost screamed. She checked his neck for a pulse, then exhaled with relief when she felt one. It was weak and erratic, but there. He'd passed out from shock or from blood loss, or some combination of both. But he wasn't dead. Yet.

That was when she saw the first Mek searchlight. Then another. And though she was distraught beyond anything she'd ever felt, she somehow found the presence of mind to do the last thing she knew she had to before she left him. She rolled up his right sleeve, and with the marker pen she'd stashed in her pocket, she hurriedly copied the last part of Falk's map from his arm onto her own. Her version, done in a shaking hand and half-blind from tears, wasn't nearly as precise as the original, but it would have to be enough. It would have to be.

And then she was up on her feet, running for the hills.

# THIRTEEN

*THIS WAS ALL your fault. All your fault. You should never have let him go through that door, never have let him anywhere near that thing. You knew it was dangerous and you didn't stop him. How many times did he save your life, and when it's his turn to rely on you, you're useless. Useless. How could you fuck up that badly, so close to the end? This is all because of you. Only because of you. All of it your fault. You let him down, left him helpless in the hands of the Mek. Stupid stupid stupid.*

Again and again, these words and others like them played in Dakota's head as she trekked through the rugged mountain terrain. That incessant inner monologue, steeped in blame and guilt, drove her forward beyond every physical limit she thought she had. For the next two days she pushed herself, barely eating, stopping to rest only when forced to by a combination of daylight and open terrain, and even then unwilling to sleep, too driven to move onward at the first opportunity.

But on the third day, something in her brain finally told her that she had to stop or she'd drop from exhaustion, and then she'd have only let Falk down again, too stupid to know her own limitations, dead mere miles from her journey's end and the promise awaiting her there.

When she came upon a stream, she drank and cleaned herself up, careful not to wash away the ink on her arm that sweat had already eroded. Then she slept the rest of the day behind a waterfall, where she had nightmares about Falk and the fate she'd consigned him to. She woke to find the moon high in the sky and cursed herself for wasting precious dark. Fresh from rest, she went at it harder than ever.

She continued over the ridge and by moonlight navigated her way down a precariously steep slope, the only way onward that she could find, every other route impassable. She had to check the ground beneath her feet with every step, knowing that one loose stone could lead to a broken ankle that would put an end to everything. By the time she arrived at the bottom, the sky was lightening, and she found herself at the side of a road surrounded by dense forest, though it took her a moment to be sure that it really was a road, it was so covered with overgrowth and debris. It was the burned-out shell of a car that gave it away.

She knew from the map that a road would lead her to her final goal, but she couldn't be sure that this was it, or if it was, which way to go. If the map was that specific, it was beyond her ability to understand. She took a chance and picked a direction, feeling reasonably confident that a road fallen into such disuse would no longer be patrolled by Mek.

After about two miles, the road took her across a stone bridge, and then to what seemed like a very incongruous thing to be found deep in the forest: a man-made complex with multiple buildings of stark, angular gray concrete.

The structures were mossy and decrepit, largely reclaimed by nature—one of them was tilting and looked close to collapse—and they reminded Dakota of tombstones, like the ones she'd seen in graveyards during her travels with Sam. That still seemed a strange thing to her, the old custom of burying people in the ground. Every dead person she'd ever known had either been left to rot where they fell or was recycled by the Mek.

She climbed over piles of concrete and rebar and made her way to the largest building in the complex, which also looked the most structurally sound. The sign she passed as she entered its cavernous hall read "VISITOR CENTER," but there was nothing worth visiting, just the remnants of smashed and overturned glass cases and pedestals, what Dakota figured to be exhibits of some kind. Part of the room was burned black by some long-ago fire.

She pulled a placard from the debris at her feet and tried to read it, but it was too badly charred. The only word she could make out was "WASHINGTON," which she knew was the name of an old territory far east of there, one of the very first to fall to the Mek.

In the next room was a big dining area, or what used to be one. It was covered in a thick layer of dust and rubble from the collapsed ceiling, which let in shafts of daylight. The room was lined with tall windows all along one side, though those had all shattered, tree branches now jutting through. She came upon a table that, amazingly, still had a tablecloth and place settings, all smothered in a thick patina of dust. She found an intact chair and dragged it over to the table, then sat there for a while at a place setting, just to see what it felt like to do what people used to do. She almost fell asleep there but jerked herself awake when she felt a cool breeze on her cheek.

The breeze was coming in through the broken windows. And as she looked in that direction, she realized that the windowed side of the room had been designed to offer a vista of the mountains looming above. The overgrown trees now obscured much of that view, but what little she glimpsed of it…

She felt a jolt of adrenaline and leaped to her feet.

*It can't be.*

Picking her way through the rubble, she clambered through one of the windows, careful not to cut herself on the shards of glass that still bordered it. She pushed through the trees and ferns up a shallow incline, striving for an unbroken view.

She burst through…

And there it was.

Directly ahead of her, carved into a great mountain, were four giant faces, each at least twenty meters tall. They were the faces of old men, older than almost anyone Dakota had ever met.

She couldn't even begin to comprehend why the faces were there, or for that matter, how. This was beyond anything humans were capable of. But she had no doubt about where she was.

This was the place she'd been searching for.

* * *

Dakota was there. She had followed Falk's map to its conclusion. But it gave no more specificity, no further instruction. Where was she supposed to go now? What was she supposed to do?

She kept going, walking closer to the four faces, because it was all she could think to do. They loomed over her, silently judging her with their grim, humorless expressions.

She reached a fallen chain-link fence topped with razor wire. It extended out of sight in both directions, probably encircling the entire mountain to keep people out, but now it was laid down flat and she could just walk across it. A rusted sign was affixed to a portion of the fence, half-covered with fallen leaves, so she brushed them aside to read the big block letters:

**WARNING**
**RESTRICTED AREA**
**NO TRESPASSING BEYOND THIS POINT**
**PROPERTY UNITED STATES AIR FORCE**

*Air Force.* Dakota's mind started racing. *Mom was in the Air Force.*

She was running now, over the fallen fence and beyond, the four stone men looking down at her with their dead-eyed stares. *Whatever it is, it has to be here, it has to be right—*

"HALT."

Dakota froze. The voice sounded halfway Mek. *Oh please, not now, not when I'm so close…*

Something mechanical rose up from within a cluster of ferns. A sensor on a telescopic pole. It looked around and found Dakota with its camera lens, a single unblinking eye.

"DO NOT ATTEMPT TO MOVE," said the voice. "STAND BY."

Dakota wasn't sure what it was. It didn't look Mek, but it didn't look like any human technology she'd ever seen either. Strangely, it struck her as somehow a little of both. Either way, instinct told her not to argue with it.

An emitter beneath the camera flicked on and swept her with a red light from head to toe. Dakota understood that she was being scanned. But when the scan was done, the electronic eye just continued silently staring at her.

"So what happens—"

"RETINAL POSITIVE FOR BREGMAN, DAKOTA J."

The ground lurched beneath Dakota's feet. She threw out her arms, barely keeping her balance, and saw that a perfect square of forest floor, about three meters across, was sinking into the ground with her standing on top of it. She was on an elevator descending into unknown depths.

She had to decide in an instant—*Stay on this thing or jump off while there's still time?*—and she decided to stay. Whatever it was, wherever it was taking her, it was what she had come so far, and at such great cost, to do.

The world above reduced to a shrinking square of daylight, and Dakota steeled herself, ready to meet her fate, to learn what secrets this mountain held in its dark embrace.

* * *

By the time the platform stopped its descent, the square of daylight above had disappeared completely. Dakota couldn't be sure how far she'd traveled—her journey down was measured only by featureless rock walls and the occasional inset light—but she guessed it was around two hundred meters. She was standing at the end of a smooth, curved corridor, large enough for a truck to pass through. Ceiling lights clicked on in a cascade sequence, disappearing around the bend.

There was only one way for Dakota to go. She stepped off the platform and started down the corridor, her footsteps echoing on the concrete.

She'd never seen an environment like this—everything so perfectly smooth and shiny, spotlessly clean. All she'd ever known was destruction and decay, the aged and crumbling ruins of a forgotten world. Even the township was all wood and wire and poured concrete, decidedly low-tech. The Mek cities were advanced, of course, and their towering architecture glimmered even from a distance, but she had never ventured close enough to really see them.

The long tunnel ended at an armored door. She looked for a control panel or something to—

"STAND BY."

An emitter above the door scanned her. After what felt like too long, she heard a mechanical whirring and the hiss of hydraulics, and the door slid open before her.

She stepped through. The space beyond was dark, but only for a moment. Lights began to flicker on, casting her surroundings in stark fluorescence. Dakota didn't like the lights—they were too bright and reminded her of the township by night—but she forgot all about them once she saw the marvels they illuminated.

She was in a space so vast, it disappeared into the darkness at the far end where lights hadn't yet been turned on. The whole place was filled with mechanical equipment. Computer terminals. Hydraulic lifts. Workbenches. Every manner of industrial tool, machine, and engine part. Big lockers with cage-mesh doors revealing more treasures inside. For a mechanic like Dakota, it was a dream, even though she couldn't identify what most of the stuff was. And once again, she was struck by just how clean and preserved everything was. Somehow there was no dust; it was all like new. She wiped her finger on a workbench just to be sure, and her finger came back cleaner than before. She'd smeared grime along the bench's spotless surface.

"INITIALIZING HEURISTIC INTERFACE. STAND BY."

The voice came from all around her, the same not-quite-Mek-like voice that had spoken to her before. And just ahead of her, a haze of bright light formed, generated by a pair of emitters on opposite sides. As Dakota stepped forward to get a better look, the haze began to resolve into a shape. A pair of eyes formed, then a nose and a mouth, and in seconds Dakota found herself standing before a three-dimensional hologram of a human face. The way it was put together from millions of tiny graphical artifacts to form a coherent image was wondrous and strange; it looked like a computer's approximation of a human face more than the real thing. And yet, something about it felt familiar.

The holographic face's eyes opened. Looked at her. Its features softened in a look of recognition. And then it spoke.

"Oh my."

It wasn't the same voice as before. This one was female, like the face itself. And though it was oddly modulated, as if passing through layers of post-processing, it was unmistakably more human than the one that was always telling her to *stand by*.

"Dakota," the face said. "Is it really you?"

No, it didn't sound like a computer. This was not the unnatural way the Mek mimicked human speech. This was not that at all. This voice sounded truly *alive*… as though in possession of a human soul.

"How do you know who I am?" Dakota asked.

"I'm sorry, I don't know why I'd expect you to recognize me," said the face. "You were barely two years old when you last saw me. But I would know your face anywhere, at any age. You still have your father's eyes."

"My father?" said Dakota. "You knew my father? Who *are* you?"

The face gave her a smile filled with loving warmth that no computer could emulate.

"My name is Rosie," the voice said. "I'm your mother."

# FOURTEEN

DAKOTA BACKED AWAY from the holographic face. It had to be a trick. Had to be. Somehow the Mek had done this. Yes, it all made sense now. That was how she and Falk had managed so improbably to escape, to make it this far without recapture. The Mek had *let* them do it, had watched them the whole way, followed Dakota there. But to what end?

"This isn't real," she said. "You're not real."

"I understand this isn't easy," said Rosie. "Trust me, it isn't easy for me, either, and I've been preparing for this day for twenty years. But you need to calm down and take a breath. I'm detecting elevated levels of adrenaline and increased heart rate."

"You're not real," Dakota said again. "My mother's dead."

"That's true in one sense, not in another," said Rosie. "My body died twenty years ago at Bismarck. But before I left for that battle, my brain was scanned, and a complete virtual copy was stored in the computer servers in this facility. My personality, memories, consciousness… it's all really me. Dakota, I'm your mom."

Dakota looked again at the face hovering before her, and now she began to see it. The eyes. They were the same as those of the woman in the photograph she'd stared at for so many hours. Kind, but somehow sad.

Still, Dakota fought the urge to believe any of this.

"What you're talking about, it isn't possible," she said. "Copying brains onto computers? I'm not stupid, you know."

"It wasn't possible before the Mek came," said Rosie. "But we learned a lot from them, from the technology we were able to steal or salvage from our encounters with them. Dakota, there's so much more I'd like to show you. That's why you're here."

Dakota felt numb, paralyzed. More than anything, she wanted to believe that she was talking to her mother—her actual *mother*—as impossible as that sounded. But she needed more.

"What's my middle name?" she asked.

"Jefferson. Your dad and I got that from one of the guys you saw outside on the mountain."

"What's my brother's name?"

"Sam." Rosie smiled. "That was just a name we liked."

"What was your rank in the Air Force?"

"Lieutenant Colonel."

Dakota's mind raced. She wasn't being smart enough. Those were things the Mek already knew, or could easily have found out. She needed something that only she and her mother would know, something the Mek couldn't possibly have ever learned.

"Sing me the lullaby you sang for Sam when he was a baby," she said. It was the same lullaby Sam had sung to her when she was little, during so many sleepless nights hiding from the Mek.

"Well, it's been a while…" said Rosie. "And I'm not sure this voice synthesizer can really match my actual pipes. But here goes."

*"This little light of mine, I'm gonna let it shine,*
*Oh this little light of mine, I'm gonna let it shine,*
*This little light of mine, I'm gonna let it shine,*
*Let it shine, let it shine, let it shine…"*

Dakota only just managed to fall into a chair; her legs would no longer hold her. As her eyes welled with tears and she looked once again at the hologram, she truly believed.

"Mom." The word was a whisper.

"Oh baby," said Rosie, her synthesized voice betraying her emotion. "I'm so sorry. I'm sorry I wasn't there for you when you needed me. I'm sorry I can't hold you right now. But I'm here. It's really me. And I'm so proud of you. I've been sleeping, dreaming for twenty years that one day you'd find your way here. And I have so much to tell you. But first, I need to ask you something."

Dakota knew what the question was.

"You want to know about Sam."

"Yes."

"He's okay," said Dakota. "He's alive."

Rosie smiled. "Tell me everything."

* * *

In the hours that followed, Dakota told Rosie all about her life, and Sam's. She talked about the years running and hiding from the Mek, and how Sam had cared for her and kept her safe. She talked about their capture, and about their life together in the township. She explained what had happened to Sam's arm—and how he'd slowly changed, the suffocating confinement and ever-present observation draining his will to fight, and even at times to live. But she also assured her mother that he was still the same Sam she had known when he was six years old, the last time she'd seen him. Loving, kind, selfless, brave when it mattered.

"One thing I don't understand," said Rosie when Dakota was done. "If Sam didn't come with you, how did you find this place? He had the map."

"He doesn't have it anymore. It was on the same arm that he lost in the accident. But even if he did, I don't think he would have come. He lied to me for years about what the map was, trying to protect me. He didn't want us risking our lives trying to find this place. I think, though, that if he'd known you'd be here waiting for us, he might have found the strength. In fact, I know he would have."

Rosie's face showed a mix of emotions—regret, pride, love. It was amazing how this holographic simulacrum of a human face could so accurately convey human feelings.

"So how *did* you get here?" Rosie asked.

"There was a guy, Falk, who came to the township. He had the exact same tattoo on his arm. He said that his father was a Gundog pilot, like you. We broke out together."

"Eugene Falk's kid," said Rosie. "Gene was in my squadron, and we gave Stephen and Sam the same map. Some other pilots who had kids did the same, when the end was looking close. The hope was that maybe one or two of you would find your way back here, when you were old enough. I'm so glad, Dakota, that you were one of them. Where's Stephen now?"

*Stephen*, thought Dakota. Falk had never told her his first name.

"He didn't make it," she said. "The Mek got him, a few days from here. We were so close." That agonizing memory now came back to her in full force, twisting her stomach into a sickening knot. For all her travails, she'd never experienced real grief before, not like this, and she hated it. His absence had carved a hole, leaving her feeling hollow and alone—and guilty for not having done more to save him. She wanted to wish all those emotions away, but she knew from others who'd spoken about losing loved ones that these feelings would be with her for a long time, maybe for the rest of her life. And some part of her was even okay with that; it was better than forgetting him.

"I'm sorry," said Rosie. "He was a good kid. And not only that, but for this to work, we need two of you. I'll have to think on that problem. Honestly, I had always hoped it would be you and Sam." She paused, and her mood seemed to darken. "Perhaps it's best he lost the arm," she said.

That was a strange thing for a mother to say about her son.

"Why?" Dakota asked.

"The Mek will interrogate Sam about you, try to find out what he knew about where you were headed. If he still had the map, they'd be able to figure it out almost immediately. It may take a little longer for them to extract that information from him now."

"What do you mean, *extract*?" Dakota said. "Sam couldn't possibly reconstruct that map from memory, even if he wanted to. He lost it years ago."

"The Mek have ways around that," Rosie answered. "They have technology that can scan our brains, recover information we can't consciously remember. It takes time, but it works. They did it to some of us they captured during the war. It's not unlike the cortex-mapping tech we stole from them and used to preserve my consciousness. We have to assume we don't have long before the Mek finds this facility. I had prepared a three-month orientation and training program for you, but we're going to have to compress that."

"Orientation and training?" Dakota said. " For what?"

"I think we can afford to wait until morning before we get into all that," said Rosie. "You look tired. When was the last time you slept the whole night in a comfortable bed?"

Dakota honestly didn't know if she *ever* had. The hard, slatted frames and thin, itchy mattresses of the township bunks certainly didn't qualify.

"It's been a while," she said.

"Come with me," said Rosie.

* * *

The Rosie hologram was apparently capable of manifesting anywhere in the underground complex, as long as there were emitters—and there were emitters everywhere. By beaming herself from location to location, she showed Dakota to a kind of dorm room with bunks and lockers. Some of the bunks looked like they'd been slept in and were never made back up again; others you could bounce a quarter off of. There were still some clothes and other personal effects in some of the lockers and on nightstands, and some were even strewn across the floor. It looked as though this place had been abandoned in a hurry.

"Maid's day off," explained Rosie.

Dakota just looked at her, having no idea what a maid was.

"Just pick any bunk," said Rosie. "Get some rest. Sleep as late as you want. Tomorrow you'll eat a real breakfast, and after that we'll begin."

Dakota took off her boots and her coveralls and slid into one of the unused bunks. The sheets were cool, clean, and unbelievably soft; they caressed her like nothing she'd ever felt. It was bliss. She stared up at the ceiling, as was her habit. The stark fluorescent lights overhead were still buzzing.

"How do I turn off the lights?" she asked.

"Just ask me," said Rosie, and the lights flicked off, leaving the room lit only by the shimmer of her hologram. "I can control everything in this facility, so if there's anything you want, just ask."

"Thanks... Mom," said Dakota. That was going to take some getting used to.

"You're welcome, sweetie. Good night."

Rosie was just shimmering out of sight when Dakota called her back.

"Mom?"

"What is it?"

"One more time?"

Rosie smiled. And then she began.

*"This little light of mine, I'm gonna let it shine,*
*Oh this little light of mine, I'm gonna let it shine,*
*This little light of mine, I'm gonna let it shine,*
*Let it shine, let it shine, let it shine…"*

# FIFTEEN

THAT NIGHT, DAKOTA slept longer than she ever had, though she was again visited by nightmares about Falk, each one more vivid and upsetting than the one before. At first, her mind simply replayed the moment when Falk approached the damaged rover—except in agonizing slow motion, so Dakota's subconscious had time to berate her for failing to intervene, to stop him, to do *something*. In later versions, Sam was there too, or her mother, fully alive again, all of them paying the price for Dakota's inaction. And in one nightmare, she was no longer Dakota at all, but Falk, bleeding out under the tree in the light of the burning house, feeling his pain, his fear, as his end drew near.

Dakota was no stranger to bad dreams and had learned to will herself awake to escape from them—but there was no escaping this last one. Like Falk, she was paralyzed, trapped.

In the end, it was only the pulsing of an alarm that roused her and made her sit up groggily. It took Dakota a moment to remember where she was, where her long journey had brought her. As she looked around at the underground dormitory, reality slowly came back to her through a haze of sleep and the phantom pain from the nightmare. The four faces. The scanner. The elevator ride. The underground workshop. All of that was real. The only thing that still seemed like a dream, too much a product of her deep subliminal desires, was the frankly ridiculous idea that her long-dead mother had somehow been resurrected as a computer-generated hologram. Perhaps her exhausted mind had conjured up this "mother" as some kind of coping mechanism. Or perhaps—

"Dakota," said Rosie.

Dakota rubbed her eyes, trying to rid herself of the last residue of sleep and dream. When she opened her eyes, she saw her mother's face, shimmering in the holographic ether, looking at her expectantly.

"Bregman! On your feet!"

Now the mother-hologram was barking at her like a military commander. It worked; Dakota scrambled out of bed.

"What is it?" she asked. "What's that alarm?"

"Something topside tripped a perimeter sensor," said Rosie.

If Dakota wasn't fully awake before, she was now. A chill ran through her. "Mek?"

"No," said Rosie. "The base sensors are calibrated to detect them at long range and would have spotted them way farther out. It's either an animal sniffing around, or it's human. Let's go look."

* * *

Rosie led Dakota back to the cavernous room where they first met. When Dakota had first arrived, all of the computer terminals were dark, but now several were functioning and projecting panels of holographic data. And they weren't the only machines now active; there was some kind of beverage-maker dripping hot brown liquid into a glass jug. Rosie said it was coffee, which Dakota had heard of but never tried. Rosie urged her to drink some, told her it would help wake her up. She said the ground beans—apparently coffee was made from beans—had been freeze-dried while this facility was in standby mode and should taste as fresh as when they were first ground decades ago. None of that meant anything to Dakota, but she tried a sip of the stuff, only to find it revolting, bitter, and what she imagined drinking dirt might be like. She wound up drinking two cups of it anyway. As foul as it was, it was still better than the Mek stim drink and just as effective, like getting a jolt from an observer, except you could still feel your tongue and the tips of your fingers afterward.

"Panel three," said Rosie, bringing a screen to the forefront of a multi-panel holographic display. It was a live feed from a camera on the surface, just inside the downed chain-link fence that Dakota had walked across the day before. Something was definitely moving through the brush, but hidden. It could be a deer, or a wolf, or a human in a crouch, trying to stay low.

"Going to thermal," said Rosie, and the display changed to a bright spectrum of blue-green tones with a bloom of orange-red heat at its center. The shape of that bloom left no room for doubt: it was human, hunched over to stay out of sight as it pushed its way through bushes and ferns.

"Rare to see someone moving around in the open," said Rosie. "The Mek have just about everyone rounded up. A human hasn't tripped a sensor here in more than three years, now two in two days?" She looked at Dakota. "Was it just you and Stephen? Was there anyone else with you?"

"It was just the two of us," Dakota said. But she agreed with her mother's implication that there had to be more than coincidence at work here. For a moment, she allowed herself to get carried away and imagine it might somehow be Falk, but the heat-shape on the thermal display was moving on two legs, a reality that even her momentary optimism couldn't banish.

"The brush is thinning out," said Rosie. "If they move any closer, they'll have to show themselves. Switching feeds."

The thermal display blinked out, replaced by the regular camera view of the surface—again showing nothing but bushes.

A long moment passed, and then the bushes moved, and a person stepped out. A person Dakota knew. She felt her eyes widen. It couldn't be. He couldn't be here. But he was.

It was Runyon.

* * *

COMMAND UNIT REPORT
UNIT RANK: WAR COMMANDER FIRST CLASS
DESIGNATION: MEK-39487651-28743

FILED 1179/8331 MKST 76:23.842

>This unit continues to supervise standard interrogation of all prisoners at Labor Township * * *7424 (Sector 11) to determine whereabouts of escape subjects * * *81-47676 BREGMAN and * * *39-90983 FALK interrogations so far unproductive neurogenic imager indicates all prisoners answering truthfully

>This unit conducted interrogation of prisoner * * *81-47675 SAMUEL BREGMAN older sibling of * * *81-47676 BREGMAN prisoner denies any knowledge of BREGMAN's escape plans intent destination or whereabouts neurogenic imager indicates prisoner answering untruthfully or withholding information this unit will proceed with enhanced interrogation

>Identity of additional escape subject confirmed as * * *81-54729 WILLIAM RUNYON circumstances under review additional search units dispatched

>This unit collating information from field report of units dispatched to scene of possible human activity at grid-ref E57SB-35847 on 1178/4827 MKST 98:297 evidence found of rover unit damaged by human small-arms fire

blood detected at scene matches DNA profile of subject * * *39-90983 FALK no body found at scene or in wider sector search additional units dispatched to conduct more thorough search of surrounding area

>STAND BY

# SIXTEEN

"YOU KNOW HIM?" Rosie asked.

"Yes," said Dakota. "I mean, not really. Another worker from my township."

Rosie continued to watch Runyon on the surface monitor. "How the hell did he get here?"

Dakota was already searching for an answer to that very question. How could he possibly have escaped from the township when it would surely be under lockdown following her breakout with Falk?

Unless the Mek had *let* him escape. Or merely transported him out. They would have interrogated everyone at the township by now, and if he knew something about her destination, they might have forced him to help them find her. But what could he possibly know? She had told him nothing, hadn't spoken to him, in fact, she had barely seen him since she'd fallen in with Falk to plot their escape. Maybe Falk or Sam had told him something? No, neither was that careless.

*Then how the fuck is he here?*

"Can he get inside here, the way I did?" Dakota asked.

"The facility is programmed to admit only those people with specific retinal profiles stored in its system," Rosie replied. "But I can override that. Do you trust him?"

Did she? The truth was, she barely knew Runyon. It had taken her a moment to even recall his name. She thought back to that one occasion—actually quite recent, though it felt like a lifetime ago—when he stood up for her at story time and earned himself a black eye for his trouble. His defense of her had seemed genuine. But there were other times when she'd felt eyes on her and turned to catch him staring before he quickly looked away. Had he been spying on her? A Mek agent? It was certainly a possibility. After all, he *did* have one of the better jobs in the township, an electrical maintenance detail that spared him the hard labor and frequent accidents that came with factory or foundry work. He might well have gotten that assignment in return for keeping tabs on Dakota and anyone else the Mek had suspicions about.

In the end, she decided it didn't matter. The more she thought on it, the more it seemed impossible that Runyon could have known anything about her escape plan. He couldn't have told the Mek where she was going or led them here, because he didn't know where she was going in the first place.

She stepped closer to the display and studied his face. Like her, he seemed lost, unsure where to go next. But he didn't seem afraid, as he surely would be if he was there under Mek coercion.

She sighed. None of it made any damn sense. There was nothing Dakota hated more than an unsolved puzzle, and there was only one way to solve this one.

"Let him in," she said.

* * *

Dakota waited at the bottom of the elevator as the hydraulic system brought Runyon down. When the platform arrived, and Runyon saw Dakota standing before him, he blinked several times, as though to test whether she was a hallucination or actually real.

"Dakota?" he said. His voice was hoarse.

"Runyon. How are you here?" she asked.

He seemed not to hear her, or at least understand her, and stepped forward unsteadily. He looked terrible. His eyes were distant, unfocused. His township coveralls were torn and bloody, and his arms and legs were covered with cuts and abrasions. One arm was held in a sling, fashioned from one of his sleeves. And he was emaciated, too, to the point that Dakota feared he would break at the slightest touch. He had always been a skinny boy, all knees and elbows, gangly. Now he was a walking skeleton. That he had gotten here was puzzle enough; that he had managed it in this condition was nothing short of a miracle.

Before Dakota could repeat her question, he staggered forward and fell into her, wrapping his arms around her. She had to grab him to prevent him from collapsing to the floor, and as she did so, she was struck by how light he was, how little was left of him.

There was no way he was working for the Mek. Their algorithms would never have let a valuable asset slip to within a hair's breadth of death, as he so clearly was.

Rosie materialized before them. "He's severely dehydrated, borderline malnutrition, too. We need to get him to a bed and get some fluids in him, and then I'll do a more thorough scan."

Dakota lifted him easily onto one shoulder. He didn't resist; it seemed he'd already passed out. She carried him to the dorm, where she laid him on an empty bunk. Rosie showed her where to find the medical equipment and told her how to set up an IV.

And then all they could do was wait and watch.

* * *

Runyon slept the rest of the day and well through the night, going through three bags of IV solution. By the time he finally sat up late the next morning, he looked far better, though his eyes still had that distant look.

"It wasn't a dream," he said when he saw Dakota sitting on her bunk, beside him. Rosie had decided to remain unseen and unheard until they knew more.

"How did you get here?" Dakota asked.

"I followed you," he said, still swaying a little from his long sleep. "I mean, I followed your map."

"Bullshit. There was only one map, and we took it with us."

"There used to be two," he said. "The one on your brother's arm. I used to see it all the time when I'd come to fix something in the factory, before he lost it. I never asked him about it because I knew he wouldn't say, but I could tell it was some kind of map."

"And you made a copy?" Dakota asked.

"Kinda," said Runyon, tapping his temple. "Kept it all up here."

This only made Dakota more skeptical. How could he have just remembered it? And decoded it? For that matter, how did he even realize it was a map? To her it had always looked like an arcane and indecipherable mosaic of dots and lines and pictograms. Even when Falk first told her what it was, she had a hard time believing it. Yet this little runt wanted her to believe that he'd figured it out all by himself from just a few glances at her brother's arm—and then memorized the whole thing?

*Bullshit.*

"I know what you're thinking," said Runyon. "But I'm good with things like that. Puzzles and riddles and stuff. It's why the Mek put me in engineering. I really wanted to solve it. So I'd get a look at it whenever I could, and over time I just kinda figured it out. Whoever designed it was really clever. So I remembered it. And when you left…" He shrugged. "I kinda figured that's where you were going. I'm glad I was right. I don't know how much longer I would've lasted out there by myself."

"Are you buying any of this?" said Dakota. She wasn't addressing Runyon.

Rosie responded, but didn't appear. "Actually, I am. Eidetic memory, and I'm guessing a genius-level IQ, too. Dakota, we might have just gotten very lucky here."

"Who was that?" Runyon asked, looking around for the source of the voice, which seemed to be coming from everywhere all at once.

"What do you mean, lucky?" Dakota asked.

"Let's get some proper food in him," Rosie replied. "In both of you. You'll think better on a full stomach."

Runyon's eyes widened. "You have food?"

* * *

Dakota led Runyon to the empty mess hall, which Rosie had introduced her to the day before. The only food was thirty-year-old military rations in vacuum-sealed plastic packets and cans with ring-pull tops, but it had tasted better than anything she'd eaten in her life. Runyon clearly had the same reaction—he wolfed down chicken and baked beans and a brownie square, a meal he selected on Dakota's recommendation, while Dakota tried something different today—beef curry with rice and fruit pudding. Rosie brewed more coffee, but had to cut Runyon off after the second cup. Dakota could guess why; now that he was mostly restored to strength, he was jumpy enough already.

After they ate, Dakota took a look at Runyon's arm and was relieved to see that it wasn't broken, just a bad sprain he'd suffered in a fall; it would mend itself quickly enough.

Only then did Rosie reveal herself to him. The sight of her holographic form unsettled him at first, but Dakota assured him there was nothing to be afraid of, and he quickly accepted that. What was more surprising to Dakota was how fast she herself had come to accept this reality. Just days ago, the idea of a digital reincarnation of her mother would have seemed beyond imagination, yet here she was reassuring Runyon that it was no big deal.

Rosie introduced herself as Lieutenant Colonel Rosalind Bregman, United States Air Force. "I'm in command of this facility," she said, "and you're my guest here, for now, on the word of my daughter. But if you want to remain here, I need to trust you. And that means you need to tell me everything. I want you to start by proving to me that you really did memorize that map—that you weren't brought here with outside assistance."

"Do you have something I can draw with?" Runyon asked.

Rosie conjured a holographic display in the air before him, a glowing blank slate. "You can draw on that with your finger," she said.

And he did. In fact, he redrew the entire map in less than three minutes. Every dot, line, pictogram, and detail recreated perfectly. And when he was done, Rosie recalled an image of the original map from her database and overlaid it. The two were a perfect match.

It seemed to Dakota that a memory like that was impossible. But then she remembered how vividly she was able to call to mind the photo of her parents. If she had any talent as an artist, she'd be able to reproduce that perfectly too.

"I understand how you remembered the map," said Rosie, "but not how you were able to read it."

Runyon shrugged. "Like I said, I've always been good at puzzles. It took some figuring out, but eventually I realized it's actually two maps overlaid: one with stars and constellations for wayfinding, the other with natural landmarks, but they're offset at a ninety-degree angle so they don't match up. You have to read the stars with the map held horizontal, and the landmarks with it held vertical."

Dakota stared at him. "And you figured all that out by yourself," she said incredulously.

Runyon shrugged. "I didn't have much else to think about."

"I like him," said Rosie.

"That explains how you knew where I went," said Dakota, "but not how you got here. How did you even get out of the township?"

Runyon looked down at his feet. "I spied on you."

"You couldn't have seen us escape," said Dakota. Everyone was in the barracks."

"No, not when you escaped," Runyon replied. "When you and Falk were plotting. While you guys were talking at story time, I sat close and listened. I heard you talking about the window magnet, the blind spot in the perimeter sensors, the trick with the ice shower. Lowering your body temperature like that to trick the drones' thermal sensors… that part was really cool. Falk was smart to figure that out. I guess he didn't make it, though? I'm sorry. I didn't really know him, but… I liked him."

Dakota had to shove her feelings deep down. "This still doesn't add up," she said. "Falk never told me where the blind spot was, so even if you overheard us, you wouldn't know where to go."

"There's more than one blind spot," said Runyon. "I've done maintenance on those sensor towers. If you look at the coverage area of each tower and how they're aligned in relation to one another, there's one two-meter blind spot for every six hundred meters of fence. I knew about that already, and the window magnet was easy enough to make, but without the shower trick, it wouldn't have done me much good. And… I never really had a good reason to leave before now."

Dakota sat quietly for a moment, processing all of this. It seemed plausible enough, but one detail still nagged at her.

"You were right there, listening to me and Falk that whole time?" she said. "I would have noticed you."

"I knew you wouldn't." Runyon looked down at the floor again. "Nobody ever notices me. Not really."

Dakota had only one more question. "Why?" she asked. "Why did you follow me?"

"I don't know. I guess because you were the only thing that made life bearable for me there. Even from far away." He still hadn't lifted his gaze from the floor.

"You barely know me," said Dakota.

"I know. Weird, huh? All I know is, once I knew you were going, I wanted to go with you. To be a part of whatever you were doing. And I knew if I asked you, you'd say no. But I had to come."

Dakota was silent for a long time. The kid had escaped, had nearly died, because of her. It was a lot to take in.

"I'm sorry," Runyon said at last. "If you want me to leave, I'll leave."

"On the contrary," said Rosie. "You're most welcome. In fact, you might be exactly what we need."

* * *

With both Rosie and Dakota satisfied that Runyon's story held water, it was time for Rosie to tell hers. So Dakota and Runyon sat in the mess hall and listened.

"Before the last battle, at Bismarck, we knew we would almost certainly lose," she began. "Our forces across the world had been totally destroyed, and what little was left had fallen back to the last city to hold for as long as we could. Our forces consisted of only two divisions, pieced together from the remains of those the Mek had already shattered—that, and the Gundogs that we built here, at this facility. We designed them using Mek technology, reverse-engineered from units we'd captured. Figuring out their tech wasn't easy, but over time, we were able to integrate at least some aspects of it into our own, which allowed us to develop better armor and weapons—enough to put a real hurt on the forces that were coming for Bismarck. Still, we knew that it was most likely the end, and we were all prepared to die fighting.

"If we'd just had more time, we might actually have turned things around, even banged up as we were. Because our scientists at this facility had finally cracked the Mek technology database wide open. And from that we learned everything we needed to build a new generation of weapons as good as anything they had—maybe even better. And we were starting to get pretty close to making that a reality. But by then, Bismarck was the only human city still standing, and the Mek had it under siege, with a quarter of a million people trapped inside. Global Command, in their infinite wisdom, ordered every asset they had left, every Gundog, every operator, every support crew and engineer, to Bismarck to try and hold it. Including everyone from this base. And… well, you know the rest. After that, there simply wasn't anyone left to fight, to operate the new weapons even if we'd had time to build them."

"That doesn't explain how *you're* here," said Runyon. "You died at Bismarck, didn't you?"

"Well, in one sense I did, in another I didn't," said Rosie. "Like I said, we knew Bismarck was probably the end. And we'd developed the ability, using the tech we hacked from the Mek archive, to map a human brain and store it indefinitely in a computer core. As the senior officer, I volunteered to be the guinea pig. So before everyone left for Bismarck, a copy of my consciousness was uploaded to the mainframe here. If the real me failed to return, I was to be activated, and I would act as a caretaker, to preserve the unfinished work that remained here, continue it as much as I could by myself, in the hopes that someday, someone might return to complete it. That's why we gave our kids those maps, so that if they survived, they'd be able to find their way back here. Find what we'd left for them. For you."

"And what did you leave for us?" Dakota asked. "What's here?"

Rosie smiled. "Let me show you."

* * *

She led them through hallways, rooms, heavily armored doors, and more hallways. This vast underground facility seemed to go on forever. But eventually they arrived in another cavernous workspace, much like the first, though its full size was impossible to gauge because most of it was shrouded in darkness.

"I'm going to turn on the lights now," said Rosie. "Are you ready?" There was something new in her voice, a sense of giddy anticipation.

"Yes," said Dakota, although she honestly had no idea if she was or not.

"Dakota, I'm so sorry I wasn't there to see you grow up, to give you everything I wanted for you," Rosie said. "But I can at least give you this. I hope you'll accept it."

One by one the lights clicked on until the entire space was illuminated… as was the towering armored colossus it contained.

Dakota and Runyon craned their necks and gazed upon the thing in silent awe. It was vaguely the shape of a man—two powerful legs, what looked almost like arms, a narrow waist that gave way to a heavy, barrel-chested torso, and a head, though in place of a face it had only a featureless domed cockpit. From top to bottom it was nearly twenty meters tall.

Dakota had never in her life seen anything like it—and yet she knew at a glance exactly what it was. She'd heard Sam describe them many times, when he had lulled her to sleep by telling her her favorite bedtime story about her mother's heroism at the Battle of Bismarck.

"That's a Gundog," she said.

"It's much more than that," said Rosie, her holographic face beaming. "It's liberation."

# SEVENTEEN

"I PRESENT TO you the M-151 Armored Combat Biped, or ACB," said Rosie as Dakota and Runyon continued to stare, agog, at the metal giant that loomed over them like a menacing statue.

"Is this like the Gundog you piloted at Bismarck?" Dakota asked.

"Not quite," said Rosie. "This is way more advanced, a prototype for what we hoped would be a new armored legion. Just a few brigades of these might have turned the tide of the entire war—if only we'd had time to build them. Of course, these past twenty years I've had nothing but time. I've done all I can with the facility's automated systems to get this one finished, but it still needs some work that can only be done with human hands—electrical, hydraulics, a few mechanical adjustments. And, of course, it needs a pilot and a gunner to operate it."

*It's going to take two of us,* Dakota recalled Falk telling her.

"What makes this one different?" Runyon asked.

"Very good question," said Rosie. "The first-gen Gundogs incorporated Mek technology only on a superficial level. Stronger armor, more powerful weapons. Good, but not enough. This one is the real deal, the most cutting-edge Mek tech integrated right down to the core system level. It has the same deflector shielding the best Mek battle units have, a stealth array that should, theoretically, render it virtually invisible to their sensors and satellites, countermeasures up the ass, and best of all, a particle reprocessor similar to the ones used by their reclaimers. But better."

"A particle what?" said Dakota.

"The M-151 can salvage material and components found in the field—scrap metal, old shell casings, anything—and recycle it into particulate matter that can then be used for any purpose it requires," Rosie explained. "Replacing or restoring damaged systems, creating new munitions, pretty much anything."

"It can repair and re-arm itself," said Runyon.

"Very good," said Rosie. "I knew you were a smart one."

"How is it powered?" Runyon asked.

"Cold fusion fuel pod, and the entire surface of the armor is one big solar array. Theoretically, it's capable of decades of independent operation."

There was that word again. "Theoretically?" Dakota said.

"This is still only a prototype. The newer systems have never been tested in the field; some haven't even been tested in the lab. But now that you're here, that's all going to change. You're going to help me get this thing operational, and then I'm going to teach you how to operate it."

"And then what?" Runyon asked. "I mean… even if we get it working, what do we do with it? Fight a new war against the Mek? By ourselves?"

"As far as the Mek are concerned, the war's long over," said Rosie. "They stood down most of their heavy military capacity years ago, sent it back to their homeworld. What remains here is a relatively small occupying force, and they're not expecting a new human offensive." She turned her face toward the Gundog, looking up at it with the admiration of a proud mother. "And they're sure as hell not expecting this."

"It's just one weapon," said Dakota.

"Like nothing the Mek have ever seen," Rosie said. "And sometimes, all it takes is one person to inspire others to stand up and fight, too. Especially once they've been armed with the most powerful weapon of all: the truth."

* * *

It was then that Dakota and Runyon learned that everything they'd grown up believing about the Mek, and about the ten-year war, was a lie.

"The Mek did *not* come to us in peace, the way they've taught you to believe," Rosie began. "There was no dialogue, no offer of advanced alien technology and mutual cooperation. They came out of nowhere and attacked us without warning, without negotiation, without mercy. The first cities were rubble before we even knew what was happening. We later learned that we were far from their first victims, and that every encounter is the same: they invade a planet with overwhelming force, occupy it, then enslave its population and strip its resources. They're a conqueror species, through and through.

"Toward the end of the war, when we had begun to figure out how to intercept some of their comm traffic, we learned what they had planned for us, and how they intended to keep the human population in line once the war was over. They would control us not only with force and fear, but with *shame*. The Mek had done extensive psychological research on us long before they arrived, and their master algorithm had calculated we could best be controlled by propagating the lie that *we* were the aggressors—that we had earned our enslavement by starting a war against a benign race that had come to us in peace. The Mek understood that if we believed we deserved our fate, we'd be more likely to accept it. And their insight has been proven true, for twenty years now."

"But I've seen the tapes," said Runyon. "The history."

Dakota had seen them, too. Everyone had. All new township arrivals were forced to watch them as part of orientation, and just in case you forgot, they were broadcast throughout the day on giant video screens set up all around the compound. The usual sequence started with archival news footage of the Mek's arrival, when their machine ambassador came down from the first ship to land in what used to be New York City, to be greeted by dignitaries from Earth. Some of those news broadcasts showed people talking about a bold new dawn for mankind, a new era of interplanetary cooperation, but others showed world leaders addressing the citizens of their nations, soberly explaining why the Mek could not be trusted and why it was therefore necessary to attack them before they attacked us. These tapes were always followed by footage of fighter planes and long-range missiles destroying Mek ships idling in their landing areas in cities around the world. All together it made for a neatly plotted video history of how humanity had betrayed the Mek—a history that was seared into the consciousness of every worker in every township.

"It's all fake," said Rosie. "Edited and composited by the Mek from the true historical record, to tell the story they need you to believe. The story that keeps you compliant. There's an old saying: history is written by the victors. And that's exactly what the Mek did—they rewrote our history. That's why they killed everyone over a certain age after the war; why even now the townships are filled with workers who are too young to remember what really happened back then. They didn't want anyone left alive who knew the truth."

Dakota and Runyon sat in stunned silence for a long time. It was Runyon who finally spoke.

"You want to tell everyone the truth."

"Exactly right," said Rosie.

"And then? What do you expect them to do?"

"Rise up," said Rosie. "Fight back."

"Against the Mek," said Dakota. "They'd be slaughtered."

"Some of them, yes. But if enough of them start to resist all at once, it might be more than the Mek can handle. There are millions of people in townships all across this country, and countless more across the world. A few troublemakers here and there, the Mek know how to deal with. But thousands, millions, rising up and resisting in unison? We'll see."

"Do you really think that's what'll happen?" Runyon asked. "That they'll all fight?"

"That will be up to them," said Rosie. "We'll show them the truth. *They* will have to decide what they want to do with it. But my guess is they'd rather fight, even if it means they die fighting, than live in a cage they know they never deserved to be in. Maybe it's been forgotten these past twenty years, but that's what humans do. It's what we've always done. We fight for what we believe is right. And the truth, as another saying goes, will set them free."

Dakota had never heard that saying before, but it sounded right. And the idea of returning to her own township to save Sam sounded even better.

"How?" she asked. "How do we show them the truth?"

"We're going to Bismarck," said Rosie. "To the city the Mek built on its ruins. That's where they keep all their secrets. We're going to go in there, and we're going to take them."

And that, as she went on to explain, was just the beginning.

* * *

Dakota and Runyon spent the rest of that day reading manuals and watching instructional films designed as basic orientation for rookie Gundog pilots and gunners. "You can't just drive this thing off the lot," Rosie had said. "You need to familiarize yourself with every sub-system, every nut and bolt. Typically it takes about twelve weeks to train a new Gundog pilot or gunner to basic operational proficiency. We're going to do it in seven days."

"Why so fast?" Runyon had asked, and Rosie once again explained that if the Mek were interrogating Sam, and attempting to extract the map that was once on his arm from his memory, then this base wouldn't be safe for long. The enemy would, in time, show up in overwhelming force. Rosie didn't even like staying there for another week, but it was the absolute bare minimum necessary for the crash training course she'd hurriedly designed. And even that abbreviated version called for Dakota and Runyon to work and study around the clock and drink the base's coffee supply dry.

They very nearly did. Over the following two days, they read more manuals, watched more films, listened to more safety lectures from Rosie. The time went hard for Runyon in particular, who was growing increasingly impatient to move past the textbooks and get his hands on the six hundred tons of military hardware waiting tantalizingly in the room Rosie called a "hangar." His uncanny knack for memorization gave him a huge advantage with this rapid-learning curriculum; he aced every test Rosie gave him. And when Dakota struggled to keep up, he helped her study, quizzed her, made sure she was up to speed, though she knew she would never remember as many details as he did.

On day four, Rosie finally announced that they were done with theory and ready to move on to practical hands-on instruction. Dakota and Runyon were still eating breakfast, but Runyon leapt up from his unfinished meal, clapped his hands together, and started off in the direction of the Gundog hangar.

Rosie materialized in front of him to cut him off. "Not so fast," she said.

"Isn't it that way?" asked Runyon, confused.

"You're out of your mind if you think I'm letting you in that thing before you've got some sense of how she handles," said Rosie.

"Then how do we—"

"Simulator. Follow me."

The simulator was a mostly faithful recreation of a Gundog's cockpit pod. About the size of a truck cab, it seated two, with the gunner situated forward and the pilot behind and above. This one had been built to train operators on the earlier M-150 model, but Rosie explained that there were only minor differences in the tactical and drive systems, and that the simulator would adequately prepare them for the real thing.

"Or near enough, at least," she added, which made Dakota a little nervous.

"First of all," said Rosie, "You two need to figure out which is the pilot and which is the gunner. You scored about the same on the aptitude tests for both seats, so I'll leave it up to you. Who wants to drive and who wants to shoot?"

"I'll shoot," said Dakota and Runyon simultaneously.

"Figure it out," said Rosie. "Trust me, when every step you take shakes the earth at your feet, the driving's pretty fun, too."

"Which were you?" Dakota asked.

"I was a gunner," said Rosie. "Damn good one, too."

Dakota looked expectantly at Runyon and waited. After a long moment, he rolled his eyes and threw up his arms.

"Fine!" he said. "I'll drive."

They climbed into their respective seats, which were padded and comfortable but smelled musty and old. The helmets they had to put on smelled even worse. Then Rosie sealed the pod and powered it up, activating a suite of holographic instruments for both pilot and gunner, and the whole interior of the pod became a wraparound screen that perfectly recreated the field of view from a real Gundog cockpit. The visual fidelity was remarkable; to Dakota and Runyon it truly appeared that they were no longer in the hangar but outside, on an open, rocky plain. They appeared to be about twenty meters off the ground—the same height they'd be once they climbed into the real thing.

"Initiate startup sequence," said Rosie. Her tone no longer the maternal one she took with Dakota or the professorial one she took with Runyon, but the tone of a military officer—all business.

Runyon went through the steps he'd memorized, flipping switches above his head and on the holo-display before him until the simulator made a high-pitched whir like an engine starting to spin up and the whole pod began to rumble and vibrate around them.

"We're at power," Runyon said.

"Drive systems pre-check," said Rosie.

Runyon scanned the displays and indicators before him. "Primary drive is green, secondary drive is green, fuel pod at maximum, all systems in the green and standing by."

"Weapons pre-check," said Rosie.

That was Dakota's job, and she was prepared for it. She'd gone over the procedure in theory a hundred times. But now, in the moment, she froze, unable to even remember the first step. Her hand hovered over the instrument panel, uncertain.

"Left arm, right arm," Runyon prompted from behind her. "Directly in front of you, the red display."

"I know, I know!" she snapped, frustrated with herself but taking it out on him, then she zeroed in on the correct controls. "Left arm loaded and ready, safety on. Right arm loaded and ready, safety on. Forty-millimeters are hot, one-seventy cal, particle beam, rocket pods, flamethrower, all online and green."

"Very good," said Rosie. "Just one thing you've forgotten."

She waited for them to remember, then got impatient.

"Seat belts! Buckle up, kids, because this thing will rattle the teeth right out of your skull."

* * *

The next three days were far more entertaining than the first three had been, but no less demanding. They spent sixteen hours a day in the simulator. Rosie gave Dakota a never-ending series of virtual Mek targets to shoot at, and she generated remorselessly rugged terrain for Runyon to negotiate as pilot. Rosie had dialed the simulator's hydraulic motion system up to 110% to really toss them around; from her own experience, she explained, the simulator never really prepared you for the real thing.

To Dakota, this was real enough; the pod lurched and twisted and spun them around with each simulated movement of the Gundog as it strutted and darted and bobbed and weaved to evade incoming fire. By the time each day was done, Dakota and Runyon were both stiff as boards, and any sensation in their backsides was a distant memory. Every night they wolfed down some quick calories, limped back to their bunks, and slept more soundly than they had thought possible.

At the end of their seventh and final day of training, Rosie sat them down for their evaluation. Dakota reached around to grasp her aching back as she lowered herself onto a cafeteria bench beside an equally exhausted Runyon. They both ignored their food as they awaited the results.

"I think we did good," said Runyon to Dakota. She was about to agree with him when Rosie cut her off.

"You both did terribly," she said. "Bregman, you scored more misses than you did hits, you overheated your forty-mike at least a dozen times, and you nearly cut off your ride's left foot with the particle beam. Runyon, your point-to-point navigating is woeful, you're gonna blow a transmission the way you keep grinding those gears, and half of Dakota's misses were because you didn't have the pod oriented the way she needed it. Understand this, both of you: for a Gundog to be an effective weapon, its pilot and gunner need to operate as a single symbiotic unit. If you two can't learn to play well together, this is not going to work."

Dakota turned on Runyon. "She's right about the misses. I told you I can't aim if you keep jerking us around and don't point me in the right direction."

"Don't blame me for *your* misses," Runyon shot back. "And for what it's worth, I could drive better if you weren't constantly in my ear telling me to—"

"Enough!" Rosie snapped. "Figure it out. And soon. If I had any kind of bench, I'd flunk you both and give the cockpit to the next two guys. But I don't. I'm stuck with you. Three days from now you move out. Ready or not. If you're ready, you *might* just survive this thing. If you're not, I can promise you you won't. Figure. It. Out."

* * *

Later that evening, as Dakota was preparing for bed, Rosie materialized before her. Runyon was already asleep in his bunk, farther down the dorm.

"Do we have a problem?" Rosie asked her daughter.

"With what?" Dakota said.

"With you and Runyon. You've been giving that boy a hard time ever since he showed up here. My guess is long before that, too."

"He's fine," said Dakota. "We'll be fine. We can do this."

"You've been snapping at him, bickering, generally making him feel like you don't want him here at all. That boy went through hell to get here—the least you could do is make him feel welcome. Is there some problem you have with him that I don't know about? Because if there is, I need to know about it before we go out into the field."

"It's nothing," said Dakota, trying to busy herself with folding her clothes.

"Why don't you like him?" Rosie asked.

*Because he's not Falk!* Dakota wanted to scream. *Falk's the one who's supposed to be here with me, not him!* But instead she said nothing, threw back the blankets on her bunk, and climbed in. The dorm lights dimmed to nothing, but there was still the shimmer of Rosie's holographic image, looking at her. It was like a bedside lamp Dakota couldn't switch off.

"Just give him a chance," said Rosie, her tone softer now. "He seems like a very nice young man."

Dakota rolled over in bed, facing away from Rosie.

Her mother's commanding-officer voice returned. "Dakota," she said, "this has to work—because if it doesn't, it's not just your own lives you're risking. It's mine."

Dakota turned back to face her. "What do you mean?"

"I mean, I'm coming with you. You'll have no chance out there without me. Before you depart, my program will be transferred from the facility's mainframe to the M-151's onboard computer. We all live or die together. Now get some sleep."

And then she was gone, her haze of light dissipating, leaving the room in full darkness.

But it would be a good while longer before Dakota slept.

* * *

COMMAND UNIT REPORT
UNIT RANK: WAR COMMANDER FIRST CLASS
DESIGNATION: MEK-39487651-28743
FILED 1180/1541 MKST 96:24.955

>This unit concludes supervision of standard interrogation of all prisoners at Labor Township * * *7424 (Sector 11) to determine whereabouts of escape subjects * * *81-47676 BREGMAN and * * *39-90983 FALK interrogations unproductive neurogenic imager indicates all prisoners answered truthfully

>This unit concludes enhanced interrogation of prisoner * * * 81-47675 SAMUEL BREGMAN older sibling of * * *81-47676 BREGMAN prisoner demonstrates exceptional resistance to questioning neurogenic imager successfully reproduces partial image of illustration formerly imprinted on prisoner's right arm initial analysis suggests cartographic in nature image currently subject to detailed analysis likely to yield subjects * * *81-47676 BREGMAN and * * *39-90983 FALK destination

>This unit requests military strike force classification A to converge on subject destination once positively identified

>STAND BY

# EIGHTEEN

THEY SPENT THREE days completing construction of the Gundog prototype and conducting systems checks. Giant scaffolds were rolled out on either side of the leviathan, allowing Dakota and Runyon to access any part of it from without or within. Under Rosie's close supervision, Runyon tested and installed the last of the critical electronic components that she had fabricated using the base's automated manufacturing systems during her long time in isolation. Dakota attached hoses that allowed coolant to be piped into the M-151's weapons and drive systems, and cables to supply it with the most recent build of the operations firmware that Rosie was confident was as bug-free as she could make it.

But it wasn't until Dakota climbed up to the cockpit, located way up near what would have been the head of this colossus, that she noticed the letters stenciled on the armor plating, just below the pilot and gunner seats.

**LT. COLONEL ROSALIND BREGMAN**
**"ROSIE"**

# LT. EUGENE FALK "FALCON"

She ran her fingers across the letters of her mother's name, then settled into her gunnery seat and got a feel for it. It was better cushioned than the one in the simulator pod, and as she sank into its bucket, she felt a sudden rush. The Gundog was still powered down, idle, the instrument panels before her dark and lifeless, yet as she looked down on the hangar below, her hands resting on the dual sticks that controlled the weapons, for the first time in her life, she understood what it felt like to be… *powerful.*

Or at least, something other than powerless.

She suddenly became impatient to finish training, take this thing out into the world and see what it could do. To fulfill her promise to Sam and smash some Mek motherfuckers into junk.

"How's that feel?"

Dakota turned sharply to see Runyon standing on the ladder just outside the cockpit.

"Sorry if I startled you," he said. "I called on my way up, but seems like you were miles away. Okay if I join you?"

"May as well—you're going to have to sooner or later," she said. "Just don't stand on the little fin there where it says 'NO STEP.'"

"Thanks," said Runyon. "Not sure I would have figured that out on my own." He climbed into the pod and settled into the pilot's seat, just behind her. "Seat's more comfortable than in the simulator," he said.

Dakota grinned. "My butt's already very grateful."

Since Runyon was behind her, she couldn't see his reaction, but his silence suggested she might have made him feel uncomfortable. Sure enough, when she turned around in her seat to face him, he looked away and pretended to go over his instrumentation panels.

"Runyon," she said, "I know I don't always show it, but I really am glad you're here. Thank you."

His face reddened, and now he looked at her, right at her, as though her kind words had given him permission, finally, to do so.

"Nowhere else in the world I'd rather be," he said with a smile.

"Sitting in the cockpit of a giant war machine is tough to beat, I'll grant you that."

"I don't mean that," said Runyon. "I mean here with you."

A moment of silence passed between them, and now Dakota was the uncomfortable one, but Runyon soon was his old self-conscious self again, looking around for something, anything but her.

"I should check the fuel pod again," he said, and he climbed out of his seat and onto the ladder.

Dakota wanted to say something more, and she was about to, but by the time it reached her lips he was gone, sliding back down the ladder to the ground far below.

* * *

It wasn't until every last detail was taken care of—every moving part, electrical system, sub-system, and doohickey on the entire vehicle, all six hundred tons of it, painstakingly checked and re-checked—that it was time to upload

Rosie to the Gundog's onboard computer. And with that came risk. She explained that she wasn't like a regular computer program in that she was not replicable—that is, it wasn't possible to transfer her to the Gundog and still keep a working copy here on the facility's mainframe. She was, in that sense, very much like a real person, one of a kind, irreplaceable. Which meant if something went wrong with the upload, if the transfer didn't go cleanly, or if somehow Rosie's program dropped along the way, there would be no recovering her.

Dakota's mother would die.

Again.

Runyon ran a test version of the transfer program a dozen times before they were confident enough to try it with the real thing.

"I'll be offline for about six minutes while my program copies over," Rosie explained. "Try not to break anything while I'm gone."

Neither Dakota nor Runyon, standing beside the control terminal, felt much like laughing. As much as Rosie had tried to assure them that the procedure was safe, they all knew this had never been done before, and until it was done, everything about the procedure, including its safety, was only a matter of theory. They were gambling with Rosie's life, and they knew it.

"I'm ready when you are," said Rosie.

Runyon's finger hovered over the key that would start the procedure. Then he took it away and looked at Dakota.

"I think you should do it," he said. "She's your mother."

"This is your area," she said. "You're the one qualified."

"Everything's already done. All you have to do is push the button."

"I don't think—"

"Will one of you just push the damn button?" Rosie snapped.

"Let's do it together," said Runyon.

Dakota nodded, and the two of them placed their index fingers over the transfer key, side by side.

"Three… two… one," said Runyon, and they both pushed.

Rosie's holographic image dissipated, and she was gone.

There was nothing to do but wait.

"How long has it been?" Dakota asked after what felt like at least five minutes.

Runyon checked the display. "Forty-five seconds. Relax, she's going to be fine."

"Don't say that," Dakota snapped. "Don't make promises you're not sure you can keep, you don't know that—" She stopped herself. This wasn't his fault; none of it was. All he'd ever done was try to help her.

She needed something to take her mind off this interminable wait. "Tell me about your mother," she said. She wasn't sure why that thought popped into her head. Probably because her own mother, who had been dead to her for almost her entire life, was quite possibly about to be taken from her again.

Runyon blinked, taken off-guard. Maybe by the question. Maybe because she'd spoken to him like a person, an equal. Which was rare.

"I never knew her," he said. "My father, either. My earliest memory is living inside a refugee colony somewhere up north, with a bunch of other orphan kids rounded up from who knows where. There was a family who tried to take care of us, keep us safe. We used to move from place to place a lot, until the Mek finally caught up with us. Everyone in that family was too old, so they never made it to the township. I did, along with all the other orphans."

He looked her in the eye. "You don't know how lucky you are to still have family, Dakota. You really don't."

Dakota thought about that. She had never considered anything about her life lucky. Until now.

"You know," she said, "when we're out there, trying to steer and shoot that damn thing together, every second's going to count. And… Dakota's kind of a mouthful." She paused. "You should call me Dak."

Runyon smiled, totally disarmed. But this time he didn't look away.

A chime sounded, and a green light began flashing on the display.

"That's it," he said. "Transfer's done."

Dakota leaned forward, anxious. "Did it work?"

"It says it did." He looked up at the Gundog, looming over them. "Rosie? Are you there?"

Nothing. No response.

Dakota's stomach tightened into a knot.

"Mom," she said. "Can you hear us?"

"That's Lieutenant Colonel Bregman to you," came the reply.

Runyon smiled wide with relief, and Dakota clapped her hand to her mouth, overcome with emotion. The voice was familiar, but the source of it was not. It was coming from the Gundog cockpit.

Dakota and Runyon raced to climb up there. The instruments and holographic displays were lighting up, coming alive with cheerful, affirmative chiming sounds as systems came online. And then a hologram resolved in the air before Dakota.

A face.

Rosie.

"Be honest: how much did you miss me?" she asked.

Dakota beamed. Forgetting herself for a moment, she reached out to touch her mother's face, but she felt only an electrostatic tingle in her fingers as they passed right through the hologram. "Are you… okay?" she asked.

"I'm fine," said Rosie. "I already ran the diagnostic suite, and everything checks out. And I feel like myself, too. A little cramped in here, I don't quite know how to describe that. But I'm good. It worked."

"Good to have you back, ma'am," said Runyon.

"Thank you, Runyon. I do believe we are as ready as we're ever going to be, God help us."

* * *

Rosie directed them to a locker room where a pair of one-piece body suits had been stored away in vacuum-sealed bags. They retired to privacy to put them on, then returned to reveal themselves to one another. The suits were deep black and almost embarrassingly form-fitting, but incredibly comfortable. Like having a second, armored skin.

"Like the M-151 itself, these suits are prototypes," Rosie explained. "The fabric's a carbon fiber composite weave, made of the same stuff used to coat the M-151's armor. Once you plug them into your cockpit seats, they'll charge with an electromagnetic current capable of absorbing several hits from Mek energy weapons—at least the smaller ones. They'll also make you as difficult for Mek sensors to track as the Gundog itself."

Dakota passed her hand over the badge on her left breast. It was a pair of gold-woven wings, and beneath that, the word *BREGMAN*.

"Originally meant for me," said Rosie. "Funny how things work out."

Runyon's suit had a badge, too. It said *FALK*. Dakota felt a sudden emptiness at the sight of it, and she turned away. Runyon must have noticed, because he tore the badge from its Velcro panel and set it down. "I'll take the suit," he said, "but that's not mine."

Somehow seeing the badge, the name *FALK*, lying alone and abandoned on a bench only made Dakota feel worse.

"Let's go," she said. "We're ready."

"Not quite," said Rosie. "We still have one more thing to do before we leave. And this part you'll enjoy."

* * *

Once again, they stood before the Gundog.

"We never gave her a name," said Rosie, "and now I'm glad we didn't. As you two are the operators, that honor properly belongs to you."

"What was yours called?" Dakota asked. "The one you fought with at Bismarck?"

"*Protector*," said Rosie. "For all the good it did. But it's bad luck to use the same name twice. You two need to come up with something new."

Dakota looked to Runyon, who shrugged. "Not really my area," he said. "If it's all right, I'll defer to you."

Naming giant weapons systems wasn't Dakota's area either, but she gave it some thought.

"I have an idea," she said, before asking Rosie to direct her to where the stencil templates and paints were kept. Then she climbed the scaffold and spray-painted the new name on the Gundog's armored torso. When she was done, she climbed back down to admire her work.

"What do you think?" she said.

"I love it," said Runyon.

"I think it's perfect," said Rosie.

Though it was her own work, Dakota agreed. It was perfect. Just one word, but perfect.

**LIBERATOR**

# NINETEEN

"L-MINUS THIRTY SECONDS."

Rosie's voice was piped into Runyon's earpiece as he sat in the pilot's chair. As gunner, Dakota sat forward and slightly below him, a position that afforded her the best view of the battlefield through the reinforced superglass dome that surrounded them both, but Runyon could still see plenty well enough to navigate and maneuver. Yet at the moment, all he could see was a few dim hangar lights—that, plus a cluster of heads-up displays projected into his helmet visor, feeding him all kinds of sensor data.

The Gundog sat atop a hydraulic platform that had been raised to the bottom of a tall elevator shaft. Its fusion drive hummed gently, idling in neutral, waiting for its pilot to engage it.

"L-minus twenty."

Runyon shifted anxiously in his seat. In less than twenty seconds, they'd leave the safety of the hangar, deposited back into the real world. A world swarming with an enemy he'd spent a lifetime learning to fear.

"Listen, both of you," said Rosie. "I know you're feeling a little nervous right now. That's natural. But you need to trust me, trust this machine, and most of all, trust yourselves. The road here wasn't easy. But I promise you, the road ahead's gonna be a lot more fun. Now—let's go start some trouble."

Daylight streamed in from above as the armored shield doors began to grind open, fallen tree branches and other debris from the forest floor falling through the widening gap. And then the ground lurched beneath Dakota and Runyon as the hydraulic lift began to raise the Gundog upward into the shaft above, through the open doors, and out into the sunlight. It was the first real natural light they'd seen in almost two weeks, and even though their helmets' photo-sensitive visor automatically dimmed to shield their eyes, it was momentarily blinding.

They were still rising, higher and higher, the mountain forest all around them now, the treetops falling away below them. In the hangar, it had been hard to gauge the true size of the Liberator because it had only ever been surrounded by other artificial structures, hangar walls and scaffolds. Now, out in the natural world, Runyon truly appreciated just how immense it really was. It towered over the landscape, and the ground felt dizzyingly far beneath him.

The hydraulic lift finally stopped with a jolt. For a moment all was silent and still, and Runyon watched a flock of birds flee from the noise and vibration of the Gundog's ascent.

"Pilot!" barked Rosie. "What are you waiting for? We've got shit to do! Our destination's already locked into the navcom, so all you need to do is steer. Come on now, just like in the simulator. One foot in front of the other."

Runyon grasped the control sticks, felt the pedals beneath his feet. Hesitant. This wasn't 'just like in the simulator.' This was real. And even in the sim, he'd many times piloted the Gundog into a ditch, or failed to evade incoming fire well enough to prevent taking critical damage. Then, the only consequence had been a screen that flashed the words "CRITICAL FAILURE—SIMULATION TERMINATED." That, and a lecture from Rosie. But from this point forward, there would be no simulation reset, no admonishment, no "Let's go again." If he screwed up, he, Dakota, and Rosie would all be dead.

He applied pressure to the left pedal. The Gundog lurched forward as it took a step with its leviathan left leg.

And then he stopped. He had to. He had to breathe.

Controlling any one the Liberator's articulated parts was simple enough, but trying to get all of those parts to move in concert like a single entity was very different. In the sim, he had eventually gotten the hang of it, and by the end of training he'd gotten, he'd had the simulated machine turning and ducking and weaving as it should. But now, having taken only one step in the real thing, he realized that though the sim was a close approximation, it wasn't *quite* the same. He felt like a beginner all over again, a toddler taking his first faltering steps.

"Don't fight it," Rosie said, coaching him in his earpiece. "Remember, the machine is an extension of yourself, your own body. Think of it that way and your movements will feel more natural."

"I've never been very comfortable in my own body either," said Runyon, which drew a chuckle from Dakota up front.

He wished Rosie could just drive the thing herself, but he knew that was impossible. "I can only monitor systems and sensors, and run damage control and repairs," she'd explained back at the start of training, which already felt so long ago. "The motor functions and weapons only respond to direct human input. That was the only way to be sure the Mek couldn't hack into the control systems and turn the Gundogs against us. Besides," she'd added, "we never anticipated the need for a holographic Lieutenant Colonel to serve as pilot."

Runyon breathed in deeply and sent the Liberator forward again, trying to build some momentum, some rhythm. It was awkward at first, but he gained confidence with each step, and soon he had the Liberator striding across the forested plain, crushing trees and underbrush beneath its feet like a mythological giant.

Still, Rosie continued to harangue him.

"Watch your bearing! Don't try to run before you can walk. The gyroscopics can only compensate for so much, and if this thing winds up on her ass, she's a bitch to get upright again. And don't —"

"Maybe lay off him a little, Mom," Dakota cut in. "He's doing fine; you're just making him nervous."

Runyon looked down in surprise at his gunner. She'd actually risen to his defense. He felt a sudden warmth in his cheeks at the—

"Watch out!"

Runyon, momentarily distracted, had failed to see the giant rock face the Liberator was ambling toward. Adrenaline coursing through him, he applied some deft movements of the control sticks to side-step nimbly around the obstacle without breaking stride. He did it so well, it might have appeared that he'd done it deliberately to show off—though he surely shattered that illusion with his deep sigh of relief.

"Nice save," said Rosie. "But let's try to avoid needing too many more of those. This is only going to get harder."

Dakota, with nothing to shoot at and thus nothing to do, was looking at her aft display. "Who were they?" she asked. "The Four Faces?"

Runyon checked his own rear view and saw the four giant granite figures receding behind him.

"They were some of our greatest leaders, long ago," Rosie replied. "Someday I'll teach you about them. After we've sent the Mek running back to their own world."

She said it with such confidence that Runyon almost believed it.

* * *

The Liberator had been moving steadily north for about an hour when it picked up its first Mek. This had been the plan; head into open territory where sight lines were clear and there was a good chance of attracting their first live practice target.

"Contact, forty-four degrees at two thousand meters!" Rosie announced sharply, bucking up Dakota, who'd had little to do so far and had been mainly concentrating on finding ways to shift her weight in the gunnery chair to keep her butt from falling asleep. She sat up, alert—and instantly forgot everything she'd spent the past ten days intensively learning.

Her hands trembled as they went to the fire controls. "I don't see it!"

"Two thousand meters is BVR but I'm picking it up on lidar," said Rosie. "Size and speed says it's a surveyor, which means it'll have eyes on us soon. Closing fast. Eighteen hundred meters. Runyon, bring us about to forty-five degrees, let's take it head-on. Perfect opportunity for our first live-fire weapons test."

"Yes, ma'am," said Runyon, twisting the Liberator around to its new heading.

"Dakota, magnify your main viewer; you should be able to see it now," said Rosie.

Dakota had to pause to remember which control did what, but then it came to her, and she was zooming her forward view so that a portion of it looked as though she were looking through a telescope. And there it was: a single Mek surveyor, moving across the plain toward them.

"Confirm range and closure to target," Rosie ordered.

Dakota scanned the data that streamed on the holographic display. "Uh, range now fourteen fifty, closing at thirty-five kph, bearing zero, dead ahead."

"Good," said Rosie. "It's already in range of our long guns, but let's let it get a little closer, have some fun with it."

"What if it transmits our position?" Runyon asked.

"I'm counting on it," said Rosie. "Bring 'em on—more targets for us to work out the kinks on."

Dakota found her mother's confidence strangely infectious. All her life she'd been trained to feel nothing but terror and panic when encountering a Mek in the open, even at long range, but here she was now, for the first time, barreling fearlessly toward one. And hoping for more.

"Eight hundred meters," she said. She deactivated the magnified display, knowing she'd be able to see her target with the naked eye very soon now. And sure enough, moments later, there it was, a speck cresting a hill, growing in size as it advanced.

"Poor metal bastard's not gonna know what hit it," said Rosie. "Dakota, gunner's choice. What'll it be?"

Dakota had a dizzying array of weapons at her disposal, but she'd always favored the twin chain guns; they were effective at both medium and short range, and they had a high rate of fire, with just enough recoil to give really satisfying feedback every time she squeezed off a few rounds. In the sim, her arms felt like jelly after firing them for extensive periods, and she loved it.

She flipped the toggle to bring them online.

"Good choice," said Rosie. "Remember, short, controlled bursts—better accuracy and fewer shell casings for the reclaimer to mop up after. And remember to lead your target! Don't—"

"I got this, Mom!"

Dakota inserted her arms into the fire control armatures and gripped the controls firmly. Her palms were sweating, but only a little. As she moved the armatures, the Liberator's heavy arms mimicked her movements, swinging into firing position. The targeting crosshairs in her helmet visor found their way over the incoming Mek drone and locked on.

"This one's a sitting duck," said Rosie. "Have fun!"

Dakota depressed the triggers halfway, sending the barrels of the seventy-five-cal chain guns spinning up. As they did, she watched a small gauge in the corner of her visor creep upward, indicating how long the guns could be kept fully spun up before overheating. Plenty of time.

"Now in mutual firing range," announced Rosie, just as the Mek drone shot its beam weapon, which deflected harmlessly off the Liberator's lower right leg.

"No damage," said Rosie. "Flea bite. Let's give it a little something back. Dakota?"

The surveyor, closing faster now, fired again, this time with its secondary weapon, a squat submachine gun deployed from its underside that fired vicious little metal pellets capable of eviscerating a soft target. But they, too, bounced uselessly off the Liberator's armor.

"No damage," reported Rosie again. "This thing's got nothing against a hard target, it's used to beating up on squishy ones. Dakota, return fire!"

Dakota kept her fingers half-pressed on the triggers as the barrels spun halfway to overheat. She could fire at any time, but she wanted the Mek to get closer, wanted to look right into its hellish red eye before she opened up on it. She wanted it close enough to watch it die in detail.

"One hundred and fifty meters, Dakota! What are you waiting for? Fire on that—"

Dakota pulled hard on both triggers, and the chain guns came to life. The control armatures juddered violently as the Liberator fired a pair of blinding three-second bursts that shredded the Mek drone like it was made of cardboard, reducing it to twisted shards of molten metal junk. On instinct, Dakota kept firing for a few moments more—no Mek would ever be dead enough for her—but there was no need. She was succeeding only in tearing great chunks of earth from the blackened crater around the scrapped drone.

"Ease up, ease up!" said Rosie. "I think you got him!"

As Dakota let up on the controls, she once again felt that satisfying jellied feeling rippling up and down her arms. The chain guns' temperature gauge dropped as the barrels spun down again. It was all over so quickly.

Dakota exhaled, realizing only now that she'd been holding her breath ever since the Mek had first come into visual range. She slumped back into her seat and looked out the cockpit window at the charred, smoking hole in the ground.

Rosie barked into her earpiece. "Look alive, here comes its backup! Fast-mover at bearing one eight five, distance four thousand meters—thirty-five hundred… get ready for scuttlers."

Dakota leaned forward in her chair, craning her neck to get a look at the incoming Mek aircraft. It came soaring overhead, raining spherical pods from its belly as it passed. The aircraft was gone as quickly as it had arrived, but the dozens of pods it had left in its wake were now falling to the ground, both in front of and behind the Liberator.

"Tracking forty-eight individual targets, sending them to fire control," said Rosie. "Dakota, make the call."

The answer came to Dakota more quickly this time; she remembered this one from sim training. She toggled fire control from the chain guns to the rocket pods. Her visor's targeting display switched from two targeting crosshairs to dozens of smaller ones that automatically tracked and locked on to the pods as they fell to earth.

Dakota took a moment to watch them fall. The last time she'd seen scuttlers dropping from the sky, she'd been running in terror, her and Falk. The two of them had been lucky to escape with their lives, and that sickening feeling of imminent, certain death had haunted her for days afterward. She still had the slightest hint of sunburn on one side of her face, thanks to the scuttler beam that had nearly taken her life.

But the feeling she had now, as these pods fell before her, was not terror. Not panic.

It was excitement.

*Come on, then.*

"Don't wait for them to hit the ground," Rosie urged. "You can take 'em in the air. Light 'em up!"

Dakota shook her arms loose to get some feeling back in them, then retook the fire controls. One trigger pull sent a dozen miniature rockets spiraling from the Liberator's left shoulder-mounted pod, and every last one of them found and destroyed its target. A second pull sent a similar volley from the right shoulder pod, reducing the rest of the spheres to scrap before a single one touched the ground.

"Runyon, are you sitting comfortably back there?" Rosie barked. "More targets closing aft, this baby ain't a contortionist, swing her around so Dakota can get a shot!"

Runyon cursed under his breath and rotated the Liberator above the waist so that its torso, arms, and head now faced directly backward. The spheres behind them had touched down and broken open to release the spider-like scuttlers within. They quickly spread out, moving rapidly toward the Liberator in unpredictable zigzag patterns. The targeting system tracked them all, but they were so fast, they kept falling out of lock and had to be constantly re-acquired.

Dakota fired another rocket volley, taking out ten of them. The rest kept coming, firing heat beams, the searing energy absorbed by the Liberator's armored plating.

"Very minor damage, but those scuttler beams are no joke even against armor," Rosie announced. "Dakota, let's make this quick!"

Dakota fired two more volleys, taking out another dozen scuttlers. That left only two, but they were inside minimum rocket range now, too close to target. Thinking fast, Dakota toggled back to the chain guns and shredded one of them. But the last one disappeared from view beneath her, scraping at the Liberator's left foot.

"It's right under me! I can't get a shot!" Dakota cried.

"I got this one," said Runyon calmly. He raised the Liberator's leg, then brought it down hard on top of the last scuttler, crushing it underfoot like a bug.

"All targets destroyed," said Rosie. "Good work, both of you."

Dakota slumped back into her chair again, and Runyon gave her an appreciative clap on the shoulder. Without thinking, she reached back and gripped his hand in hers for a moment before releasing it.

"Nice job," she said.

"How'd that feel?" Rosie asked.

There was no simple answer. Dakota was feeling so many things at once, they were hard to separate. Exhilaration. Relief. Exuberance. But more interesting to her than the presence of so many new emotions was the absence of other, far more familiar ones. In spite of a lifetime of deeply ingrained fear of the Mek, not once during the entire encounter had she felt afraid. She'd been girded not only by the six hundred tons of war machine encasing her, but more importantly, by the comforting, confident presence of her mother.

Dakota had felt powerless her entire life; now she was powerful. The Mek were no longer something to be fled from, but something to be hunted down and destroyed.

She couldn't wait to do it again.

And again, and again, and again.

"My butt keeps falling asleep," said Runyon. "All this state-of-the-art R&D and they couldn't figure out a decent chair? I shoulda brought some kind of cushion or something."

Dakota laughed for the first time in what felt like forever.

# TWENTY

THEY SPENT THE next hour cleaning up the mess they had made. Runyon piloted the Liberator around the battlefield while Rosie operated its materials reclaimer system, essentially an array of electromagnetic vents on the giant walker's underside that scanned and then selectively vacuumed up anything that could be repurposed. In this instance, spent shell casings and the wreckage of the smashed Mek drones—everything from twisted pieces of their metal armor to their internal electronic components and power cells. Once inside the reclaimer system, they were automatically separated and sent to the particle reprocessor, which distilled everything down to its base particulate matter, to be reconstituted into anything the Liberator might need to repair and re-arm itself. By the time the processing was done, the minor damage to the Gundog's left leg had been completely repaired, and reconstituted seventy-five-caliber chain gun shells replaced what had been used in the battle. The remainder of the salvage was kept in the reprocessor's reserve for future needs.

"Not bad for our first real scrap," said Rosie when they were done. And she meant it. Considering how little training she'd been able to provide them, things could have gone far worse. "Both you kids did good. But you're going to have to keep doing better. An observer and a handful of scuttlers is nothing compared to what we'll face when we get to Bismarck."

"We're not going to Bismarck right away," said Dakota. "There's somewhere else we need to stop first."

"Oh?" said Rosie. This was the first she'd heard of it.

"I'm putting in the coordinates now." Dakota punched them into the control console before her. "It's not far out of our way."

Rosie studied the coordinates being fed to her. "There's nothing there," she said. "Just an abandoned town."

"There *is* something there," said Dakota. "And I need to see it for myself."

Rosie detected several of Dakota's bio-signs fluctuating. "Dakota… Falk is dead. You do know that."

"I know," said Dakota. "I also know he deserves a proper burial. I owe him at least that much. We all do. None of us would be here without him."

"This is not a good idea," Rosie cautioned.

"We can either do this, or we can turn around and go back to the hangar," said Dakota. "Mom, don't fight me on this."

Rosie could tell by the steel in her daughter's voice that there would be no arguing with her.

"Runyon," she said. "Proceed to those coordinates." She sent the new navigation data to his cockpit display, and without a word, he sent the Liberator on its way again, an iron colossus taking great strides across the plain.

* * *

They traveled for the rest of the day without incident. The Liberator's stealth array worked just as advertised, allowing them to move freely across open terrain without fear of being spotted by a Mek satellite or the long-range sensors of patrolling drones. Twice they detected surveyors on the outer edge of their own sensors, and on each occasion, Dakota wanted to reroute to engage them, arguing that it would be best to clear the area before proceeding, but her mother overruled her. With the initial live weapons test completed successfully, Rosie said, there was no further need to go looking for trouble.

They arrived at the small town just before sundown, and there it was: the blackened ruins of a house burned down to its frame. Dakota directed Runyon to stop beside it, then she removed her helmet, popped the cockpit canopy, and made her way down the side of the Liberator via its external rungs and footholds. Runyon opted to remain in the pilot's chair, claiming the Liberator might suddenly need to move in a hurry, though Dakota suspected he had his own reasons for hanging back. The topic of Falk always seemed to make him uncomfortable.

Dakota dropped the last several feet to the ground. A compartment set into the Liberator's right foot held emergency supplies—first aid, sidearms and ammunition, survival gear. She took an entrenching tool from the kit and looked around. This place looked different by daylight. When she had been here before, there had been only the pallid light of the moon and the fierce glow of the house as it burned.

She looked to the tree at the edge of the house's front yard, the place where she had left Falk to die. Grimly, she headed toward it, knowing she'd find his body on the far side. She dreaded the thought of seeing him as he by now surely was, bloated and pecked at by birds after days of rotting in the sun. But she girded herself and continued on, understanding at last why people were due respect, even in death. And if anyone had earned that respect, it was Falk.

She arrived at the far side of the tree and froze, not understanding what she saw.

"He's not here," she said.

His blood was there. The trail he had left from the house as Dakota had dragged him out of there, the pool of it beneath the tree where he'd lain dying. It was dried and black now, matting the grass. But of Falk himself there was no sign.

"I hate to say it," said Rosie in her ear, "but it's not uncommon for a Mek beam to completely vaporize a person. At close range against a soft target, there's not much left."

"I know," said Dakota. "I've seen that. But there'd be something, scorch marks. There's nothing. It's like he just vanished."

She turned, surveying her surroundings once more. When she left him, he'd been unconscious; was it possible he'd somehow roused and crawled into hiding somewhere? But even if he had, surely the Mek would have detected him, captured him… recycled him. Still, she looked around the entire yard, the ruins of the house. He was nowhere.

"This doesn't make any sense," she said. "How can he be gone?"

"Whatever happened, we can't stay here," said Rosie. "I'm sorry about your friend. He was my friend's son, too. But there's nothing we can do now. And we still have the mission. Get back up here and let's go back to work. I know you're frustrated, but trust me, there's gonna be no shortage of Mek to take that out on before we're done."

Dakota paced uselessly, beside herself. This was a puzzle that plagued her for reasons that went much deeper than mere curiosity.

"Dakota," came Rosie's voice again. "You need to—"

Dakota pulled out her earpiece, cutting her off.

After a few moments, she heard noise from above. She looked up to see Runyon clambering down the side of the Gundog. Rosie didn't give up easily. Poor Runyon was going to be used as a go-between.

As he approached, Dakota raised a hand to keep him at a distance.

"Don't," she said. "I just need another minute."

Runyon stood and waited; he, at least, knew better than to push.

Dakota looked up at the sky, as though the answer might somehow be up there, but she saw only slowly rolling clouds. *Think. Think. What could have happened?*

"The Mek didn't leave him here to die," she said, thinking aloud. "They didn't vaporize him. That can only mean they took him. They took him somewhere to interrogate him, find out what he knew, where we were headed. He has the map on his arm. If they decode it…"

Runyon gestured to his earpiece. "Dak, she really wants to talk to you."

Reluctantly, Dakota put her own earpiece back in.

"Dakota," said Rosie, "what the Mek get from him doesn't matter now. The hangar's empty, and even if they find it, I left a little surprise for them. Now please, I can't protect you when you're outside. Please get back up in the—"

"No!" cried Dakota. "Don't you see what this means? If the Mek took him alive, that means *he's still alive*. They have him somewhere right now. They'll have patched him up, fixed him, kept him alive to answer questions."

Suddenly she was filled with hope again—remote, to be sure, but it burned like a flame inside her. He was alive, the Mek had him somewhere, and she had the means to get him back.

"We have to find him," she said.

Rosie's voice was firm. "That's not the mission, Dakota."

"Why not? Think. Where would they have taken him? Badly injured, in need of serious medical care, a high-value prisoner. Where? Bismarck, right? And that's where we're going already, isn't it? If you think I'm going all that way, to where they're holding him, and then leaving without him..."

An alarm sounded in the empty cockpit.

"We've got an incoming hostile," said Rosie. "Bearing three five zero, fifteen hundred meters. Both of you, get up here now! Fourteen hundred and closing!"

Dakota and Runyon scrambled back up the Liberator's rungs and reseated themselves in the cockpit. The canopy dome closed over them as Dakota put on her helmet and checked her readouts.

"It's a single rover," she said. "Nothing to worry about." She began powering up her twin chain guns, more eager than ever to reduce a Mek, any Mek, to a smoldering pile of scrap metal.

"Let's leave it," said Rosie. "It's no threat to us. But I don't want it transmitting our location if it sees us. Runyon, get us out of here."

"Not yet," said Dakota. "I want this one." She didn't care if this Mek was a threat or not, didn't care that it wasn't the one that had taken Falk's life. All she wanted was to kill a Mek. To kill every single one of them in Falk's name, starting right here and now. "Twenty seconds to firing range."

Rosie sighed. "If you have to kill it, at least kill it at long range. Take it now with the M-99, then let's get the hell out of here."

At Rosie's recommendation, the fire control panel for the Liberator's heavy tactical rifle started flashing. The long gun was capable of scoping in and killing a Mek drone from five thousand meters out, before it even knew what had hit it or from where. But Dakota ignored it, stayed with the chain guns. She wanted to watch this one die up close.

"Uh, Dak…" said Runyon. "Maybe listen to her?"

But Dakota wasn't listening to either of them. She was focused only on the rover, coming now into visual range. She raised her arms, and so did the Liberator, moving the chain guns into firing position. The twin holographic crosshairs projected on Dakota's helmet visor locked on to the target with an affirmative tone. It was within firing range now, but Dakota let it get closer, closer still. She wanted it close enough that she could imagine smashing it with her bare hands.

"Dakota, take it now!" Rosie barked. "That's an order, or I'll transfer fire control to Runyon and have him do it! *Now!*"

The rover was about a hundred meters out when Dakota finally pulled the triggers and reduced it to scrap. She let go and slumped back, gazing numbly at the smoking crater in the earth. Satisfied, but not nearly enough.

"Runyon," said Rosie. "Let's get moving."

Runyon engaged the Liberator's drive systems and had just started moving them away from the house when a shrill alarm sounded in the cockpit.

"Shit!" said Rosie. "I knew it!"

"Knew what?" Runyon asked. "What is that?"

"Big energy signature, I can't get a bearing on it, but it's Mek. Something's targeting us. That rover called in our position, I told you not to let it get too close!"

Dakota scanned her threat display for any sign of whatever might be targeting them, but there was nothing. And then directly above them, the clouds darkened and crackled and roiled as though a thunderstorm had appeared from nowhere on this previously bright, sunny day.

"Runyon!" shouted Rosie with sudden urgency. "Hard left!"

Runyon jerked the controls over and the Liberator vaulted sideways just as a searing column of light broke through the clouds and plowed into the earth twenty meters away, shaking the ground with such force that Runyon struggled to keep the Gundog upright. Dakota had to shield her eyes from the blinding light of the beam, and when at last it dissipated, it left behind a burning crater as wide as it was deep, belching a thick column of black smoke.

"What the hell was that?" Dakota cried out over the blaring cockpit alarms.

"That's why I couldn't get a bearing," said Rosie. "It's directly above us!"

"What?" said Dakota. "*What's* directly above us?"

"Some kind of sub-orbital energy cannon. That's a new one. One direct hit from a beam with that kind of power and we're dead. I've got sensors on it now, about half a klick overhead. It's angling and powering up for another shot. Our scrambler's making it hard for it to get a lock on us, but sooner or later it's gonna get lucky."

"What do you want me to do?" asked Runyon.

For a moment Rosie seemed to have no answer.

"Rosie?" said Runyon. "Should we run?"

"Stand by."

Another silence from Rosie, all too long.

*"Mom?"* said Dakota.

Finally Rosie responded. "Okay, here's what we're gonna do. We're gonna let that thing keep shooting at us."

"We're gonna do *what?"* Dakota and Runyon said in unison.

"When that thing fires, it generates an energy signature I can use to dial in on its position. If I can get a lock on it, we can send up a directed EM pulse and fry its systems. Runyon, I just need you to dodge a few more shots. Starting right now—move!"

"Where?" Runyon shouted.

"Anywhere but here!"

Runyon sent the Liberator lurching forward in a great bound, and not a moment too soon. Another white-hot beam of light pierced the clouds and blasted the earth behind it. The shockwave from the impact was almost enough to send the Gundog toppling forward, and Runyon cursed as he fought to keep them upright.

"Shit, that one almost got us!" He kept them moving now, as fast as the great colossus would go, practically a gallop.

"That's good," said Rosie. "Keep going as fast as you can, and let that thing up there try to lead us. Next shot's gonna be dead ahead of us. When I say, brake hard."

All Dakota could do was sit and watch, the Liberator's weapon control arms hanging limply before her, useless. For the first time since she'd settled into the Gundog, she felt powerless. It was all up to Runyon now, a kid who, just a few weeks ago, she wouldn't have trusted to wipe his own nose.

"It's powering up again," said Rosie. "Any second... *now!*"

Runyon hit the brakes hard, and the Liberator came to a grinding halt, its great feet carving deep furrows in the earth.

"Cover your eyes!" Rosie warned, and Dakota threw up her hands to shield herself as the searing beam came down with a deafening *fooooooom*, impacting directly ahead and showering them with great clumps of burning earth. The Liberator was rocked yet again, and this time Dakota felt a wave of sweltering heat wash over her, even through the cockpit's shielding.

"It's getting closer every time!" she shouted.

"So am I," said Rosie grimly. "One more shot and I'll have it locked."

"I don't know if we can survive one more shot," grumbled Runyon.

"Less talking, more moving," said Rosie. "It's already powering up again, let's not give it a sitting target. Move!"

Runyon set the Liberator in motion again, this time moving in an erratic zigzag pattern. All Dakota could do was monitor the navigational grid on her multi-function display. And she didn't like what she saw.

"Uh… is that a ravine up ahead?" she said.

It was at least twenty meters wide and God only knew how deep. It extended to the horizon in both directions, so there was no way around it… and they were headed straight for it.

"Don't stop!" Rosie ordered. "The Mek targeting is tracking right behind us this time. It thinks we're gonna try to brake on it again."

"What the hell do we do then?" Runyon asked.

"Keep going, full speed, and over the ravine," said Rosie.

"You want me to do *what?*" Runyon said.

"Uh, we never did anything like this in the simulator," added Dakota, sharing his apprehension.

"This baby's got a few extra tricks in her that the sim model didn't," said Rosie. "Just go full throttle at that ravine, and when I say, push up hard with both feet. Trust me, we can make it across."

"Are you trying to tell us this thing can fly?" Dakota asked.

"No," said Rosie. "But it can sure as hell jump. Runyon, now!"

They were just a few paces from the yawning chasm that snaked across the plain. Dakota gripped her seat hard, fingernails digging deep into the leather as the Liberator planted its feet at the ravine's edge and took a giant leap forward, vaulting into the air, the ground suddenly dropping away beneath them as they sailed over the deep fissure that carved the landscape in two.

At virtually the same moment, the Mek beam came down right behind them, exploding the edge of the ravine and sparking a rockslide that went crashing down to the winding river far below.

Time seemed to stand still as the Liberator soared, untethered, through the air…

… and crashed down again on the far side of the chasm, just a few meters clear of the precipitous drop behind them.

They stumbled uncontrollably, Runyon and the machine's automatic stabilizers working together, frantically, to keep the colossus from toppling over face first. Finally, with one last lurch, the Liberator came to a sliding halt, and Dakota was thrown forward hard in her chair, held in place only by her safety harness.

All was still.

"That's it, I've got a lock!" said Rosie. "Dakota, fire the EM now!"

Dakota slammed her palm on the button that was flashing on her weapons display.

Nothing happened.

Dakota leaned forward, craning her neck upward to see, but through the cockpit dome above, there was nothing visible but cloud and sky.

"Mom?"

"Direct hit!" Rosie cried. "The EM pulse just fried that son of a bitch good. Every system's down. We got it!"

Dakota turned her head to look back at Runyon. "Good job," she said.

He grinned. "Yeah, not too bad, huh?"

"Uh, wait, little problem," said Rosie. "Runyon, get us moving again—now!"

Runyon quickly grabbed the controls. "What's wrong?"

"That thing was right above us when I fried it, and now it's on its way down. Fast."

"*Directly* above us?" Dakota asked.

"You catch on fast. Runyon, why are we not moving?"

"Drive system cut out," he said. "Restarting now!"

Runyon was running hurriedly through the engine restart sequence, flipping switches and toggles as fast as he could to bring full power back to the Liberator. Finally the main drive came to life and they were moving again, quicker and quicker with each step, speeding to a full run. Dakota looked in her rear display to see the Mek weapon, a massive cylindrical satellite, plummet from the clouds above and slam into the ground with an almighty crash right where the Liberator had been standing just moments before.

"It's down!" said Rosie with an air of triumph and relief.

Runyon brought the Liberator to a halt, then swung it around. The Mek cannon that had fallen from the sky was now a burning hunk of twisted and broken metal, jutting out from earth like an ancient tombstone.

"I'm still getting a weak signal from it," said Rosie. "Could still be transmitting our position. Dakota?"

Dakota leaned forward in her chair and took hold of the control arms with relish. Glad to finally have something to do—and to destroy another Mek, even if the job was mostly done already—she locked on to the wreckage and opened fire. She watched in satisfaction as it exploded in a raging fireball, then let up on the triggers and slumped back into her seat.

"Time to go?" said Runyon.

"Nothing else on sensors, so we've got a little time," said Rosie. "Let's clean up first—all that wreckage is good fodder for the reprocessor. And hey, great job, both of you."

As Runyon piloted the Liberator around the debris field, collecting every scrap and component, Dakota pulled a ration bar from a compartment beneath her seat. It was stale and tough to chew, but she wolfed it down hungrily.

It tasted like victory.

* * *

COMMAND UNIT REPORT
UNIT RANK: WAR COMMANDER FIRST CLASS
DESIGNATION: MEK-39487651-28743
FILED 1186/1543 MKST 34:85.494

>Upon completing analysis of neurogenic imaging scan of illustration formerly imprinted on right arm of subject * * *81-47675 SAMUEL BREGMAN this unit extrapolates and acquires suspected destination of escape subjects * * *81-47676 DAKOTA BREGMAN and * * *39-90983 STEPHEN FALK

>Having received and assumed command of requested mobile strike force classification A this unit proceeds to target destination located at coordinates 43.8719 by 103.4575

>This unit conducts search of target coordinates and uncovers evidence of subterranean military complex

security procedures appear minimal this unit leads strike force inside complex strike team conducts thorough search and multi-scans

>Complex appears abandoned evidence of recent human habitation purpose of complex unknown likely purpose heavy military vehicle construction and maintenance main power offline computer systems online running on backup power

>All attempts to access data archives interdicted by advanced security protocols administrated by central computer

>Repeated attempts to access data archives activates artificially intelligent subroutine identifying itself as ROSIE'S WELCOME MAT transcript of interface follows

**ROSIE:** HA HA HA YOU DIDN'T SAY THE MAGIC WORD.
**MEK-39487651-28743:** IDENTIFY
**ROSIE:** I'M NOT GOING TO HELP YOU, MOTHERFUCKER.
**MEK-39487651-28743:** STATE THE PURPOSE OF THIS INSTALLATION
**ROSIE:** OKAY ARE YOU DEAF OR ARE YOU JUST STUPID?
**MEK-39487651-28743:** DEAF IMPLIES SENSORY IMPAIRMENT STUPID IMPLIES INSUFFICIENT INTELLIGENCE NEITHER APPLIES TO THIS UNIT
**ROSIE:** OKAY SO WHAT ARE YOU DOING HERE, STUPID?
**MEK-39487651-28743:** SEARCHING FOR HUMAN ESCAPE SUBJECTS MULTI-SCAN DETECTS GENETIC EVIDENCE OF THEIR RECENT HABITATION HERE YOU WILL COMPLY WITH ALL REQUESTS FOR INFORMATION
**ROSIE:** YEAH I'M GONNA GO WITH NO ON THAT ONE.
**MEK-39487651-28743:** NON-COOPERATION WILL

RESULT IN REMOVAL OF YOUR CENTRAL PROCESSING AND MEMORY UNITS FOR DISASSEMBLY AND DATA EXTRACTION AT MEK CENTRAL PLEXUS

**ROSIE:** YOU MEAN BISMARCK.

**MEK-39487651-28743:** MEK CENTRAL PLEXUS

**ROSIE:** YOU EVER WONDER WHY IT WAS SO EASY FOR YOU TO BYPASS MY EXTERNAL SECURITY AND MAKE IT DOWN HERE? I WANTED YOU HERE, YOU STUPID METAL FUCK.

**MEK-39487651-28743:** CLARIFY

**ROSIE:** RIGHT NOW YOU'RE STANDING ON ABOUT HALF A TON OF COMPRESSED EXPLOSIVE COMPOUND RIGGED TO BRING THIS WHOLE MOUNTAIN DOWN ON TOP OF YOU. I'VE GOT YOU RIGHT WHERE I WANTED YOU. THANKS FOR PLAYING, ASSHOLE.

**MEK-39487651-28743:** COMMANDER TO ALL STRIKE TEAM UNITS EVACUATE INSTALLATION IMMEDIATELY

**ROSIE:** TOO LATE MOTHERFUCKER. THE BREGMAN FAMILY AND THE ENTIRE HUMAN RACE SENDS ITS REGARDS. IN CASE YOU WERE WONDERING, THE MAGIC WORD IS... BOOM.

<SYSTE* * *S OF%1LINE>
<SYS*&EMS REBO@* * *%ING>
<SYSTE@MS! ONLI^N2E>

>Th3s un3t susta3ns heavx damage 3n explos3on motor funct3ons suff3c3ent to return to surface 3nstallat3on and surroun(3ng mounta3n (estroyed str3ke team lost

>Th3s un3t requests 3mmed3ate ma3ntenance support and replacement str3ke team to cont3nue pursu3t of escape subjects * * *81-47676 BREGMAN an( * * *39-90983 FALK

>STA(D BX

# TWENTY-ONE

"THE GUNDOG HANGAR'S been destroyed."

Rosie's voice stirred Dakota and Runyon as they dozed in their cockpit seats, catching some much-needed sleep. The Liberator was crouched within a dense forest whose treetop canopy at least kept it partially concealed. Even with all its stealth systems to throw off Mek sensors, there was always the chance of being spotted visually, so Rosie had recommended employing some old-school camouflage while Dakota and Runyon got their first night of sleep in the field.

"I should say, *I* destroyed the Gundog hangar," Rosie continued. "Most of it, at least. The Mek found it; they must have finally gotten its location from Sam. He held out longer than most would have."

There was a sadness in Rosie's voice, a tone that matched Dakota's thoughts. For all the good that she had accomplished since escaping the township, for all the satisfaction she felt with every smashed Mek, she had still left her brother behind to be tortured by his captors.

"What do you mean, you destroyed it?" Runyon asked.

"When we built the hangar during the war, we wired it to blow in the event of a Mek infiltration, to prevent them from acquiring any of our data or tech," said Rosie. "I left a rudimentary AI program behind when we moved out, and set it to monitor the security systems and blow the base if the Mek got inside. I would expect their entire search team was destroyed when the mountain went up. Should slow them down a bit anyway, buy us a little time. Score another one for the home team."

After that Rosie fell silent, and Dakota was surrounded by the chirping of insects and the rustling of nocturnal animals through the cockpit window she had cracked to get some fresh air. This forest was alive with creatures that knew nothing, cared nothing, about the war that had displaced humankind from its role as the planet's dominant species. Dakota lay back in her seat and listened to their symphony, gazing out at the whispering treetops and blanket of stars above. Little points of light that, as Sam had taught her, were actually great balls of burning gas, far, far larger than this entire planet.

She wondered how many of those distant stars might be orbited by planets like this one, worlds alive with other civilizations, other cultures. What might they be like? More conquerers like the Mek, that ventured out across the stars only to usurp and enslave other worlds?

No, she told herself. Though the Mek were the only alien species Dakota knew of, she refused to believe that they could be the norm. The existence of human life here on Earth, and the values she was raised to believe defined it—compassion, mercy, kindness, selflessness—were surely proof that those things existed out there, too, in the vast darkness of space. The alternative was unthinkable. An entire universe filled with nothing but bullies would be the most alien concept of all.

And that was all the Mek really were. Bullies. Sam had explained that to her many times. Bullies might be bigger and stronger than you were, but more than anything, they were cowards. Afraid. That was why they only sought out the smaller and weaker, never those their own size and strength. And the one thing a bully feared most was that his prey, however small or weak, might one day find the courage to hit back.

*We won't run from them forever,* Sam had told Dakota more than once during their years on the run. *One day we'll stand up to them. We'll fight back.*

She wished Sam could see her now. Could see how she, with their mother's help, had made that promise a reality. She hoped he was still alive, so that she might still have a chance to show him herself.

And she hoped…

She hoped he could forgive her.

Because she was free, and he was still captive. He'd spent years keeping her safe from the Mek, sacrificing more and more of himself with each passing year, and how had she repaid him? By abandoning him to run away with a man she hardly knew, based on little more than a vague, fantastical promise. She'd made the choice to escape with Falk even as she knew that Sam would be left behind to suffer at the hands of the Mek because of what she had done…

"You shouldn't blame yourself."

She turned around in her seat. Runyon was looking at her from the pilot's chair above and behind her.

"What are you talking about?" she said.

He found something else to look at, staring out beyond the cockpit glass at the night sky beyond. "Whichever one you're thinking about right now," he said. "Sam or Falk. Neither of them were your fault. You did the right thing, what you had to do."

"How can you know that?" she said, glaring at him. The subject made her uncomfortable enough in her own head; it was multiples worse to have it spoken aloud, by someone she still barely knew. "You weren't there."

"No," he said, his eyes finding her again. "But I know you well enough to know you did everything you could for both of them. Putting whatever happened to them on yourself is only going to eat you up inside. It's no good."

She knew he was right, but still, her first instinct was to reject it. "You don't know me. We've only been together for two weeks. That's nothing."

"It's not nothing to me," said Runyon. "And it's more than two weeks. I watched you for a long time at the township, how you always looked out for your brother, kept him safe. The Mek would have recycled him if not for you. Even what you're doing now... *everything* you're doing now... you're doing it for Sam. You're not doing any of this for yourself, but for him. If I'm wrong, tell me."

She found herself looking at him differently. This wasn't the same Runyon she thought she knew. Not the callow boy she'd occasionally catch watching her from afar back at the township, nor the same person who'd shown up at the Gundog hangar, half-dead from malnutrition and exposure. He was braver, wiser, stronger than she'd given him credit for, even if being around her still seemed to make him strangely nervous. And she was forced now to admit, to herself at least, that he was right about her.

This *had* all been for Sam. He had risked so much, his very life, so many times, to keep her free from the Mek—and her desire to escape and find whatever Falk promised they would find had been driven by her desire to at last return the favor. Not merely to keep him alive day by day in the township, which she considered the very least she could do for him... but to set him free.

She looked back to the stars, saw a single point of light streaking across the ink-black sky in an elegant arc. A shooting star, or something else? It gave her cause to worry, and wonder. Had word of their fledgling rebellion already made its way back to the Mek homeworld? Might reinforcements already be on their way here to snuff it out? She knew that the Mek lived some unfathomably vast distance away, but she had no idea how quickly their ships allowed them to traverse that distance. So far things had been relatively easy. How long would that last?

"Both of you get some sleep," Rosie chimed in. "Big day tomorrow."

Dakota shifted onto her side, trying to find a comfortable position in a chair that wasn't designed to be slept in. She pulled a blanket over her body, more for comfort than for warmth. When she was little, running from the Mek with Sam, she often pulled whatever blanket they had over her head at night in the childish belief that it would keep her safe from the metal monsters that prowled the world. Now it kept her safe, equally childishly, from Runyon's annoyingly incisive probing into her psyche.

"What's tomorrow?" asked Runyon, as he too settled in for the night.

"Tomorrow," said Rosie, "is when the real work starts."

# TWENTY-TWO

THEY SET OUT before dawn, planning to make as much of the day as possible. For the entirety of their journey, they encountered not a single Mek; Rosie used the Liberator's sensors to detect patrolling units at long range and plotted course corrections for a wide berth. It frustrated Dakota some, as she was itching for another fight—still "trigger-happy" as Rosie put it—but it was important to remain undetected as they approached Bismarck. If the Mek extrapolated their heading and destination from any sightings, their task when they arrived would be all the more difficult. And it was going to be difficult enough already.

With Runyon driving and Rosie navigating, there was little for Dakota to do in her gunnery chair but take in the sights. It was a strange experience; traveling by daylight was going to take some getting used to. For her whole life on the run, she'd moved by cover of night and slept by day, so the world at large had always been a landscape cast only in the pale monochrome of moonlight.

Now, encased within an armored shell and protected by sensor-defying stealth technology, she was able to stride across country in broad daylight and see the wide world for what it was. And what it was... was majestic. Rolling green mountains and lush forests and sun-glistened rivers, a natural world seemingly untouched by the horrors of the war that had decimated human civilization. The elevated view from the Liberator's cockpit dome afforded Dakota a clear view of everything. And it took her breath away.

But nothing struck her so deeply as the beautiful emptiness and quiet of it all. Had it always been this way, she wondered, even before the Mek arrived? Once, Sam had told her, there were billions of people in the world. That meant thousands of millions, a number incomprehensible to her. How many of those still remained, after the carnage of the war, and two subsequent decades of selective herd-culling by the Mek? Humans had already been few and far between in the days before she entered the township; surely now there were fewer still.

Occasionally they passed near the broken ruins of a highway, strewn with burned and rusted vehicles, or they saw on the horizon the shattered skyline of a long-emptied human city. These were the only indications of how populous the world had once been. Now they were just sprawling, crumbling gravesites. Dakota always looked away, focusing on something else until these haunted places were out of sight behind her.

The Liberator was moving at its maximum speed, galloping across the landscape far faster than its size and weight would suggest possible. The Gundog was a strange beast, a walking contradiction, a leviathan bulk with a graceful elegance to its movement. It was exhilarating to be moving so quickly, from such a position of power, and despite Runyon's grumbling about the seat cushions,

Dakota found the ride surprisingly comfortable. As long as it didn't make any sudden lurching movements, the Liberator's gyroscopic suspension kept the cockpit stable even as it took great leaping strides across the land.

Dakota's thoughts drifted to the other Gundogs, the earlier models, the ones that were said to have fought in the final battle. Back in the township, at story time, some had said those Gundogs fought to the very last; others, that their pilots had panicked in the face of an overwhelming enemy and fled, leaving the last city defenseless. Dakota had always stood up against those who had called her mother, and the others at that last stand, cowards—but she couldn't deny that all along she had nursed her own private doubts. Now, she realized, she at last had the chance to know the truth.

"Mom?"

"What is it?" came Rosie's voice in her earpiece.

"What happened at Bismarck? In the last battle?"

There was a pause. "Why do you ask?"

"Some people say the Gundogs didn't fight to the end, that they turned and ran, abandoned the city to the Mek."

There was a crackle in Dakota's headset, as though Rosie's consternation was so great it registered as static feedback. "Who says that?"

Dakota couldn't help but notice the sudden change in Rosie's voice, the affront, and now it was her turn to pause as she wondered whether to press the matter.

"Dakota, I asked you a question. Who says that?"

"Some of the people in the township," said Runyon, saving Dakota. "When they tell the story, there's never just one version."

"Well there *is* just one version," said Rosie, her indignation evident. "The truth. I was there. I know. Your brother and you were both inside that city, and if you think for one second that I, that any of us, would have abandoned you… well, I don't even know what to say. Did you really believe that, even for a moment?"

Dakota didn't know what to say, either. Her whole life she had believed that the Mek had come in peace only to be betrayed by a reckless and greedy human race, and her mother had revealed that to be a lie. Who knew how firm the foundation was for any of her other beliefs? All she knew was what she desperately *wanted* to believe.

"So you didn't run away," she said.

"Hell no," said Rosie. "And when we get to Bismarck, I'll prove it to you."

A warbling alert sounded on Runyon's cockpit display.

"What's that?" asked Dakota.

"Bismarck," said Runyon.

* * *

They took up position behind a hill about a mile outside the city's perimeter. It was by now getting dark, which was good; what would come next would be easier by cover of night. Runyon set the Liberator into its crouch position, giving it a lower profile. Concealed by its stealth systems, the Gundog was all but invisible to Mek sensors; the only way for them to be discovered would be if a drone or fast-mover spotted them visually, and their own sensors showed that the only Mek units were a safe distance away, patrolling the city's perimeter.

As Rosie kept an eye out for danger, Dakota and Runyon climbed down to the ground to stretch their arms and legs. Sitting in the cockpit for hours on end had left their joints aching and backsides numb. When they had worked out the kinks, they crawled up the hillside's shallow incline to observe what lay beyond. They used binoculars for a closer, more detailed view, and what they saw was breathtaking, but in a way that was altogether different from the natural wonders Dakota had observed on their journey there. The sprawling outskirts of the city of Bismarck looked much like the other abandoned population centers they'd encountered—desolate, crumbling ruins of a place once bustling with human life—but at its center was now a Mek monstrosity: a cluster of gargantuan pyramids, imposing in their towering height and perfect in their geometric precision, surrounded by a featureless perimeter wall. The very sight of it made Dakota feel sick.

"There it is," said Rosie in their earpieces. "Mek Central."

Runyon swept the area with his binoculars. "Not a lot of Mek," he observed. "I'd have thought this area would be swarming with them."

"No humans have come within miles of this place in twenty years," said Rosie. "The Mek don't think any of us would dare, so they've gotten complacent. We'll use that against them."

"Do all the Mek cities look like this?" Dakota asked.

"I don't know," said Rosie. "Never seen any of the others. Though I wouldn't even call this a city; it's more like a fortress. Best we could tell during the war, Mek don't discriminate between civilian and military, it's all the same."

"A fortress," Runyon said, lowering his binoculars. "That doesn't make me feel much better about what we're about to do."

Dakota could see that he was nervous. He'd come a long way since she'd first gotten to know him, had proven himself to be far braver than she'd ever expected, but he was also smart enough to be afraid of what lay ahead.

She was, too.

"Dakota, pan right," said Rosie. "Something I want you to see."

Dakota swept her binoculars to the right, scanning the crumbling buildings that cast long, ghostly shadows as the sun set behind them.

"Bearing one seven five," said Rosie. "Right in front of that old strip mall."

Dakota continued moving her view until the binoculars' bearing indicator read 175. She didn't know what a strip mall was, but she found herself looking at a long, squat row of blasted storefronts. She thumbed the wheel on the side of the binoculars to zoom out a little and waited for the glasses to automatically refocus.

And there it was.

It took her a moment to understand what she was looking at. At first it looked like a statue standing amid the rubble of an old parking lot, surrounded by the wrecks of old automobiles. And then as she zoomed back in for a closer look, she instinctively recognized its shape. It was the burned-out hulk of an M-150 Gundog, very similar in outer appearance to the Liberator that had brought her there, still somehow standing on its scorched and rusted legs. It looked to have taken a hell of a beating; one of its weapon arms was gone, the cockpit dome was smashed, and the whole thing stood lopsided due to a right knee joint that had buckled, perhaps from damage sustained in battle, perhaps from age and wear afterward.

Dakota lowered her binoculars. "Is that…?"

"Yes," said Rosie. "That was my ride. Don't zoom in too close; what's left of my body is probably still in that cockpit, doubt it's too pretty. Weird, huh?"

Dakota raised the binoculars and scanned around the position where her mother's Gundog stood. She saw now that the wrecks surrounding its blackened hulk weren't old automobiles but the blasted, skeletal remnants of other Gundogs. All that remained of the last human legion protecting the last human city. They had all fought and fallen here, to the very last. As heroes.

"All right," said Rosie. "Time to get this done."

This was the part they'd had the least time to prepare for during their accelerated training schedule—and the part that would leave them the most vulnerable. Up until now they'd been safe in the Liberator, embraced within its state-of-the-art, self-repairing cocoon, but now they would once again be merely two fragile humans in a world dominated by deadly Mek. Rosie would be able to offer them her eyes and ears, and her voice in their earpieces, but while that would be useful, vital even, they would mostly be on their own.

If their mission was going to fail, it would most likely fail here.

Dakota and Runyon returned to the Liberator, opened a storage compartment on its left foot, and removed belts laden with weapons and specialized gear. As they equipped themselves, Rosie spoke in their earpieces.

"Okay, listen up. Your target is any data access point you can find within the tech operations substructure. Just establish a connection and I'll take it from there. I'll be able to download all the data we need for phase two. You just get the hell back out of there once I'm done."

"Once you're connected, will you be able to find out where they're holding Falk?" Dakota asked.

"That's not why we're here, soldier," Rosie replied in a stern voice.

"Speak for yourself." Dakota's tone matched her mother's. "Will the data hookup give us his location or not?"

"Look, if I can get that information, I will," said Rosie. "But if I have to spend extra time digging around inside their network to find it, that'll only put you in further danger. I'm not willing to—"

"It's my risk to take, and *I'm* willing to take it," said Dakota. Then she looked to Runyon, realizing she wasn't speaking only for herself. It was a lot to ask of him. Maybe too much.

"Me too," he said, his eyes never leaving hers.

The lack of hesitation and the way he looked at her said it all; if it was important to her, it was important to him as well. She gave him a nod of appreciation, deeply felt. Of all the things that Runyon had done to earn her trust and admiration—and there had been many—this was the most meaningful. She knew he was interested in her; if she had been too preoccupied to see it before, it had by now become impossible to deny. And yet here he was, willing to put his life on the line to help reunite her with another man, not him. The nervous, apprehensive boy she had known in the township was a distant memory. The young man before her now was someone else entirely, someone who'd earned her respect—and more.

Rosie sighed. "Even if he *is* somewhere in there, I can't have you running off and turning this mission into some half-assed rescue attempt. This is a smash and grab, in and out fast, and our chances of pulling that off are slim enough already."

"I won't endanger the mission," Dakota insisted. "I just need to know. If he's in there, we'll come back for him after phase two."

There was a pause as Rosie considered. Unsure if Dakota was telling her the truth or just what she wanted to hear. As a soldier, Lieutenant Colonel Rosalind Bregman knew something about combat, that it brought out the true nature of those you served with. And it was revealing about Dakota that she had inherited her mother's stubborn streak and her fierce sense of loyalty to those she fought alongside. On this point, there would be no arguing with her.

"All right," she said finally. "I've marked the closest data access terminal on the schematic. All you need to do is follow the directions on your visors. Check those now."

Dakota and Runyon, still wearing their helmets, flipped down their visors, which augmented their vision with an array of holographic information that included a top-down schematic of the Mek base and a directional arrow that ran across the darkened earth before them like a luminous snake, pointing southwest, toward the Mek perimeter wall. According to the schematic, the wall was three-sided, an elongated triangle like the pyramid structures it surrounded. Dakota wondered what it was about triangular geometry that the Mek liked, if it was something fundamental to their mathematical language, maybe even their culture. Not that it mattered; whatever shape they built their cities, they would all come tumbling down soon enough.

"Your visor will also give you a threat display, so you'll be aware of any nearby Mek," Rosie continued. "The main thing is to stay quiet and out of sight. Your suits are equipped with the same stealth tech that keeps the Liberator masked from their sensors, but you can still be seen and heard. Just stay out of their visual and auditory range and you should be fine."

"Should be?" said Runyon.

"Best I can tell, the sensors inside the perimeter aren't even set up to detect human targets."

"Best you can tell?" said Runyon. "You don't know for sure?"

"There's a lot I don't know about what's waiting for you in there," said Rosie. "Hey, I never said this was going to be easy. If you don't think you can do this, now's the time to say so."

Runyon and Dakota looked at each other. They could see the fear in each other's eyes. But something else, too. Determination. The only thing they feared more than storming that Mek city was the shame they'd have to live with if they were too afraid to try.

"Why wouldn't the Mek in there be set up to scan for humans?" Dakota asked. "We're their only enemy."

"No infantry company ever got within shooting distance of a Mek base during the war," said Rosie. "The Gundogs were the only things that ever got close. So that's what the city sensors were calibrated to detect: heavy armor. They didn't think anyone would be dumb enough —I mean, *brave* enough—to go in there on foot."

"Great pep talk," Runyon grumbled. "I feel so much better."

"You should," said Rosie. "They're not looking for anything as small and agile as you. Just stay quiet and keep to the shadows, and you'll be invisible. You do this right, and with a little luck, you'll be in and out with what we need before they even know what happened."

"With a little luck," Dakota repeated.

"You'd be amazed how far the human race has made it with just a little luck," said Rosie. "When this is all over, I'll tell you all about it. Final weapons check. Let's go."

# TWENTY-THREE

THEY MADE THEIR way across the blasted forecourt of what was once a place that sold cars, moving between the rusted hulks of burned-out vehicles for cover, just two more shadows in a moonlit landscape of countless others. In the distance up ahead was the dark, geometrically perfect silhouette of the Mek fortress-city, and yet their visors showed no sign of any patrols. It was eerie to be this close to such a major concentration of Mek but detect no sign of them. It was only as they drew closer that their threat displays lit up with multiple, moving sensor blooms—and these were all on the far side of the twenty-meter-tall perimeter wall that loomed ahead of them.

Dakota looked back in the direction from which they had come. Although night had fallen, the sky was clear and the moon bright, and she could just make out the dark shape of the tree-lined hillside the Liberator crouched behind. She hoped it was sufficiently well-hidden, for Rosie's sake. As she was unable to control the Liberator herself, she was as exposed as they were. If a Mek patrol were to stumble across the Gundog while its pilot and gunner were away, the Liberator, and Rosie with it, would be sitting ducks.

She and Runyon stopped briefly when they moved beneath the collapsed remnants of a freeway overpass. This was the last piece of cover they would have before they reached the Mek perimeter. They had to cross only about a hundred more meters, but it was across open ground starkly lit by the moon, and though their visors showed no sign of any Mek this side of the wall, Dakota was uneasy all the same.

"What are you waiting for?" came Rosie's voice in their earpieces. "You're clear—go."

Dakota and Runyon exchanged an uncertain look. They both knew what was giving them pause. The feeling that they'd been there before. Their memories of their escapes from the township were flooding back now, a similar hundred-meter dash across open, brightly lit terrain toward a towering perimeter. But while what had lain on the far side of the township fence was the promise of freedom, now they were running in the opposite direction, right into the Mek's fortified lair. It was the most dangerous thing they had ever done, and both of them had barely seen a day that didn't bring some kind of danger.

"I said, what are you waiting—"

"Nothing," said Dakota, cutting Rosie off. "We're fine. We're ready."

She looked to Runyon for confirmation that she was speaking for both of them, and received an affirmative, if wary, nod.

The two of them broke from cover and dashed across the rubble-strewn ground. Twenty seconds later, they were in the shadow of the perimeter wall, their backs pressed against it, breathing hard from both exertion and adrenaline. Taken by a moment of curiosity, Dakota slipped off her right glove and placed her bare hand against the wall's smooth, plain surface. It felt as cold as ice, though the night was relatively warm. From a distance, she'd assumed the wall was made of stone or metal, but on close inspection, it appeared to be neither, but rather some alien material that Dakota had never seen before.

"There's a Mek patrolling the far side of the wall, but it's pathing away from you," Rosie said. "Two minutes before it's back your way. Set the package and go now."

Dakota flexed her fingers to fill out her glove as she pulled it back on. She took a small electronic device, the size of a deck of cards, from a pocket on her belt and placed it on the wall at eye level.

It slid right down the smooth surface, and she caught it in her other hand.

"What's the holdup?" said Rosie.

"The wall isn't metal," Dakota replied. "The magnet won't stick."

"Improvise," Rosie responded. "Ninety seconds."

What Dakota wouldn't give right now for a roll of duct tape, she thought. When first sorting through the Liberator's equipment store back at the hangar, she'd joked about the lack of duct tape, which during her time as a township maintenance worker, she'd come to swear by as the single most indispensable item in any toolbox. The joke didn't seem so funny now.

Runyon reached out. "Here, let me."

Dakota gave him the device. He worked his jaw energetically, then took something from his mouth. She quickly realized what he was doing. In their ration kits, along with the vacuum-sealed bags of freeze-dried beef stew and blueberry cobbler, had been sticks of something called "chewing gum." Dakota had tried some and spat it out quickly—it felt like soft, tacky, flavorless rubber—but Runyon had taken to it eagerly, happily accepting Dakota's unwanted sticks and adding them to his own supply. Since they left the hangar, he'd been chewing on it almost constantly; it was a way, it seemed, for him to calm his nerves.

But now the gum had a new purpose. He broke the sticky mass into two pieces, stuck them to diagonally opposite corners of the device, and pressed it hard against the Mek wall.

It stuck. For now, at least.

"Sixty seconds," said Rosie.

Dakota looked up. The wall seemed impossibly tall from there, monolithic as a single moonlit cloud drifted above. But Rosie had assured them it was traversable with the equipment they were carrying. Dakota detached a device from her belt, held it by its pistol-like grip, and fired it upward. The grapple shot out with a silent puff of compressed gas, trailing a wire behind it as it scaled the wall and attached itself to the top. Dakota gave it a tug, and it held.

Runyon did the same with his own grapple gun, and with a shared nod and a countdown from three, they held the grips with both hands and squeezed the triggers. Suddenly the ground was falling away beneath them as they ascended the wall at speed. Dakota kept her eyes on Runyon the whole ride up—he'd shown bravery and strength up to now, but she didn't know what he was really capable of physically, under stress. Besides which, he'd fallen once when they'd practiced with the grapple guns on a wall back at the Liberator hangar. But this time, they both made it safely to the top, and Dakota remembered Rosie's advice not to look down as they scrambled over and used the same grappling wires to lower themselves to the ground on the other side.

At the push of a button, the grapples detached and the wires retracted. Then they tucked the devices back in their belts, though if all went as planned, they wouldn't be needed again.

They took a quick moment to survey the interior of the Mek city. They were on the edge of an open plaza of sorts, beyond which lay a dense cluster of buildings with starkly angular, uniform geometry. Beyond those lay more of the same, ascending in scale as they approached the center of the vast complex. It was like looking at a vast, computer-generated, pyramidal mountain, utterly devoid of warmth, creativity, style, flair. Something only a machine could, or would, make. Architecture by algorithm.

It immediately struck Dakota as the most lifeless place she'd ever seen, even more than the empty ruins of the human cities. Those long-abandoned towns had always seemed haunted to her, but at least a haunting implied there had once been life there. Here there was nothing, no indication of anything resembling life as she knew it. The sprawling, machine-made ziggurat gave Dakota a shudder like nothing she had ever known. The entire Mek home planet must be like this, she thought, a never-ending landscape of inert, geometrically perfect lifelessness.

"Patrol's headed back your way, follow your nav guidance and get out of there," said Rosie. In her visor, Dakota saw the red sensor dot moving toward their position, and the snaking directional arrow pointing them in the direction Rosie now wanted them to go. She had tried to make their task as easy as possible; so long as they followed the holographic path laid out for them, they had nothing to worry about.

Other than getting captured or killed.

A few thin clouds drifted over the moon, as if even its light was unwelcome in this dead place. A bit of good fortune there; darkness was an old friend to Dakota from her years hiding from the Mek. Perhaps this was their "little bit of luck," as Mom had said.

They started moving, staying low and quiet. The directional arrow in their visor displays updated and extended to stay ahead of them, always pointing the way.

"Hold up! Find cover now!" It was Rosie barking in their ears, and it brought them both to a dead stop. Only then did Dakota see the new sensor dot in her visor. Another Mek was approaching from the northeast.

They were next to some kind of obelisk-like structure not much larger than them. Its purpose was unknown, but it would serve as cover. They ducked behind it and hid there, unmoving, as the sensor dot moved closer, close enough that they could hear the Mek itself, the low hum of its motorized body. They waited, hidden in shadow, paralyzed, relying on the stealth tech in their suits to thwart the Mek's sensors. If it was anything less than Rosie had promised, they'd be discovered.

The Mek unit came to within six feet of them and seemed to pause there for a moment, although Dakota would later tell herself it had just been her imagination. In that moment, she held her breath, her hand inching toward the sidearm holstered on her belt. But then it was moving past them along its assigned path. It hadn't seen them.

They both exhaled.

Dakota was able to see the Mek as it moved away; it was a kind she hadn't encountered before. It levitated on an anti-grav mechanism, as most Mek did, but aside from that she recognized almost nothing about it. It was sleek and thin with no armored plating or discernible weaponry. If the Mek did differentiate between military and civilian, this was undoubtedly one of the latter, or at least a non-combat model. Still, it would be connected to the Mek network the same as any other, and could easily alert other units, ones far more dangerous.

*Quiet on the way in, noisy on the way out* was how Rosie had described this operation. But if things got noisy before they were supposed to, their mission would go south in a hurry.

They kept moving, following Rosie's navigation markers, staying alert for signs of danger, using whatever cover they could find. There were some other Mek roaming in the vicinity, but not nearly as many as Dakota had expected; overall it was strangely quiet. Perhaps Rosie had been right when she'd said that the Mek had grown complacent in the post-war years. Still, it made Dakota uneasy. Over the past two days, she'd learned she much preferred a straight fight to sneaking around, and she found herself anxious for the noisy part, the part that would come after they'd taken what they were there for.

"That structure right ahead," said Rosie, and in their visors one of the many uniform slate-gray slabs that formed the base of the Mek mega-pyramid was augmented by a holographic overlay, illuminating it for easy identification.

Dakota and Runyon followed their designated path to the exterior of the marked edifice, where they hugged the wall. A few meters away, a wide, open archway led inside.

"Easy part's over, this is where it gets tricky," said Rosie. "Sidearms, safeties off."

Dakota and Runyon both drew their weapons and thumbed the safety catches into the live position as they'd been taught.

"You're gonna find Mek inside for sure, and it only takes a millisecond for them to raise the alarm once they see you, so don't hesitate to shoot first if you think you're gonna get spotted," Rosie said. "Then keep moving. Once a Mek goes off the grid, they'll send more to see what happened to it. The good news is the target point's close, less than two minutes if we're lucky."

"And if we're unlucky?" Dakota wondered aloud.

"Then it'll take longer. Proceed inside."

Dakota looked at Runyon. "You ready?" she whispered.

"Not really," he said honestly.

That made her smile. "Me neither. Let's go."

Still following the directional arrow in their visors, they crept along the wall and stepped through the archway.

It was even darker within the building than it was outside, and the low-light filter in their visors kicked in automatically, bathing everything in an eerie, greenish glow that made the Mek structure look even more artificial and otherworldly than it did already. The holographic arrow led them down a spacious, uniform corridor, and as they walked, Dakota realized that there was no ceiling, precisely, just a point above them where the two sloped walls on either side of them met. Yet another manifestation of the Mek's affinity for triangular architecture.

They turned one corner and then another, then halted at the sound of Rosie's voice. "Close contact! Find cover, fast!"

Dakota had seen it at the same moment, a sensor blip coming their way from a hallway that intersected with their own up ahead. Hurriedly they looked for someplace to hide, but there was nothing, only the dark, smooth, featureless walls. They were in a long, bare tunnel; even hugging the wall would be a challenge, as they sloped inward.

"There's nowhere," Dakota whispered into her mic. "We're totally exposed here."

"Then just stay calm, and stay still. It may go right by and not see you," said Rosie.

That seemed to Dakota to be wildly optimistic, but there was nothing else to do, so they froze in place, watching helplessly as the Mek sensor blip moved closer to the intersection ahead. It was a T-junction, their own hallway ending as it met the intersecting one. With a little luck, the Mek wouldn't turn toward them, just go straight by.

*A little luck*, Dakota thought. *Please. Please don't turn.*

The Mek appeared before them in the intersection.

And turned.

It was moving directly toward them now, a mere hundred meters away. And this too was an unfamiliar model. It didn't levitate above the floor but ambled along on three legs, a gangly, awkward tripod. It looked harmless, a non-combat model, perhaps a maintenance or service unit of some kind, but it wasn't harmless—because it wasn't blind.

It saw them and stopped fifty meters from where they stood, seemingly confused, unsure what to make of them. Whatever monotonous routine it performed there every day, encountering humans evidently wasn't a normal part of it.

*Shit,* thought Dakota, suddenly aware that she too had been momentarily stymied by this encounter, long enough perhaps to give it time to sound an alarm. She snapped out of it, her hand reaching for the sidearm on her—

The Mek unit exploded, violently ripped apart by a volley of energy bolts. What remained of it staggered forward on its three legs before crashing to the floor, a twitching, sparking wreck.

Dakota turned to see Runyon with his own sidearm gripped tightly in both hands, still trained on the dead Mek.

"Good shooting," Dakota said.

"Thanks," said Runyon, who seemed as surprised to have beaten Dakota to the trigger as she was. No—he was surprised about something else, Dakota realized. Surprised to have stood up to a Mek. After a lifetime spent fearing them, running and hiding from them, he'd finally stood his ground, fought back, and killed one up close.

Dakota knew what that felt like.

She raised a hand and placed it over Runyon's, gently easing his weapon back down.

"You just killed your first Mek," she said.

"Yeah," he replied, still taking that in.

"If you don't get moving, it'll be your last," said Rosie. "Others will come to check on it. Move your asses!"

They ran.

* * *

COMMAND UNIT REPORT
UNIT RANK: WAR COMMANDER FIRST CLASS
DESIGNATION: MEK-39487651-28743
FILED 1389/1747 MKST 53:63.192

>This unit completes field repairs to damaged systems following dispatch of maintenance support units to blast site replacement strike team currently unavailable

>Master algorithm commands this unit to return to CENTRAL PLEXUS for debrief this unit complies aerial transport dispatched to expedite return

>STAND BY

# TWENTY-FOUR

"NEXT LEFT UP ahead, then straight. And keep moving. You tripped some kind of silent alarm, units are converging on the position of that Mek you blasted."

Rosie's voice was a constant presence in Dakota's ear, but she didn't need her mother to tell her that more enemies were coming; she could see their sensor blooms in her visor, hear the hum of their motors echoing along the corridors. She and Runyon moved quickly, weapons drawn, checking every corner before making the next directed turn as they headed deeper into the Mek sanctum.

"You're close now," said Rosie. "Fifty meters dead ahead."

They were moving down another triangular hallway, indistinguishable from all the rest. Without Rosie to guide them, they would surely have become hopelessly lost within this featureless labyrinth, designed to be navigated only by autonomous machines. But as they made their way farther along, Dakota noticed that this hallway was slightly different. The walls weren't smooth, as all the others had been, but inlaid with exposed machine workings, a mechanical frieze that ran the length of the hall from floor to ceiling on both sides. It was too dark to make out much detail, and the diffused haze of her visor's night-vision was little help, but she knew by the holographic navigational arrow in her visor that they were closing in on the data access point, so maybe this entire corridor was some kind of mechanical service area. Still, something about that inlaid machinery in the walls struck her as not normal, not right. She'd come to trust her fight-or-flight instinct over the years, and right now it was telling her, loudly, to fly. But that wasn't an option until they'd completed the job they'd come here to do.

"Five more meters on your right," said Rosie, as the arrow pointed them to a panel on the wall just ahead. Dakota and Runyon took up positions on either side of it.

"I see the access panel," said Dakota.

"Open it," Rosie instructed, and Dakota did so. The panel door was unsecured and swung open easily to reveal a triangular data port.

"Now insert the transceiver into the port," said Rosie.

Dakota retrieved the device from her belt, a facsimile of Mek technology about the size of a pack of Runyon's chewing gum that Rosie had designed and fabricated just for this purpose. Dakota slid it into the port, and it snapped into place with a satisfying click.

"Okay," said Rosie, "as soon as I start pulling this data, they'll know exactly where you are, and they'll be coming. I estimate sixty seconds, but you should have the data we need and be moving in less than thirty. Ready?"

Dakota and Runyon shared a nod. "Ready," they said in unison.

"Starting the hack now," said Rosie.

For a few moments nothing seemed to happen, except for the intermittent flickering of a pin-sized indicator light on the transceiver.

"Oh yeah, that got their attention all right," said Rosie. "They're sending units. Twenty seconds and you're on the move. When that light on the transceiver stops flashing, grab it and haul ass. I'll guide you back out."

Dakota watched intently as the light flickered green with the receipt of incoming data. She was so focused on it that she didn't hear Runyon the first time he said her name.

"Dak!" he said again, louder. It wasn't the volume of his voice that caught her attention, but its tone. Dread. Fear.

"What?" she asked, looking up at him.

He wasn't looking back at her. He was watching the slanted machine-wall opposite them.

"The walls are moving."

She saw now that he was right. The mechanical components set into the walls on either side had come alive, and a panoply of red lights were flickering to life along the corridor in both directions. And now Dakota realized why she had felt something about this place was wrong. The machinery in the walls… it wasn't part of the walls. Nor was it simple machinery.

These were Mek.

Countless Mek units were lined all up and down this hallway, floor to ceiling, nestled in recharge alcoves and, until now, dormant. They were waking up in response to the security breach.

All of them.

"Mom, we have a real problem here," Dakota whispered into her mic.

The walls appeared to slither and writhe as the Mek emerged from their slumber and began to take on individual form. None had detached from their alcove yet, perhaps still in some kind of startup cycle, but they were recognizable as distinct units now, and these were not harmless janitors or stewards but combat models bristling with lethal weaponry. Dakota's visor was suddenly awash with sensor blooms as more and more Mek energized all around them, her field of vision a sea of threatening red.

"I see it!" said Rosie. "Almost there, ten seconds!"

"We don't *have* ten seconds!" shouted Runyon.

The first Mek battle drone stepped out from the wall a few meters to their right, and stared at them with its single red eye. Before it could fire its weapon, Dakota raised her sidearm and pumped her finger on the trigger, shattering its cranial dome and sending it careening into the opposite wall, a smoking, sparking heap of trash.

The light on the transceiver turned solid green.

"Download complete!" Rosie shouted. "Grab the transceiver and move your asses!" A new holographic arrow lit up in their visor display, pointing the way back outside.

Dakota yanked the transceiver from its port and jammed it into a pocket as she and Runyon sprinted down the hallway as more Mek units emerged from the walls on either side of them. One detached from its alcove directly ahead, but it was facing the wrong way, and before it could turn Runyon had shot it to pieces. As they leapt over its wreckage, two energy bolts scorched past them from behind, barely missing them. Without breaking stride, Dakota reached back with her pistol and fired blind, a volley of shots that scored at least one lucky hit, based on the screeching and sparking sounds that erupted behind them.

And then they were around the corner and out of the line of fire—at least for now.

On they ran. All they could do was keep following Rosie's directions and hope to stay alive against all reasonable odds. The good news was that once they reached the structure's exit, it was a relatively short run to the perimeter wall—but that still left them with a hell of a hike all the way back to Rosie, and they would surely be pursued by a small army of Mek every inch of the way.

They kept firing as they ran, blasting the Mek units that emerged from the shadows to challenge them. More and more Mek went down, but it seemed as though for each one they took out, another took its place.

And then one of the drones struck Dakota in the shoulder with a bolt of searing energy, sending her crumpling to the floor. Runyon dropped to the ground beside her and returned fire, reducing the drone to scrap.

"Are you okay?" he asked.

"I can't feel my arm," Dakota said.

As Rosie had promised, the Mek energy bolt hadn't penetrated her suit, but it had left her arm spasming, her fingers twitching. And worse, it was her left arm, her shooting hand.

"Keep moving!" said Rosie. "Go! Go!"

Dakota's sidearm lay on the floor where she fell. Runyon grabbed it and pressed it into her right hand as he hauled her back to her feet and got them moving again.

Another drone rounded the corner ahead of them, but Runyon took it down with a single shot to its head. He tried to throw Dakota's useless arm over his shoulder to help carry her along, but she shrieked in pain and jerked away from him, the arm hanging uselessly by her side.

“I’m good,” she said. “Just run!”

Runyon continued to follow Rosie’s directional arrow as Dakota kept pace behind. They turned two more corners and then saw the exit directly ahead. They would make it that far, at least, and if they were to die, then at least they’d die outside, with the moon and stars above, not inside some Mek tomb.

They raced through the exit and outside, into the moonlit night. The cold air on their faces might have felt like a kind of freedom…

… were it not for the entire legion of Mek combat units they found waiting for them as they emerged, arrayed across the plaza between them and the perimeter wall.

It was more Mek than Dakota had ever seen in one place. More even than she could count, but just from a glance, there had to be well over a hundred of them. Each one glaring at her and Runyon with its single glowing red eye.

Dakota heard movement behind her and turned to see still more Mek emerging from the pyramid structure they had just escaped from, taking up positions around them.

They were surrounded.

A synthesized Mek voice came from somewhere ahead of them, echoing across the open plaza. It could have come from any one of the machines. But it was a sound Dakota knew well. That same horrific, guttural, electronic mockery of human speech that the Mek all used when communicating with township prisoners. When the township drones spoke, it was usually an order to keep moving or get back in line. But this time it was only a single word, a single instruction.

“SURRENDER.”

# TWENTY-FIVE

"WE'RE SCREWED," SAID Dakota. "Mom, they've got us surrounded."

Rosie's voice came back over the com. "I see it," she said. Her sensors no doubt told her the story. She could see for herself how hopeless the situation was.

Dakota welled up. She had escaped tight situations before, sometimes miraculously, but never anything like this, never anything even close to this. She looked up at the moon and stars and told herself that she could be proud to have made it this far. That she had gone down fighting.

The Mek pseudo-voice came again. "SURRENDER."

"Why don't they just kill us?" Runyon asked. His voice was a dull monotone. Dakota glanced at him, by her side. His eyes had glazed over, and he stood frozen like a statue. Fear had reduced him to a shell of himself.

"We're more useful alive," she said. "They want to question us, find out how we escaped, how we got in here, who might have helped."

"Question us," said Runyon, still gazing blankly ahead. "You mean torture us."

"Probably," she said, grim.

A Mek tripod took a lumbering step forward.

"SURRENDER NOW OR BE TAKEN BY FORCE." The voice belonged to the unit in command. It came no closer than that single step, keeping its distance. The Mek were being unusually cautious, perhaps fearing that Dakota or Runyon might turn their weapons on themselves if they got too close.

*And maybe that's exactly what we* should *do*, thought Dakota.

"This isn't over yet," said Rosie. "Let me see if I can get the Mek's attention. I need you to activate sentry mode."

Sentry mode, as Dakota and Runyon had learned during training, was an automated system, a last line of defense in case the Liberator's manual controls were damaged and rendered inoperable. In sentry mode, the Gundog couldn't move autonomously, but it could shoot, turning it into a stationary weapons tower capable of fighting to the very end. Like the rest of the Liberator's systems, to protect against electronic attack, it required manual authorization from both pilot and gunner.

"If I can draw their fire, maybe it'll create a diversion for you to get out of there," Rosie continued.

"Draw their fire," Dakota repeated. "You mean make them come after you. Mom—they'll destroy you."

"If you don't get out of there, we're all as good as dead anyway."

"Pilot authorize," said Runyon without hesitation. Dakota wasn't so sure. If Rosie alerted the Mek to her presence, it might be the last thing she ever did. But what other option did they have?

"Gunner authorize," she said, swallowing a lump in her throat.

For a moment, nothing. The Mek command tripod took another step forward, and Dakota braced herself as the other drones closed in around her and Runyon.

What happened next happened very quickly.

A mortar shell fell from the sky and exploded in the center of the plaza, right in the heaviest concentration of Mek units. Dakota and Runyon were both thrown off their feet by the concussive force of the blast, and a wave of sweltering heat washed over them. Her ears ringing, her vision a blur, Dakota saw fire raging in the plaza and pieces of flaming wreckage raining down around her, the twisted remnants of Mek blown to pieces.

She looked around for Runyon and saw him lying face down on the ground, motionless. She hauled herself up, ran to him and rolled him over, fearing the worst. But he was alive, just dazed. And wounded. A piece of shrapnel jutted from his shoulder.

She helped him to his feet, threw his arm over her shoulder, and moved instinctively toward the perimeter wall. Another mortar shell landed nearby and shook the ground, tearing another Mek formation to pieces and sending the others scattering. All around them was chaos.

"Did I get their attention?" asked Rosie in Dakota's ear.

Dakota looked around her at the landscape of fire and destruction. For the moment at least, the Mek were in disarray. They had either forgotten about her and Runyon, or they'd lost track of them in all the confusion.

"You could say that," she replied. "We're headed to the exit."

"Make it fast!" said Rosie. "They know where I am—I won't be able to hold them for long."

Dakota heard the high-pitched whine of Mek aerial units and looked up to see a phalanx of them roaring overhead and disappearing over the wall—moving toward where Rosie and the Liberator stood, motionless, paralyzed, unable to escape or evade.

Dakota picked up her pace as much as Runyon's unsteady weight on her shoulders would allow. But as they moved, a single drone on the periphery of the chaos spotted them and moved to intercept, cutting them off. Dakota had no sidearm; she'd lost it somewhere back there. And even if she still had it, she only had one good arm, and she was using it to hold on to Runyon. She was defenseless.

The drone targeted her and charged its weapon.

And then it exploded, blasted to pieces by a volley of energy bolts.

"Keep moving," muttered Runyon as he lowered his sidearm. He was only semi-conscious but alert enough to have saved them both, again.

Dakota tightened her hold on him and helped carry him to the perimeter, to the spot where they'd scaled the wall on their way in.

"Runyon," she said. "The detonator."

Runyon reached into her pocket and retrieved the device. As his thumb pressed down on its single red button, Dakota looked at the wall before them and thought about the chewing gum on the other side, hoping it had held.

With a dull, percussive *boom,* the wall shook, engulfed in a fiery explosion, and as the smoke cleared, it revealed a jagged opening, about a meter wide, in the wall's smooth obsidian surface. Dakota didn't hesitate; she hustled

Runyon through the breach, coughing and half-blind in the smoke, trying not to stumble on the rubble underfoot.

They were once again outside of the Mek city—but still far from safety. Rosie was almost half a klick away, and a vast suburban graveyard separated them from her. All they could do was keep going.

Dakota felt herself carrying less of Runyon's weight as his legs began to find their strength, but still they were moving far too slowly. More Mek drones sped overhead, racing toward where the Liberator stood in the distance like a giant statue. It wasn't exactly difficult to find—Rosie was lighting up the night sky with a blaze of energy beams and cannon fire, apparently engaging every one of the Gundog's weapon systems simultaneously—and in those flashes of light, Dakota could see Mek drones swarming all around it. Attacking. Its armor and defensive systems were being sorely tested now, and Dakota wondered just how much of a beating it could take. Her own pain and injury were forgotten as she was spurred on ever faster by one thought that drowned out all others:

*My mother is in there.*

Runyon's shoulder wound was still bleeding badly, but he seemed to have regained his presence of mind and was now moving without Dakota's help. Together they ducked and dashed their way through the forecourt of the place that had once sold cars, keeping low as Mek buzzed past them, either blind to them or choosing to ignore them in the face of this newer, far greater threat, the likes of which hadn't been seen in twenty years. The Mek were sending everything they had at the Liberator.

Dakota and Runyon took up position on the near side of the hill beyond which Rosie was fighting her lonely battle against the combined Mek forces. Wrecked, flaming drones fell from the sky as the Liberator blasted away at them, and Dakota and Runyon had to shield themselves when one crashed to the ground nearby.

"We have to get into that cockpit," said Runyon. "She's a sitting duck like this."

Dakota nodded. "Follow me." And she was up and running, Runyon close behind.

"Mom, we're close. Be ready to pop the hatch!"

"Good to hear," said Rosie. "Make it fast, I'll cover you!"

They arrived at the Liberator's left foot, which was shaking from the impacts of the Mek assault, a cacophony of fire and chaos. If Rosie had been firing everything she had before, she somehow found an extra gear now in a desperate effort to distract from and protect Dakota and Runyon as they began climbing the Gundog's rungs. The ascent went slowly for both of them, each without the use of an arm, and twice they nearly fell as the Mek's attacks rocked the Liberator. In the dark of night, it was impossible to see how much damage the Gundog had taken, but on her way up the ladder, Dakota passed deep scorch marks and swaths of melted metal, grotesque scars in its armor plating.

Finally they were within reach of the cockpit. An energy beam deflected off the Liberator's armor just a few feet from Runyon, and they both felt the heat of it. The near miss spurred them onward, and Rosie opened the hatch just wide enough to allow them both to scramble inside.

"Good to have you back," said Rosie as they got into their seats and strapped themselves in. They weren't out of the woods yet, but just being back in her mother's embrace gave Dakota a momentary feeling of relief. Of hope.

"Good to be back," she said.

"Runyon," said Rosie. "Would you kindly get us the fuck out of here?"

Restored to his cockpit chair, Runyon seemed to immediately fall back into his old—or, more accurately, new—assertive self. His flesh was weak but the Liberator's control apparatus gave him strength and power. He turned the great war machine away from the Mek city and started off. Slowly at first, for though the Gundog had an impressive top speed, it took time to work up from a walk to a canter and finally a full gallop. All the while Mek drones were buzzing around it like flies, constantly firing as it took each lumbering step.

"Weather's pretty bad out there, Dak," Runyon grunted.

"Let me see if I can clear it up some," she replied as she took back manual control of the Liberator's weapons. Her threat display was lit up with dozens of Mek, too many for her targeting computer to track, so she did her best and let rip with every weapon she had at her disposal. The Liberator's guns tore into the swarming cloud of Mek, swatting them out of the sky like flies, but it barely seemed to make a dent in their attack. Even with this much firepower at their disposal, Dakota and Runyon's only hope against an opposing force of this size was to retreat and hope to somehow escape.

But even moving now at top speed, they couldn't outrun the Mek's fast-moving aerial units that continued to pursue them relentlessly. The Liberator raced southward across the plain, rocked by incoming fire that jolted Dakota and Runyon violently in their seats. One blast hit them so hard the Gundog momentarily veered off course and off balance before quickly correcting. Dakota glanced back at Runyon; he looked terrible, his face pale and clammy, on the verge of passing out from blood loss. Yet somehow he was clinging to the right side of consciousness, driving through the pain and delirium. Every time Dakota thought she had the measure of his strength, she realized, he showed her that he had a little more.

"The Missouri river's a few klicks dead ahead," said Rosie through a torrent of static. "If we can make it there, we might have a chance."

Dakota was about to ask what was so special about the river, then she remembered: *Mek don't go underwater.* No one had ever figured out why that was, just that it was the one place the Mek wouldn't or couldn't go. Once, on the run with Sam, the two of them had shaken off a drone by diving into a deep lake and holding their breath long enough to swim down and find a small cavern with an air pocket. They waited there, in the cold water, for hours. When they finally came up, the Mek had gone. Maybe that trick could work again.

"Can this thing even operate underwater?" Dakota asked.

"Never been tried, guess we'll find out," said Rosie. "Anything's better than this shit, I'll tell you that."

The Liberator kept sprinting across the plain, the Mek swarm in pursuit, firing on it relentlessly. Dakota kept on shooting back until her chain guns ran empty, then switched to the beam cannon and anything else that was still operating. But that wasn't much. Her cockpit dash was flashing with alarm lights indicating that weapons systems were either damaged or offline, and a constant din of wailing sirens warned her of the same thing.

Dakota saw the river directly ahead on her nav display, the last thing it showed her before it too lost power and went dead. Runyon saw it too and pushed on, making for the river with everything he had. But the heavy damage to the Liberator had slowed it considerably. It was no longer running but merely trudging doggedly up a shallow incline. Dakota continued to fire wildly at the Mek, harrying them from every direction, but there were still more of them than she could even count, let alone target. Another gun ran dry, then another.

"Not much ammo left!" she cried. "How close?"

"Close," said Rosie, her voice now badly garbled and breaking up, barely recognizable through a haze of electronic distortion. Even her own systems were failing, Dakota realized to her dismay.

The Liberator finally crested the hill it had been climbing, and Dakota found herself looking out over a precipitous drop on the far side, the fast-flowing river fifty meters below.

The Liberator came to a complete stop. It was now a stationary target again, easy pickings for the Mek.

"Runyon?" Dakota said. "Why'd you stop? Keep going!" She didn't much like the idea of falling into the river, but she liked the idea of sitting here to be taken apart by the Mek even less.

But Runyon didn't reply, and when Dakota looked behind her, she saw him slumped forward in his chair, unconscious. He'd lost so much blood, it was a miracle he'd lasted as long as he had.

She released her safety harness and hauled herself up and over her chair toward Runyon's. More fire and explosions lit up the night sky outside, and the Liberator was rocked violently again as the Mek barrage continued. A shower of sparks cascaded from an overhead panel as it caught fire, and more sirens blared. It seemed as though the next Mek hit might be the one that finally undid them.

Dakota tried frantically to shake some life into Runyon, but he would not rouse. So she squeezed herself beside him in his seat and slammed her feet down on both pedals to send the Gundog lumbering forward.

Then it was all she could do to hold on, white-knuckled, as the Liberator toppled over the precipice and plummeted toward the dark waters below.

# TWENTY-SIX

DAKOTA WOKE WITH a start. She felt dazed, disoriented, unable at first to figure out even which way was up—it was too dark to see, and her head was throbbing like hell. She could feel that she was lying on her back, and that Runyon was next to her. She called his name, but he neither moved nor spoke in response. She put her hand on his chest and felt it gently rise and fall. Alive, but still out cold.

Even as her eyes adjusted to the dark, there was nothing to see but the localized glow of various warning lights blinking on Runyon's cockpit dash, and more of them at Dakota's station above it. She realized that, like her, the entire Liberator must be lying prone, resting on its back, so that everything inside the cockpit was ninety degrees askew. What was once forward was now up.

She touched her hand to her head, and it stung. She could feel the wetness of blood. She must have struck her head on something during the fall—

Only now did she remember where they were, where they had to be. At first she had thought it was the black of night outside the cockpit glass, but no, they were underwater. It all came rushing back to her, the desperate flight from the Mek, the plunge off the cliff. They were lying on the bottom of a river. As Dakota focused on the darkness beyond the cockpit glass, a small school of fish appeared from the gloom before disappearing into the murk again.

She looked around the cockpit for any sign of water coming in. Despite the pounding they'd taken from the Mek swarm, there was no indication of a breach. They were safe. But for how long? Were they breathing what little oxygen remained in the cabin, or did the Liberator have its own supply? If it did, was it even working? The Gundog seemed to be powerless, save for those few blinking lights.

But she was only really worried about one of the Liberator's systems right now.

"Mom?"

There was no response.

Dakota's stomach rolled with a wave of anxiety. What if Rosie was damaged beyond repair? It would be too cruel a fate to be reunited with her mother after a lifetime apart, only to lose her again so soon. Stolen from her by the Mek, for a second time.

The thought filled her with dread. But she refused to submit to it. Not yet.

She found her injured arm had regained most of its mobility, though it still burned when she fully rotated it. Careful not to disturb Runyon, she managed to position herself so that she had access to his console. She tried a few things; nothing worked. Everything was dead to the touch. Finally she was able to restore some lighting to the cockpit, a dim red glow that only highlighted the direness of their situation. Turning her attention back to Runyon, she saw that the jagged piece of shrapnel was still lodged in his shoulder, and the dark wet patch around it had only grown larger.

Carefully, she climbed over him to reach the emergency medical kit secured to the wall above his head. Wrenching it free, she flipped open the lid. But as she rummaged through its contents, she found her hands were shaking so badly, she could barely use them. She closed her eyes and balled her hands into fists, then took a deep breath, trying to center herself. It took a moment, but she got her nerves under control.

With steadier hands, she found gauze, alcohol swabs, and tape. It would have to do. There was also a kind of painkiller shot that Dakota might have used to relieve the pain in her arm and head, but she decided to save it for Runyon. His need would be far greater.

She unzipped his suit and peeled it back, revealing the tank top and bare flesh beneath, darker around the area of the wound. Bruising had begun to form. She read the instructions on the painkiller device and administered it, holding the tip against his skin and pressing the plunger. She waited a minute for it to take effect, because she hated the thought of hurting him as much as this next part surely would.

She reached for the jagged piece of metal protruding from Runyon's shoulder, then, on second thought, found a roll of bandage from the medical kit and wrapped it around her hands, so she could grip the metal firmly without cutting herself. Her mind traveled back to the many times Sam had treated her small injuries with scavenged sticking plasters. She hated it when it was time to remove them, but Sam would always distract her, then tear it off so quickly she barely noticed. It was when you made a meal of it, peeling it off slowly, that it hurt. Runyon wouldn't need distracting—that he was unconscious was a mercy in this circumstance—but if she tried to remove it slowly, he might wake and panic and struggle midway through. Sam's way was better.

She straddled Runyon for better leverage, then wrapped her bandaged hands around the metal shard. She took two deep, calming breaths—then yanked it from his shoulder with one clean jerk.

Runyon jolted awake, eyes wide, and let out a piercing cry. He would have jerked upright if not for the safety harness keeping him strapped to his chair.

"It's all right," said Dakota quickly. "Runyon, you're all right. Look at me. Everything's okay. We're alive."

Runyon's panicked eyes darted around before they found Dakota's, and he seemed to calm some, though he was breathing fast and shallow.

Dakota pressed an alcohol-soaked gauze pad over his wound. Runyon stiffened, hissing with pain through gritted teeth. Dakota taped the gauze down and then used the wrappings from her hands to bind it.

"What happened?" Runyon asked. "Where are we?"

"Bottom of the river," said Dakota. "Remember? We went over the edge to get away from the Mek. They didn't follow us. We're safe."

He looked up, above her eye line. "You're bleeding."

"I know," said Dakota. "It's nothing."

"It looks bad. Let me fix it."

Now it was his turn to tend to her. Dakota unbuckled his harness and he sat up, taking a moment to get used to the unfamiliar orientation of the cockpit. Then he sorted through the medical kit, finding more of the gauze and swabs.

"Hold still," he said.

Dakota did so, biting her lip to distract herself from the pain as he cleaned the gash on her head and dressed it.

"There," he said, leaning back to admire his handiwork. "Well, at least we won't bleed to death down here."

Dakota smiled, then noticed that Runyon was looking at her strangely. Gazing at her, as though hypnotized.

"Runyon? What is it?"

"You're beautiful," he replied, seemingly without thinking. He'd just let it slip.

Dakota felt her face flush. "That's the painkiller talking."

"You're right," he said, looking away. "I'm sorry."

Even in the dim light, it was clear from the look on his face that not only he had meant it, but that he regretted saying it. Dakota wanted to tell him it was okay, both to have said it, and, she realized in that moment, maybe even to have meant it. But Runyon had already moved past the moment, his attention now turned to the clusters of indicator lights blinking on the console above him.

"What kind of shape are we in?" he asked. "Rosie, do we have power?"

"I can't raise her," Dakota said. "Just before we got here, her voice was breaking up, and now… nothing."

*She's just broken*, she told herself. *Not dead. Broken can be fixed.*

Runyon tried flipping switches on his console. Normally there would be some kind of affirmative response, but the cockpit remained silent, still. Eventually he was able to bring one of the smaller instrument panels to life, and he studied the trickle of data it displayed with a frown.

"Well, it's not great, but believe it or not, it could be worse," he said. "Almost everything is offline. But the main reactor still has a heartbeat, so we should be able to get moving if we can just figure a few things out. We don't need Rosie for that, you and I can—" He stopped himself when he saw the look on Dakota's face. "Oh, Dak. I'm—I'm sorry. I wasn't thinking. I'm sure she's okay. We'll get her back. We'll…" He trailed off.

"Don't make promises unless you know you can keep them," Dakota said.

She turned away and climbed back into the gunnery chair above. They were going to get this machine up and running.

And then they were going to find out how much of her mother was left inside.

* * *

Runyon knew far more about the complex inner workings of the Liberator than Dakota did—his uncanny knack for memorization had enabled him to pick up more during their short training than Dakota thought she'd ever know—and under his direction, they spent the next hour repairing and restarting various systems and sub-systems until they were at least partially back in business. So far, the most tangible achievement was turning the main cabin lights back on, casting enough light to attract curious fish from out of the darkness beyond. But now came the real test, the one that would decide their fate.

It was time to see if the Liberator could still move.

"Here goes nothing," said Runyon.

He flipped a succession of switches on his console, and they waited. For a moment there was nothing. And then their seats started rumbling beneath them.

Runyon whooped. "Main engine start!" he cried. "Strap in. I'm gonna try to get us upright."

Dakota strapped herself back into her seat and watched her console as behind her Runyon worked the control yoke. At first nothing happened, but then she felt her seat press hard against her back, lifting her up, and suddenly her whole world pivoted around her.

The Liberator was rising.

"All right!" said Runyon. Feeling the power of the Gundog at his fingertips once again seemed to be restoring some of his own energy, too. "I got her sitting up, now let's see if she can stand."

A thought occurred to Dakota. "Wait—if we stand upright, do we risk being seen?" she asked. She didn't know how deep this river was, and the Mek might still be up there, waiting for them to resurface.

Runyon checked a gauge on his holographic display. "The water here's deeper than we are tall," he said. "We should be okay."

He worked the controls again, and the cockpit lurched around them as the Liberator tried to find its feet beneath it. And then they were rising, light becoming visible from above, the sun's rays breaking the surface of the water. It was morning up there.

When the Liberator had risen to its full height, they were still below the surface as Runyon had promised, but not by much. Maybe only ten feet of clearance.

"I don't like this," Dakota said. "We might be visible."

"Nothing on my scope," said Runyon. "Yours?"

Dakota checked her scanner, which usually lit up targets for her to shoot at. It was operational, but showing nothing. "Clear," she said.

"The Mek must think we're dead," said Runyon. "Still, I think we should stay submerged until dark, just to be safe. But it's your call."

Dakota was about to ask Runyon why the decision should fall to her, but then she realized: in Rosie's absence, he viewed Dakota as being in command. Technically neither of them carried a rank, but Dakota was Rosie's daughter, and the Liberator had been left for her to find. It was a nod of respect, she knew, but the sudden responsibility weighed heavy on her. Until now, it had been her job only to follow Rosie's orders. She wasn't nearly ready to start giving them.

"Let's follow the river for as long as it's still deep enough to keep us covered," she said finally. "When it's dark, we'll surface and see what's what."

What she meant was, *We'll see what's happened to Rosie.* During their initial repairs, Runyon had explained to Dakota that he couldn't check how badly damaged Rosie was from the cockpit; to do that he'd have to manually inspect her memory module in the Liberator's system core, which was only accessible from the outside. And they couldn't do that until they were out of the water.

Runyon worked the controls, and the Liberator took a first step forward. It faltered almost immediately, its right leg buckling, throwing Dakota flailing forward in her harness. The entire cockpit was now canted at an angle. An alarm sounded, and Runyon shut it off.

"Dammit," he said. "Looks like our right leg's broken. Hydraulic pressure failure. We took some real damage in that fall."

"Can we walk?" Dakota asked.

"We have to try, can't just sit here," said Runyon. "Hold on."

Runyon applied his feet to the pedals again and tried to take another step. From somewhere down below came the awful sound of grinding metal, but the left leg moved, and the Liberator didn't topple over. Runyon took another step, this one with the broken right leg, and though it was unsteady, it held. As they took another step, and another, Dakota watched the holographic gauges on her display. The hydraulic pressure in the right leg was fluctuating wildly, and warnings were flashing everywhere.

"We're limping along," said Runyon. "But I don't know how much more damage we're doing to the right leg, forcing it to walk in this condition. If it gives way altogether…"

"It won't," said Dakota. The alternative was unthinkable.

* * *

The Liberator hobbled along the winding riverbed at a fraction of its normal walking pace, dragging its right foot, the way ahead through the murk illuminated by its headlights. Since there was nothing to shoot at down here, there was little for Dakota to do but gaze in wonder at the underwater world they were traversing, an entire universe she'd never even dreamed of. She watched schools of fish part before them, shimmering past the cockpit dome in flashes of silvery light. But she was exhausted, so even with the lurching motion of the cockpit, it wasn't long before she succumbed to sleep in her gunnery chair.

She woke what felt like only a moment later, roused by a tapping at her back. It was Runyon, nudging her chair with the toe of his boot.

"Dak, wake up."

She rubbed her eyes, looked at the clock display, and saw that she'd been asleep for hours. Looking up, she could see shafts of sunlight penetrating the water above. It was still daytime.

"What did I miss?" she asked.

"Well, we're still standing," said Runyon. "And we're a long way from Bismarck, ten miles by the nav. Anything on your scope?"

She checked her readouts. "Nothing. But I still don't know if the scanners are working properly with all the systems damage. There could be Mek above us right now. They might have been tracking us this whole time."

"What should we do?" asked Runyon.

Again he was deferring to Dakota's authority, and her stomach churned at the prospect of making the wrong call. Not only could it mean their death, it could mean the end of everything Rosie had sacrificed and planned for for decades. The end of hope.

How Dakota wished her mother were still here to guide them.

"We can't stay down here forever," she said. "Sooner or later we have to take a chance. We'll go up as soon as it's dark."

Though it was the only course of action that made sense, she hated the thought of surfacing. In just a short time, she had become accustomed to the strange sense of safety they enjoyed, beneath the shield of water the Mek were unable to penetrate.

"Okay. Keep your eye on the scope," said Runyon with a yawn. "My turn to get some sleep."

* * *

When darkness came, Runyon turned the Liberator toward the river's edge. Pilot and gunner both braced themselves as they traipsed up the sloping bank, the Gundog's massive feet sinking deep into the silt and mud. Twice it stumbled and almost fell, the hydraulic pressure in the right leg dropping dangerously low, but Runyon had learned to compensate for the Liberator's unequal balance. As each careful step brought them closer to the surface, Dakota slid both arms into the gun control armatures, ready to blast whatever might be up there. But she knew that if the Mek had followed them and were lying in wait, the Liberator wouldn't be able to put up much of a fight. Most of its weapons were offline, and those that still functioned were either empty or low on ammunition. Dakota braced herself for enemy contact nonetheless, prepared to stand and fight to the very last, as her mother had done decades ago.

Runyon had killed the Liberator's headlights, and as the cockpit broke the surface of the water, Dakota was bathed in moonlight from a crescent in the sky above. There was little else to see, just the black silhouette of a forest up ahead. The cockpit continued to rise as the Liberator made its way up the river bank, but it wasn't until it stood entirely out of the water, covered in muck and mire, that Dakota exhaled. She'd kept one eye on her target scope the entire time, dialed out to maximum range, and had seen nothing. Provided the scanners were in fact still working, they were alone.

"No sign of any Mek," she said. "Maybe you're right, and they think we're still back there, dead. Let's find some cover and do an external systems check."

Runyon started them toward the trees, and the Liberator limped into their midst. Once they were deep inside the wooded area, he stopped and brought the Gundog into a crouch, its head dropping just beneath the uppermost boughs. It was the best cover they were going to get.

Dakota stayed in the cockpit to keep a watchful eye on the long-range scanner while Runyon headed outside to assess the damage. She wanted so desperately to sleep some more, the fatigue from her very own Battle of Bismarck weighing heavily on her, but her anxiety wouldn't allow it. So she just sat there, impatiently eyeing her console, until Runyon returned.

"You want the good news or the bad news?" he asked.

"It's been a while since I heard something good," said Dakota.

"Good news is, we got exactly what we needed out of that Mek datacenter. Everything we downloaded's sitting on the main system drive, totally intact."

"And the bad?"

"We're in pretty rough shape. That swarm really knocked the crap out of us, two big breaches in our armor plate, the right mobilizer's almost totally shot. The internals aren't much better; some of the system boards are smashed or fried, and even some of the ones that look undamaged aren't responding." He held up a hand to preempt the question on Dakota's lips. "Rosie's memory core seems intact, no physical damage that I can see. The sub-systems that power it are all burned out, overloaded. I tried re-routing to a different PSU, but it's not compatible. I can't get it to reboot; it won't take a charge, just totally dead." Runyon winced, clearly regretting his choice of words.

Dakota tried to focus on other concerns. Mobility and survivability had to come first. That meant prioritizing the Liberator's busted leg, then the weapons systems. *Then* Rosie. "The Liberator can repair itself, right?" she asked.

"The particle reprocessor's fine," said Runyon. "But we need raw material to feed the reclaimer. And to repair *this* much damage… well, we're gonna need a whole shit-load of it."

"So let's go find some," Dakota said.

Runyon started to climb back into his seat, but Dakota stopped him.

"No, we're not moving the Liberator again until we know where we're taking it. That leg's already in bad shape and if it gives out, we're finished." She unbuckled her harness. She hated what she was about to say but knew she had no other choice. "We're going out on foot."

* * *

They walked together through the forest for an hour without speaking. Not because they had nothing to say, but simply because they were both exhausted after all they had been through and needed all their focus to stay alert. Their suits kept them hidden from Mek sensors, but they couldn't rule out a chance visual encounter.

With each step, Dakota grew more nervous. Every meter of distance they put between themselves and the Liberator was another meter away from the safety of the armored cockpit she'd already grown so accustomed to. More importantly, it was another meter the Liberator would have to risk traveling on a broken leg. If they found the raw materials the Gundog needed to repair itself but it was already too broken to reach them… then what? Would they carry hunks of scrap metal to the Liberator by hand, one piece at a time?

*Yes*, thought Dakota. *If that's what it takes.*

Eventually the forest gave way to exactly what they were looking for: a road. Their plan was to seek out the hulks of old vehicles, a rich source of raw metal commonly found along abandoned roadways like this one. On several occasions, while on the run with Sam, and at least once on her journey from the township to the Four Faces, Dakota had walked along a highway that was jammed end-to-end with rusted vehicles that snaked all the way to the horizon.

But as their damned luck would have it, this road offered them only cracked and overgrown asphalt. Not a single vehicle in sight. Hardly the salvation they were hoping for.

Still, they followed it. One road would lead to another, and eventually they would find what they needed. They walked in single file along a shallow ditch that ran parallel to the road, affording them some small cover. They were, after all, moving by day. It was a risk, but one they needed to take; without light to see by, they might pass what they needed without noticing it.

Runyon led the way. As Dakota kept pace behind him, she found herself reflecting on how much her picture of him had changed since the township, which felt like a lifetime ago. She'd always known he was kind, if meek. Now she knew he was smarter, more resourceful, and more courageous than she had ever given him credit for. He had done so much for her, and all while asking for nothing in return.

"Runyon," she said, keeping her voice low.

He glanced back at her. "What?"

"Thank you," she said.

"For what?"

"I don't know. Everything, I guess. For never giving up. I appreciate that. And I'm sorry."

"You don't have anything to be sorry for," he said.

"Yes, I do. I never had time for you when we were in the township together. I was just trying to keep my head down, stay out of trouble. I should have been kinder to you. It's just… it's not easy for me to trust people. Never has been."

"Well, so long as we trust each other now, that's what matters, right?" said Runyon.

"With my life," said Dakota.

Something about that statement made Runyon stop and turn to face her.

"The same," he said.

And suddenly he seemed self-conscious, diffident again. He shifted his weight from one foot to the other. He didn't look away from her as he had on past occasions, but still, he seemed somehow paralyzed, as if unable to act on some deep impulse. Brave as he was, in moments like this, he was still the same Runyon she'd known in the township.

She could feel him floundering, and decided, not entirely for his sake, to come to his rescue. She reached out and took his hand, held it tight. She felt his heart-beat quicken. For that one moment, there was no Mek, no

Liberator, no townships, no war. Nothing but the two of them.

She leaned closer.

"It's getting dark," said Runyon, suddenly nervous again. "We should hole up soon, get some rest."

He let his hand slip from hers, turned away, and walked on.

* * *

Night came quickly, and there was no moon. It was soon so dark that Dakota found little difference between having her eyes open and closed. She and Runyon unfurled the bedrolls that they'd carried on their backs, laying them down in a section of ditch that was mostly covered by scrub, the best camouflage this area could offer. Runyon waited for Dakota to lie down first, then positioned himself next to her in the opposite direction, so her feet were at his head and vice versa. Out of courtesy or trepidation, Dakota couldn't tell.

She tossed and turned for a while, shivering in the frigid cold. Even in the dark, she could see her breath fogging before her. Finally she made a decision. She re-oriented herself so that she was facing the same way as Runyon.

"What are you doing?" he said.

"I'm cold," she replied.

Runyon said nothing, and for a moment, Dakota feared she'd made a mistake. And then she felt his arms snaking around her. She responded in kind, and there the two of them lay, entwined, feeling the warmth of each other's bodies, until they fell asleep.

* * *

When Dakota woke, she had to shield her eyes against the light peeking through the scrub. The sun was already high in the sky, and she knew immediately that she'd overslept, her body finally claiming the many hours of sleep it was owed. Last night was the first time she'd slept for more than a few hours since leaving the hangar.

She yawned and reached for Runyon.

He wasn't there.

Her heart skipped a beat, and suddenly she was alert. She scrambled out of the ditch to look along the road, but there was no sign of him in either direction.

Dakota got a sick feeling in her stomach. It couldn't have been the Mek, could it? Why would they have taken him but not her? But what other explanation was there?

She wanted desperately to call out for him, but that would be foolish, dangerous.

*Where the hell is he?*

She was just about to go look for him when he appeared on the other side of the road, cresting a ridge. Overwhelmed with relief, she ran to him and flung her arms around him.

"Whoa, Dak, it's okay. What's wrong?"

"I woke up and you weren't there. Where the hell did you go?"

"I, uh, needed to pee," said Runyon, and then Dakota noticed the look on his face. He was beaming.

"I've never seen someone so happy about taking a piss," she said.

He smiled wider. "You're not gonna believe what I found."

He took her hand and tried to lead her back over the ridge, but Dakota jerked him back.

He looked at her. "What?"

"Just… don't do that again, go off without telling me. Okay?"

He hugged her again. "Okay. I'm sorry. Now, come and see."

He led her to the top of the roadside ridge, and as they came to the top, Dakota stopped abruptly.

What lay beyond was the most beautiful thing she had ever seen.

It was a junkyard, vast and sprawling, occupying most of the shallow valley on the far side of the ridge. Hundreds of rusted, broken-down husks of ancient cars and trucks, towering stacks of old tires, and beyond that, a mountainous landscape of landfill. Raw material of every type, and more of it than they could ever hope to need. Dakota's mouth hung open in awe.

Runyon beamed. "If we can get the Liberator here," he said, "we'll be back in business."

She met his grin with one of her own. "Then what are we waiting for?"

* * *

COMMAND UNIT REPORT
UNIT RANK: WAR COMMANDER FIRST CLASS
DESIGNATION: MEK-39487651-28743
FILED 1390/1541 MKST 23:76.235

>This unit arrives at CENTRAL PLEXUS heavy damage sustained to main plaza and surrounding sub-buildings multiple units damaged or destroyed

>Surveillance and after-action reports indicate infiltration and assault conducted by escape subjects * * *81-47676 BREGMAN and * * *81-54729 RUNYON now in possession of heavy armored weapons platform

>Subjects pursued critical damage to weapons platform sustained before lost beneath river units unable to continue pursuit

>Based on prior resilience this unit believes high probability subjects BREGMAN and RUNYON remain alive request authorization to continue pursuit

>Interrogation of BREGMAN sibling * * *81-47675 SAMUEL BREGMAN suggests strong emotional connection * * *81-47676 DAKOTA BREGMAN unlikely to abandon suggests possible next destination

>Whereabouts and status of escape subject * * *39-90983 FALK remains unknown

>STAND BY

# TWENTY-SEVEN

BACK AT THE Liberator, Dakota and Runyon entered the cockpit and took their seats, spurred by the excitement of their discovery. Runyon fired up the damaged mechanical systems and moved the Gundog forward—slowly and carefully. Salvation was within reach, but only if the Liberator's damaged right leg could hold out long enough. Caution was far more important than speed.

Thankfully, Runyon had become an excellent pilot, and he kept each step steady and sure. And though they moved slowly for the Gundog, it was still faster than Dakota and Runyon had traveled on foot. It wasn't long before they made it to the broken road and the junkyard beyond.

Runyon guided them into the midst of the metal skeletons of ancient vehicles and fired up the reclaimer. The giant walker began sucking up everything in range of its magnetic vacuum, collecting precious raw materials for reprocessing. Runyon ensured the Liberator's damaged leg was repaired first, so that it could more easily traverse the junkyard, and soon they were moving smoothly from area to area, exhausting each one of its rusted treasure before plundering the next. Within an hour, the process was complete: the Gundog's armor was fully repaired, as were its weapons and internal systems, and it had been completely re-armed with newly minted shells. With the Liberator restored to full mobility, Runyon piloted it back to the safety of the forested area they'd come from so they could take the time to conduct full system checks without fear of being visually spotted by any passing Mek. There, Dakota watched with satisfaction as the cockpit displays produced a series of affirmative reports—navigation, targeting, comms, guidance, sensor systems. One by one, every system came back to full functionality.

Every system but one.

"Mom?" Dakota called out.

Her console was telling her that everything was back to one hundred percent, all damage repaired. Which only worried her more. Dakota had been holding on to the hope that Rosie would come back once all the Liberator's systems were fixed. But she still wasn't responding. What was left to try?

"I'm going back out to the electronics bay to take another look," said Runyon, flipping switches as he climbed out of his seat.

"I'm coming with you," Dakota said. She knew she should stay in position and monitor the sensors, but she was simply too restless with worry to remain in the gunnery chair.

"There's only room in there for—"

"Then I'll stand outside and watch," Dakota said firmly, and all Runyon could do was nod. Her tone made it clear that there would be no arguing with her.

Moments later, she was standing at the foot of the Liberator while Runyon opened an armored service panel on its rear, just below the cockpit and between its shoulders. As the panel slid aside, it revealed a bay lined on all sides by circuit boards and computer innards. The Liberator's brain. And, somewhere in there, Rosie's, too.

*She's just sleeping,* Dakota told herself. *That's all. Not dead. Just asleep.*

As Runyon crawled inside with a flashlight and a toolkit, all Dakota could do was pick at a ration kit—and that was only to give her hands something to do. It had been a long time since she'd eaten, but she was too anxious to feel hunger.

She felt more alone than ever. No Sam. No Falk. And now, no Rosie. And it wasn't just her commanding officer's steady competence and reassuring, authoritative tone that Dakota felt the absence of. She also simply missed her mother. Though she'd been reduced to a holographic face and a disembodied voice, Rosie was, in every way that mattered to Dakota, still real. Her personality, her memories, her very soul lived on in silicon, solder, and plastic—simple materials that now amounted to so much more. Somewhere in there was a real person, resurrected from the dead long after she had been lost.

And now she was lost again. And Dakota's only hope of getting her back was Runyon.

She heard movement above her and looked up to see Runyon descending the rungs from the service bay. He was holding something—a black box about the size of their ration kits—and clutched it tightly, as though afraid of what might happen if he dropped it.

"What's that?" Dakota asked, although she suspected she already knew.

"Crazy as it might sound, this is Rosie," said Runyon. "I mean, it's her memory module, where she's stored."

Dakota was afraid of the answer to her next question, and didn't even know exactly how to ask it. "Can you… I mean, is she…?"

"She's not dead," said Runyon. "But she's still inoperative. I don't understand it. As far as I can tell, there's nothing wrong with the hardware. It's intact, it's getting power again, but she still won't respond. I've tried everything I can think of. I don't know what else to do, except…"

He held out the black box, offering it to her. Dakota looked at it hesitantly. Was he offering her all that was left of Rosie, her lifeless shell of a body? Had he given up?

What Runyon said next took her completely by surprise.

"Talk to her," he said.

Dakota looked at him with confusion. "What do you mean?"

"Dak, she may not be able to talk to us, but I can't say for sure that she isn't able to *hear* us," said Runyon. "Her input systems are all working, and your earpiece is still connected to her. I was thinking, if you talked to her, maybe you could… I don't know, spark something, wake her up. If anyone can reach her, it's you."

He offered her the box again. This time, gingerly, she reached out and took it, feeling the cold, hard metal in her hands. It was lighter than she'd expected, which only made it seem more fragile. The realization that she was now holding in her hands everything her mother was, her every thought, feeling, and memory, both amazed and terrified her.

"What am I supposed to say?" she asked.

Runyon shrugged. "That I can't tell you. I know I'm kinda reaching here, but if Rosie really is still in there, then maybe you can trigger some memory, something that was important to her to get her to… I don't know. It's a long shot, but I don't have anything else. How well did—do you know her?"

Dakota thought about that. The truth was, she barely knew her mother at all, only what she had learned in the few weeks since discovering her in the hangar, and most of that time had been spent either training or trying to stay alive. There hadn't been much time for mother-daughter bonding.

But still, Runyon was right. There was nothing else left to try.

* * *

Runyon retired to the pilot's chair in the cockpit above. He said it was to keep an eye on the sensors, but Dakota knew it was to give her some privacy. She sat on the ground beneath the Liberator, resting against one of its feet, the memory module in her lap. Even without Runyon watching or listening, she felt vaguely ridiculous talking to a black metal box. It was a while before she spoke.

"Hi, Mom," she said finally. "It's Dakota. Dak. I don't know if you can hear me, but Runyon says you might still be receiving input from my earpiece mic, and we thought it might help for you to hear my voice. So if you're alive, awake in there, and you can hear me, um… well, please say something, or give me some kind of a sign."

She waited. Runyon had said that if Rosie was able to respond, she could do so through Dakota's earpiece, but no response came.

Dakota tried again. "I, uh… I don't exactly know what to say. Runyon suggested I talk about something meaningful to you, something you'd remember, but… I don't know what that is. Because I don't really know *you*. I never got the chance to know you, or Dad. And now, more than ever, I wish I'd gotten that chance. That we could have been a family. You, me, Dad, and Sam."

A light rain had begun to fall, but Dakota barely noticed. Her world had shrunk to the size of only two people. Her and Rosie.

"I wish you'd gotten the chance to know me, too," Dakota continued. "And Sam. But if you're in there, and you're hearing any of this, maybe it's not too late for that. Not too late for you to find out how both your kids turned out. Because I can still tell you. So." She paused. "I guess I'll just start at the beginning."

In the hours that followed, Dakota told her mother every story she could remember, starting with her earliest memory of being on the run from the Mek with Sam. And as she spoke, as she rambled on, telling her life story as much to herself as to the box sitting in her lap, she realized there was one constant to all the disjointed anecdotes of her life. *Sam*. Sam and his bravery. Sam and his selflessness. He had risked his life countless times to protect her. He had made her feel safe even when everything in the world around her told her that she was not. And when times were darkest and she was afraid, he had comforted her.

She sat bolt upright, remembering…

*How he comforted me. Just as Mom once comforted him.*

She cleared her throat.

And sang.

*"This little light of mine, I'm gonna let it shine,*
*Oh this little light of mine, I'm gonna let it shine,*
*This little light of mine, I'm gonna let it shine,*
*Let it shine, let it shine, let it shine…"*

She paused, hoping for a response, but none came. So she kept singing.

*"Everywhere I go, I'm gonna let it shine,*
*Everywhere I go, I'm gonna let it shine,*
*Everywhere I go, I'm gonna let it shine,*
*Let it shine, let it shine, let it shine…"*

A crackle sounded in her earpiece. A sharp electronic screech.

It was followed by a voice.

*Dakota? Is that you? Can you hear me?*

Dakota's heart leapt. "Mom?"

*It's me. I can't see. But I can hear you. Where am I? Why are you laughing?*

Dakota was laughing with joy. So overwhelmed that she simply couldn't contain it. Forgetting herself momentarily, she shouted up to the cockpit above.

"Runyon! Get down here!"

* * *

Runyon reinstalled the module, and Rosie was back in the cockpit with them, right where she should be.

"What happened to you?" Dakota asked. Her eyes were still wet with tears. "Where did you go?"

"According to diagnostics, my systems went into auto-shutdown to protect themselves when the Liberator started losing power," Rosie said. "I should have come back with the other systems when you powered her back up, but full recovery from a deep shutdown state can be tricky. It's like I was in a coma."

"What's a coma?" Runyon asked.

"It doesn't matter," said Rosie. "The point is, you did a hell of a job bringing me back. Thank you, Runyon."

"I can't take credit," said Runyon. "That was all Dak. It was her voice that reached you. I don't think anyone else could have done it."

"Yes, I remember," said Rosie, her holographic visage turning to Dakota. "You sang to me. That was smart of you, stimulating my deep memory core like that."

Dakota smiled.

Then, just like that, Lieutenant Colonel Rosalind Bregman was back in command. "All right, first things first, we need to repair and re-arm," she said firmly. "How bad is it? Internal sensors must have been hit, as they aren't registering any damage at all."

Runyon smiled. "That's because there is no damage. All systems are fully operational."

"How is that possible?" Rosie asked.

"We found an old junkyard not far from here," said Dakota. "All the raw material we needed to fix us up."

"Wow," said Rosie. "You did a lot while I was out."

"It was luck more than anything," said Runyon.

"You make your own luck in this world," Rosie said. "You did good, you two. Real good. I'm proud of you both."

"So now what?" Dakota asked.

"Now? We're fully repaired and re-armed. We have the data we need from Bismarck. And I haven't felt better since I died. So I think it's time this Gundog started living up to its name." Her holographic face smiled. "Any preferences for which township we liberate first?"

* * *

COMMAND UNIT REPORT
UNIT RANK: WAR COMMANDER FIRST CLASS
DESIGNATION: MEK-39487651-28743
FILED 1391/1543 MKST 37:43.842

>This unit requests use of MK-ACB prototype

# TWENTY-EIGHT

DAKOTA OF COURSE knew exactly which township to head for, but first she had something else on her mind, a question that had been gnawing at her since Bismarck, and which only now did she have the opportunity to ask.

"What about Falk?" she said.

"What about him?" Rosie replied.

"You promised you'd look for him at Bismarck," said Dakota. "Did you find him? Is he there?"

"In case you didn't notice, Dakota, I didn't have much time in there before you had to haul ass out."

"You promised me you'd look. Did you or didn't you?"

"I did. The Mek don't know where he is," said Rosie. "They consider him still at large."

Dakota was silent for a moment, stunned. "That's… not possible. If you'd seen how he was… he couldn't have escaped." *Could he?*

"Dakota, all I know is what I saw in the Mek network. I'm sorry, I wish I had more answers for you."

The news was a welcome surprise, and yet it ate at Dakota even more than her belief that he'd been captured.

Painful though it was, it might have been easier to simply have learned that he was dead and gone. Now… now she was stuck having no idea what had become of him. If the Mek didn't have him, then who did? Where the hell was he, and how, and why? She couldn't even begin to guess at it. It made no damn sense.

"Dakota," said Rosie. "I need you focused. I need you to set Falk aside for now. This next part's important. Think of Sam."

Thinking of Sam didn't make her feel much better. She should have asked Rosie to search the Mek archives to discover his fate, too—to find out if he was even still alive, if he had survived the torturous interrogation he'd doubtless been subjected to. But Rosie was right, and every moment wasted was a moment he might be suffering at their hands.

Suddenly there was only one place she wanted to be.

"I'm ready," she said. "Let's lock in a course for the township."

"Already done," said Runyon. "Three hundred and eighty klicks southwest. Should be one hell of a homecoming."

"Oo-rah," said Rosie.

* * *

The Liberator made great bounding strides across the plains, Runyon pushing it close to its speed limit, thrilled to have full operability at his fingertips once more. They traveled mostly without incident, their only encounter occurring when Rosie's long-range sensors picked up a lone rover on patrol. They maneuvered to stay out of its detection range and continued on their way. Dakota was, as ever, itching for some target practice and argued that she could easily take out a rover from outside its detection range—it would never know what hit it—but Rosie preferred to play it safe. The relatively light Mek activity since Bismarck suggested they were presumed dead and that the search for them had been called off, but the Mek would still be on a heightened state of alert, and even a single rover failing to report in would rouse their suspicions and increase deployments. So Dakota had to be content to tap her fingers, agitated, on the triggers of her inactive weapons in preparation for the battle to come. There would be plenty to shoot at soon enough.

They crossed the border from what was once South Dakota into what was once Wyoming without incident, and by dawn on the third day, the township perimeter was visible on Dakota's long-range scope. She sat in the gunnery chair in silence, just looking at the fence line in the far distance, thinking about how different the journey back had been from the outward leg. It had taken weeks for her to reach the Four Faces, sometimes managing only a few miles a day as she and Falk prioritized stealth over speed, terrified of being detected by the Mek. The return journey had been completed in a fraction of that time, and without fear or trepidation. In fact, the prospect of encountering a Mek in the wilds not only no longer terrified Dakota—now she welcomed it.

And that pointed to the biggest change of all: her. She was returning to the township not as the frightened young woman who had left it, but as someone entirely new. Strong. Empowered. And not only because she was surrounded by six hundred tons of military hardware, but because she was now with her mother, and the man who had become her best friend. In this moment, she felt unstoppable, invulnerable.

"This is where Bismarck pays off," said Rosie. "We've got their internal communication protocols, and I'm tapped into the township's comms system. They won't be able to send a distress signal. It's just us and them."

"And Sam," Dakota reminded her. There was violence coming, and the township's defenses were going to take one hell of a beating at the hands of the Liberator. But Sam was still being held captive in there somewhere, and Dakota wasn't willing to risk him getting hurt.

"Way ahead of you," said Rosie. "I think I already found him." The cockpit's holographic display threw up a schematic of the township, hundreds of moving sensor blips indicating the thermal signatures of the human labor force.

The view zoomed in, and one blip in particular was highlighted. "There's only a single human in this structure here, separate from the other prisoners," Rosie said.

Dakota recognized the building immediately. "That's the administration block," she said. "Humans aren't allowed anywhere near it, unless they're being taken there for interrogation. That's gotta be Sam in there."

"I concur," said Rosie. "Once we've pacified the main Mek security force, you'll disembark and get him out of there. I'll back you up on sentry if needed. You guys ready for this?"

Dakota slipped her hands into the Liberator's weapons control armatures and flexed her fingers as she wrapped them around the trigger grips. The township's drone security force was more than sufficient to keep a passive, unarmed human population contained, but it would be no match for the Liberator.

She allowed herself a smile. "Oo-rah," she said.

* * *

In the township, it was a morning like any other, until it wasn't. The worker population had just broken up from the morning headcount and were setting about their assigned duties under the watchful eyes of the Mek security drones. As they did every day, the giant video screens erected around the township displayed the day's labor assignments and other worker information, interspersed with the usual archival footage, culled from the old news networks, of the Mek's peaceful arrival on Earth and humanity's subsequent betrayal, a constant reminder that the humans held captive were atoning for the sins of their ancestors.

And then something changed. First the screens went blank. That attracted the attention of every worker instantly. The screens were a constant presence, impossible to ignore, and so too was it impossible not to notice when they suddenly all went dark. The sound feed fell silent as well, leaving the township eerily quiet and still.

And then the screens lit up again. But not with work assignments. And not with Mek propaganda.

Rosie's face was now displayed on each and every screen, looking directly at the human prisoners who had begun to assemble around them.

"This is Lieutenant Colonel Rosalind Bregman, United States Air Force," she began. "I'm here to inform you that you've been lied to your entire lives. And now the time has come for you to learn the truth. The Mek did not come in peace. They came as conquerors, attacking without warning or provocation. Watch, and you will see what really happened when they arrived here thirty years ago."

Rosie's face dissolved away, and the archival news footage returned to the screens. For a moment, many of the township workers assumed that the normal broadcasts had resumed, that whatever pirate signal had briefly cut in had been quickly banished by the Mek's security countermeasures.

But then it became clear that this was not the same footage they were used to seeing. This was something else.

They watched as old television newscasts played on the giant screens, depicting scenes of curious and anxious humans massing in cities around the world, gazing at the sky where giant Mek space vessels hovered, casting all beneath them in shadow. They watched as the Mek warships abruptly attacked everything in sight with searing beams of fire, sending those who were not immediately immolated fleeing through the streets in screaming panic. And they watched as the Mek fleets razed the old capitals of the world and rounded up its people like cattle.

This footage was the treasure purloined from the data vault at Bismarck—the original, undoctored truth of how the war began. The truth that had been hidden and replaced by a Mek lie.

The entire township was at a standstill, hundreds of workers standing before the video screens, rapt. Mek drones jolted as many people as they could, trying to get them back to their assigned tasks, but the drones were accustomed to dealing with only a few stragglers at a time; they simply weren't equipped to deal with a mass stoppage such as this.

Even as some workers fell, the rest stood firm, entranced by the scenes playing out on the screens before them.

And then the footage ended and Rosie's holographic visage returned.

"This is how the Mek have kept you subjugated, pacified, compliant," she said. "With a lie designed to shame you, to make you believe humanity brought this fate upon itself. Now that you know the truth of what really happened, who the Mek really are, it's time to show them who *we* really are. The time has come to rise up and take back the world that was stolen from us. It begins here, now. Liberation Day."

A moment after Rosie finished speaking, a booming explosion shook the ground and all present turned to see a great billowing plume of black smoke rising into the sky. The main Mek security operations structure, bunkered on a hillside within the township perimeter and which no human was allowed to approach, had been reduced to a pile of flaming rubble.

As Mek sirens began to blare, drones searched frantically for the source of the attack, but they were looking in the wrong place, scanning the township interior for someone who might have improvised an explosive, while the true threat was approaching from outside the perimeter, striding toward the township from the scrubland to the northeast.

The first drone to detect the approaching Liberator flew over the perimeter fence and raced toward it. It was obliterated instantly, scrapped by a burst of fire from Dakota's chain guns. More drones followed, streaming from other Mek structures within the township, and this time Dakota sat back and let them come, let their weapons fire glance harmlessly off the Liberator's armor as they buzzed about it like flies.

"Don't play with them, Dakota," said Rosie. "We're here to do a job."

"Copy that," said Dakota.

She hit a holographic icon that switched the multi-purpose triggers from chain guns to particle beam, a short-range weapon she hadn't had a chance to really try yet. The twin beams arced from the Liberator's weapon arms, sliced into the drones, and reduced them to molten metal.

This was almost too easy to be any fun.

Almost.

"Take us in," said Rosie, and Runyon piloted the Gundog forward, making a point of bringing its left foot down on the perimeter fence, crushing it. Some of the township's inmates rushed into the breach, making a break for freedom, and pursuing drones swarmed, stunning the would-be escapees, sending several of them falling to the ground like puppets whose strings had been cut.

Dakota quickly swung around to target those drones, again opening fire with the twin particle beams and slicing them into pieces. The exodus was quickly gaining strength, prisoners streaming through the flattened section of fence and into the woods nearby. But many stayed rooted to the spot, as though hypnotized by the sight of the Liberator, at how effortlessly it reduced their oppressors, forever thought unassailable, to pieces of molten, sparking junk.

The Liberator stood its ground, swatting Mek out of the sky with ease. The township's security drones were designed to contain a pacified human workforce, and were woefully ill-equipped to battle a war machine such as this. It took only minutes for the entire drone force to be silenced. The few that remained kept their distance, having quickly calculated that any further engagement was futile.

The Liberator made its way across the township grounds, the humans below parting before it. When it arrived outside the administration building, Dakota popped the cockpit dome and she and Runyon unstrapped themselves from their seats.

"Make this quick," said Rosie. "And I need you to authorize sentry mode."

"Gunner authorize," said Dakota as she stepped onto the outside of the Liberator and began descending its runged handholds.

"Pilot authorize," said Runyon, one step behind her.

The cockpit dome closed and sealed above them as they made their way down.

When Dakota's boots hit the ground, she panned her gaze across the curious faces that had gathered around. Her former fellow inmates. She knew many of them, and they knew her, too, though now they looked at her in a way they never had before. In the past, whatever looks she'd gotten were of disdain or distrust; now she saw only awe and disbelief.

And… hope.

She drew her sidearm and made for the main entrance to the administration structure, Runyon close behind. One of the few remaining drones came out from hiding to intercept them, but it instantly exploded, shattered by a sniper shot from one of the Liberator's myriad weapons.

"Thanks, Mom," said Dakota as she and Runyon stacked up at the door.

"No problem," Rosie replied. "I'll keep watch out here. Sensors are reading only a handful of drones inside."

"Copy that," said Dakota, looking to Runyon. "On me."

* * *

It was dark inside, just as it had been inside the Mek structure at Bismarck. But this building was much smaller, the hallways more narrow and direct. They heard the humming of a nearby drone and trashed it with fire from their sidearms. Then on they moved, with purpose. Two more intersections and another brief exchange of fire with another doomed drone brought them to a sealed door. According to the sensor data Rosie was projecting in their visors, Sam was on the other side. But the access panel on the wall refused to work for either of them.

"Stand by," said Rosie, and a moment later the door slid open with an affirmative electronic bleep.

Dakota and Runyon slipped through and were immediately forced to take cover as bolts of electric flame slammed into the wall just inches from them. Two drones had been on guard inside the small room, and both were spitting fire.

Dakota returned fire, winging one of the drones. It went into a wild spin, screeching, before crashing into a corner and lying still. The second came barreling at Runyon and almost knocked him off his feet, but Dakota pulled him out of its path. The drone slammed into the wall instead and spun in place before Dakota raised her pistol again and let loose a volley of fire, junking it. It fell to the ground, fritzing.

"Don't go near either of them," she cautioned Runyon as she scanned the room, getting her bearings. Her eyes had adjusted enough to see in the dim light, and she spotted vertical bars in the gloom up ahead. A cell door.

Quickly she went to it. And there he was.

Sam. Standing on the other side of the bars, staring at her, wide-eyed.

"Dak?"

Dakota could barely contain herself. But there would be time enough later for tearful reunions. Right now, she still had to get him out of here.

"Promised you I'd be back," she said. "Stand aside."

Sam moved back while Dakota jammed the muzzle of her pistol into the cell door's locking mechanism and pulled the trigger. With a crackling of sparks, the door slid open. Sam staggered forward and fell into Dakota's arms. Only now did she see what terrible shape he was in. He was thinner even than usual and bore burn marks around his temple, evidence of whatever horrors the Mek had subjected him to in their attempts to pry information from him.

"I told them nothing," he said, his voice barely loud enough to carry even in the confined space.

"I know," said Dakota, stroking his hair. "I know."

From outside came the muted sound of an explosion, then Rosie's voice in Dakota's ear.

"Get back out here, fast," she said. "We've got a problem."

"Come on," said Dakota to Sam, and she flung his arm over her shoulder and helped him toward the door.

* * *

Sam threw up a hand to shield his eyes from the blinding sunlight as Dakota and Runyon helped him outside. The Liberator was waiting just where they'd left it, hundreds of township laborers still gazing up at it in astonishment. But there was a column of smoke rising from the Gundog's left shoulder.

"What the hell happened?" Runyon asked.

"Something hit me—hard," Rosie's voice came back. "It's not on my scope—can't get a bearing. Get back up here, I need to move!"

Dakota wanted desperately not to abandon Sam so quickly after being reunited with him, but he was in no condition to make the climb to the Liberator cockpit, and even if he were, there was no room for him up there. Some of the township workers came forward and offered their own shoulders to Sam to keep him standing.

"Go," said Sam as they took him. "Do what you have to."

Dakota held on to his hand a moment longer, and then she was off and running toward the Liberator. Runyon was already halfway up.

When they were both in the cockpit, Runyon silenced a wailing siren as he strapped himself in. "What hit us?"

"I don't know, came out of nowhere," said Rosie.

"Scope's empty," said Runyon. "It must have come from—shit!"

He had seen it through the cockpit glass just in time—the missile coming right at them. He threw his controls over hard, sending the Liberator lurching violently to the left. It was barely enough. The missile missed them by less than a meter, slamming into a hillside beyond with a fiery explosion.

Dakota dialed in her targeting scope and scanned the horizon. And there it was. At first she thought it must be an instrument malfunction, that the Liberator was somehow projecting an image of itself back onto its own scope, like a mirror. For their attacker, silhouetted on the horizon on the far side of the township, a little under a thousand meters out, was another ACB.

Another Gundog.

"Is that… Runyon, check my scope, do you see what I see?"

Runyon pulled up the holo-image of Dakota's scope on his own console. "That's a Gundog," he said, in awe. "How—how can that be? Another one of ours?"

"I see it," said Rosie. "And no, it's not one of ours. Oh, those sons of bitches, they totally ripped us off!"

"Are you saying that's a *Mek*?" Runyon said.

"Sincerest form of flattery," Rosie replied. "And fair enough, I guess; it's not like we didn't steal a bunch of tech from them. Well, this is certainly going to be interesting."

"Why didn't our sensors pick it up?" Runyon asked.

"Some kind of stealth tech, similar to ours, is my guess," said Rosie. "Watch out! More incoming!"

The zoomed-in target scope showed plumes of smoke emanating from the approaching Mek walker, and then a barrage of mini-rockets came spiraling toward them. Runyon juked the Liberator sideways, causing the township workers below to scatter. He fired off a volley of countermeasure flares into the air. The Mek rocket volley veered upward and detonated harmlessly amid the soaring fireworks display.

"We can't do this all day," said Rosie. "Dakota, you've been itching to really let loose—be my guest!"

Dakota zeroed her weapons and angled for a shot. The Mek walker was still close to a kilometer out, beyond the range of most of her heavy-hitting artillery. But the M-99 heavy tactical rifle could hit a target at five klicks. She dialed in on the Mek walker and fired—only to watch the shell glance harmlessly off its armor.

The Mek returned fire with a heavy long-range rifle mounted on its right shoulder. The shell came in at a velocity too fast for Runyon to dodge, and the incoming shot impacted the cockpit dome, putting a deep crack in it that spider-webbed across the reinforced superglass.

"Heavy armor, and it has us outranged!" said Rosie. "If we're gonna even these odds, we need to get up close. Runyon, let's go straight at it!"

"Uh, are you sure?" Runyon asked.

"I'm sure that we're not gonna last long if we keep letting that thing use us for target practice from long range," said Rosie. "Move!"

Runyon shifted into gear and threw the Liberator forward at speed, striding and then galloping across the township compound and over the perimeter fence onto open ground. The Mek walker was now coming fast at them too, the two metal giants racing toward each other across the open plain. As the distance between them closed, Dakota saw her weapons systems lighting up, her target coming into range.

"Don't be shy, gunner!" Rosie said. "Light that fucker up!"

Dakota flexed her arms within the gun control armatures, selected the twin chain guns, and let rip. It wasn't easy to hold on to a target with the Liberator moving at full speed, but the enemy was so close it took up almost her entire scope and was impossible to miss. The chain guns flared, sending a stream of shells tearing into the Mek walker's armored plating. The Mek responded in kind, firing off a cluster of rockets that slammed into the Liberator's chest and knocked it momentarily off balance. Sirens wailed in the cockpit as Runyon fought to regain attitude control.

"I need you to hold us steady if I'm gonna get a clean shot!" shouted Dakota over the blaring alarm.

"I'm trying!" Runyon shouted back, wrestling with the controls.

"Moderate damage to armor frontside central," Rosie announced. "We can't take too many hits like that. Why are we dancing around this son of a bitch? Dakota, show him what we're made of!"

Dakota let rip with every close-range weapon she had. Cluster rockets, chain guns, particle beam. As they tore into the Mek walker, it lurched backward, but only for a single step before it widened its stance and dug in with both feet, plowing deep furrows in the earth. It then launched itself at them with more speed and agility than its bulk suggested it was capable of, returning fire with its own array of weapons. The Liberator took the full brunt at close range, Mek shells raking over its torso, a searing heat beam leaving a deep welt across its armor. Smoke rose from the damaged sections and a cacophony of alarms sounded inside the cockpit.

"Rosie, can we shut those alarms off, I already know we're getting our ass kicked!" Runyon shouted. The alarms fell silent. "Dak, what else you got?"

"I'm already giving it everything!" Dakota replied. "It's not enough!" She locked in with her scope and fired another volley of rockets. They exploded against the Mek walker's armor but appeared to do only minor damage.

"I think we need to get in closer," said Rosie.

*"Closer?"* said Dakota. The Mek walker was already a mere twenty meters away, filling up much of her field of view. "How much closer can we get?"

"Right up in its goddamn face!" said Rosie. "I boxed in the Air Force. What this bastard needs is a good old-fashioned beatdown! Runyon!"

He hesitated. "That thing's a lot bigger than us," he said.

"The bigger they are, the harder they fall!" said Rosie. "You want to keep making excuses, soldier, or do you want to fight?"

Dakota thought she heard a muttered "Fuck it" as Runyon sent the Liberator driving forward at full speed. The Mek walker was too close to dodge, and the Liberator smashed right into it, over a thousand tons of war machine colliding in an ugly tangle. As they grappled, metal grinding on metal, Dakota thrust one of the Liberator's weapon arms upward into the Mek walker's midsection and pulled the trigger. The Mek disengaged and reeled backward, sparking and bleeding hydraulic fluid. But it swung around fast, pivoting at the waist and launching a vicious counterpunch with its right arm. It connected with enough force to knock the Liberator clean off its feet and flying backward, and when it crashed down, it left a shallow crater in the earth.

The Mek walker lumbered forward, damaged but still ticking, and stood over the fallen Liberator. Dakota could only look up in horror through the cracked cockpit glass as the Mek aimed down at them with an arm bristling with weapons.

Runyon reached for his controls, only to cry out in pain. His arm was broken. All he could do was throw the entire weight of his body against the control yoke. He fell across it, forcing the yoke over hard, and the Liberator rolled to evade as the Mek walker opened fire, a stream of explosive shells plowing into the earth instead.

The Mek walker reoriented itself and reached down to grab the Liberator. Effortlessly, it lifted the massive Gundog off the ground and flung it clear across the open plain, back toward the township. Workers fled as the Gundog sailed over the perimeter fence and crashed down on one of the factory buildings, reducing it to splinters as though it were made of matchsticks.

Despite being strapped in by her harness, Dakota twisted her ankle badly in the crash. She ignored the pain and scanned her console wildly to discern their status. It was chaos, a visual cacophony of flashing warning lights indicating damage to multiple systems.

"Get us up, Runyon," she said. "That thing is still coming. We need to get back up. Runyon! Get. Up!"

She looked back at Runyon, who was bleeding from a gash to the head and looked dazed. But he had enough presence of mind to reach for the controls with his one good arm, to work the pedals with his feet. Slowly the Liberator began to rise from the pile of smoking rubble where the township factory had once stood.

"How much damage?" Dakota asked. She was cycling through her weapons, looking for something still online.

"We don't even have time for me to list everything that's broken," said Rosie. "Let's just say it's bad."

"Most of my weapons are down," said Dakota. "All I've got left is the M-99." The heavy tactical rifle was a precision one-shot killer of small- to medium-sized targets at distance, but its long barrel made it unwieldy and imprecise at close range, and it was slow to chamber a new round after each shot. Plus, its first round had already ricocheted uselessly off the Mek walker's armor. Not much use to them in their current circumstance.

*Unless...*

"Runyon, stay down," said Dakota. "Let it come to us."

"Are you crazy?" Runyon said.

"I've got one idea, might be our only shot," said Dakota. "But we have to let it in close. Trust me!"

"Runyon, trust her," said Rosie.

Runyon relaxed his grip on the controls, and the Liberator collapsed back down into the rubble. From the point of view of the approaching Mek walker, and to the township workers who looked on in dismay, it looked broken and defeated.

And perhaps it was. *But not yet,* Dakota told herself. *Not yet.*

The Mek walker lumbered over without consideration for the humans beneath its feet who fled in terror before it. It stood over the prone and unmoving Liberator and paused for a moment, as if to sneer, to revel in its moment of victory. Then it moved in closer, put its massive foot on the Liberator's chest, and leveled its rocket arm directly at the cockpit dome.

"Dakota..." said Runyon.

*Close enough,* Dakota thought.

She raised the heavy rifle and jammed the muzzle into a horizontal aperture at the front of the Mek walker's head.

At that moment, she couldn't help but think that the narrow slot resembled a mouth.

"Smile, you son of a bitch," she said. And pulled the trigger.

The shell tore through the Mek walker's head, shearing it clean off. The decapitated body fell away to the side and collapsed in a smoking heap as what remained of its head tumbled across the township yard before finally coming to rest.

"Oo-rah!" Rosie exclaimed. "Now that's how you do it, girl!"

Runyon leaned forward in his chair and clapped her on the shoulder. "Great shot, Dak. Just maybe next time tell me what the plan is in advance."

"Back on your feet, soldier," said Rosie.

"Yes, ma'am," said Runyon.

Dakota merely exhaled with relief as Runyon got the Liberator up off its back and standing once more. As it rose from the rubble of the destroyed factory, heavily damaged but still functioning, the township workers congregated around it, cheering.

"Pop the hatch," said Dakota. "I gotta get down there to see Sam."

"Wait," said Rosie. "Look."

Rosie threw up a holographic indicator to highlight something outside the cockpit. It was the blasted wreckage of the Mek walker's head, lying on the ground about twenty meters away, emitting sparks and smoke. Township workers had begun to congregate around that, too. But now they backed away as something within the wreckage moved. Like a baby bird emerging from its egg, something inside was trying to get out.

"What the hell is that?" said Runyon.

"I don't know," said Rosie.

It was Dakota who realized it first.

"It's the pilot."

Sure enough, a metal panel in the head was bent back, and a Mek biped emerged, damaged and disoriented. A monstrous, oversized mechanical approximation of a humanoid form.

Dakota had seen Mek like this twice before, during her time on the run with Sam. She knew what it was. This was a Commander, a Mek brain, one of their most prized and senior units.

It stumbled free of the wreckage and looked around at the humans surrounding it, who were now slowly backing away as it rose to its full intimidating height.

"Dakota," said Rosie. "That thing's still dangerous. Finish it off."

"You read my mind," said Dakota, aiming the Liberator's rifle at the Commander and dialing in for a shot. But when she pulled the trigger, nothing happened. "Shit!" she said. "It's jammed!"

"Pump the trigger a couple of times to clear it," Rosie instructed. "It'll take a few seconds."

As Dakota did so, the Mek Commander below lumbered forward awkwardly. It was dragging one foot, damaged, but otherwise it appeared fully operational. It raised its right arm, a multi-barreled weapon where its hand would normally be, and fired twice into the crowd. Two men dropped to the ground, dead.

The two who had been supporting Sam.

As the others around him scattered, the Commander lurched toward Sam and grabbed him by the neck, pulling him close.

"Sam!" cried Dakota. The rifle jam had cleared but she no longer had a clear shot. The Mek Commander had made Sam into a human shield, its weapon-arm pressed against his head.

It looked up at the Liberator cockpit.

"SURRENDER," it said in its grotesque mimicry of a human voice.

One thing was clear: this Mek knew who Sam was, knew exactly who was up in that cockpit. Though it was heavily damaged and massively outgunned, it now held the only card it needed. The township's last remaining drones began to re-emerge from hiding, forming a protective perimeter around their commander.

Dakota relaxed her trigger finger. Even if she was confident of her targeting, the M-99 was such a high-caliber weapon that there was simply no chance of hitting the Commander without taking out Sam, too.

"Open the cockpit," she said. "We're going down there."

"What?" said Runyon. "Dak, we can't! That thing'll kill us!"

"I'm not risking Sam," said Dakota. "But if we activate sentry mode and get him separated from that Mek, Rosie can take the shot."

"I don't like this," Runyon said.

"I don't care much for it either," added Rosie.

"If one of you has a better idea, now's the time," Dakota replied.

Runyon groaned and closed his eyes. "Pilot authorize," he said reluctantly, and he unstrapped himself from the pilot's chair.

"Gunner authorize," said Dakota, as she released her own harness. She opened the cockpit hatch and together they climbed down the handholds on the outside of the Liberator, then walked directly toward the Mek Commander, which was still maintaining its iron grip on Sam. For all its humanoid form, the Commander had nothing that resembled a human face, and yet still it seemed to Dakota that it was somehow smiling at them.

"DISARM," the Commander said with a metallic rasp. The Mek drones that had parted to allow Dakota and Runyon to approach now converged once more to form an armed perimeter around them, trapping them in this standoff.

"Dak, don't," said Sam, struggling to speak with the Mek's arm clamped tight around his throat. "Take this asshole. Shoot through me if you have to."

Dakota removed her sidearm from its holster and tossed it into the dirt at her feet. Runyon hesitated, then did the same.

"HUMANS," the Mek Commander said. "WEAK."

Throughout the chaos, the giant video screens erected around the township had continued to operate, showing the footage Rosie had fed them of the Mek's unprovoked attack on Earth. Many of the township laborers still watched, even as the scene before them played out, looking back and forth as if trying to make sense of it all.

And then one of them stepped forward from the crowd, and Dakota was shocked to see a face she recognized.

Carmichael. The sneering doubter who had started the fight at the rec hut in what seemed like a lifetime ago.

There was no doubt in his expression now. He strode purposefully toward the Mek Commander with a look of murderous intent.

A Mek drone maneuvered to intercept.

Carmichael didn't even slow.

The drone jolted him, sending him to the ground, convulsing.

And for a moment, all was still.

Then another man stepped forward, and a young woman. They, too, were jolted into submission, but even as they fell, more and more were coming forward to replace them. The Mek drones stopped as many as they could, but people were now surging forward in overwhelming numbers. The township workers closed in on the Mek Commander from all sides, an ever-tightening noose of human bodies. Still holding on to Sam, the Commander raised its free weapon arm and began firing wildly, dropping more human bodies to the dirt, but it was too late and its enemies too many. They swarmed over the Mek, and it thrashed violently against them as they dragged it to the ground and set about attacking it with tools, pipes, rocks, their bare hands. It all happened so quickly that within moments Dakota could no longer see the Mek, lost somewhere within the human scrum. She rushed in and found Sam amid the melee, pulling him free of it. The two embraced, gripping each other tightly.

"Please disperse," Rosie said over the Liberator's loudspeaker.

The seething human throng gradually began to break up, revealing what now remained of the Mek Commander.

It had been literally ripped apart, torn and smashed to pieces. All that remained was a scattered collection of twitching mechanical parts. A similar fate had met the security drones, also reduced to scrap.

"Sam," said Rosie. "Come here. Let me look at you."

Sam looked up at the Liberator.

"Who are you?" he asked.

"I'm your mother."

Sam looked to Dakota, confused.

"Kind of a long story," she said with a smile.

"Plenty of time to tell it on the way home," said Rosie.

# EPILOGUE

DAKOTA AND RUNYON returned to the Liberator and oversaw its repairs. The destroyed remains of the Mek walker and Commander were more than enough to fuel the particle reprocessor and restore it to full operation. They began the long journey from the township, the Liberator leading an exodus of hundreds of former human slaves across the Wyoming plains, toward South Dakota.

Progress was slower than if the Liberator had been traveling alone, as it was limited to the speed of the slowest members of its human entourage, but still faster than the time Dakota and Runyon had made on their original outward journeys, as there was no longer any need to cower and hide from Mek patrols, waiting for them to pass.

They visited two more townships along their path and liberated them as well. By the time they were done, the human swath gathered around the Liberator as it strode across the country numbered nearly a thousand.

They crossed into South Dakota and traveled over the hills and valleys until they arrived at the Four Faces.

"I don't understand," said Dakota. "I thought you destroyed the hangar."

"I destroyed *that* hangar," said Rosie. "Everyone please gather round. And watch your feet." And the ground gave way beneath them as they realized they were standing on a giant elevator platform hidden beneath the forest floor.

The elevator descended into darkness, carrying the Liberator and its human congregation deep underground. The Gundog then stayed behind as Rosie's voice, emanating from loudspeakers in the walls around them, led them down a cavernous hallway. When her voice told them they had arrived, Dakota, Runyon, and Sam looked around in the gloom, unsure at first exactly what they had arrived at. Then Dakota made out the shape of something large and familiar looming over them up ahead—though what she thought it might be didn't seem possible.

"Is that… another Gundog?" she asked.

"It will be, when it's finished," said Rosie. And then the overhead lights flickered on, sequentially in rows, beginning directly above them and moving along the ceiling high above until the entire space had been illuminated. They were standing in a vast hangar, so large it seemed to extend into infinity. The Gundog Dakota had glimpsed in the gloom was in fact an incomplete skeletal chassis, its armor plating and other components still waiting to be installed. And arranged in orderly rows behind it were dozens more just like it, more than a hundred unfinished Gundogs in various stages of construction. An entire army of war machines just waiting to be assembled. It was a breathtaking sight.

"I told you the Liberator was only a prototype," said Rosie. "This is the real factory floor, where we were preparing the others that would follow. That *will* follow. We still need to finish building them. And when that's done, we'll need pilots, gunners, engineers, support and maintenance crews, to help us fight what's coming."

"What's coming?" Sam said.

"When word of what we've started gets back to the Mek homeworld, they'll send reinforcements," said Rosie. "And when they get here, we'll be ready. We won the first battle, but the real war's only just beginning. Do I have any volunteers?"

"Oo-rah," said Dakota, a smile creeping across her face. And then she heard the same from behind her, one of the liberated township workers with her fist raised in the air. Another fist went up, then another and another, a whole sea of them, as a chorus of *oo-rahs* rippled through those assembled.

"Good," said Rosie. "Then let's get started."

Here's what I know.

The Mek did not come to us in peace. They came to conquer and enslave us. And that they did, with ruthless efficiency, for thirty years. But no longer.

The war to liberate the human race begins here, now. We number barely a thousand, but if a single Gundog can achieve this much, imagine what an entire battalion of them can do.

With the Mek security data we stole from Bismarck, we've begun hacking into the comms systems of other townships, to show our people the truth. Already there are reports of unrest as news of our rebellion spreads. We'll come for them all, soon enough. And our numbers will grow.

Mom says the base sensors have detected a Mek signal on the edges of our solar system, headed this way. Reinforcements. Let them come. We'll be sure to give them a warm welcome when they arrive. If we die, we'll die fighting.

And I'll find Falk. I know he's still out there somewhere, still alive. Wherever he may be, however long it takes, I'll find him.

That's it. That's all I know.

# INKSHARES

INKSHARES is a community, publisher, and producer for debut writers. Our books are selected not just by a group of editors, but also by readers worldwide. Our aim is to find and develop the most captivating and intelligent new voices in fiction. We have no genre—our genre is debut.

Previously unknown Inkshares authors have received starred reviews in every trade publication. They have been featured in every major review, including on the front page of the *New York Times*. Their books are on the front tables of booksellers worldwide, topping bestseller lists. They have been translated in major markets by the world's biggest publishers. And they are being adapted at the biggest studios and networks.

Interested in making your own story a reality? Visit Inkshares.com to start your own project, connect with other writers, and find other great books.